"An intriguing yarn filled with secrets and sins, including false identities, covert relationships, adultery, greed and theft. With a dollop of whimsy, a cast of eccentrics and an intricate puzzle, *Death at High Tide* will sweep you away with its sly charm, its wicked wit and its artful trickery."

—*Fredericksburg Free Lance-Star*

"*Death at High Tide* took me away to a new and beautiful place. I have no idea when I'll get a chance to travel to the Scilly Isles, but in the meantime, I'm definitely going to enjoy this series set there."   —Donna Andrews

"A blend of all my favorite things: the Scilly Isles . . . the joys and trials of sisterhood, fun characters, and of course Hannah Dennison's witty prose. If you love Doc Martin, this is for you! A complete delight."   —Rhys Bowen

"A delightful new mystery series featuring a truly unique setting, wonderfully eccentric characters, a thoroughly intriguing plot, and the most fascinating cat in the world. Do not miss this fast-paced, funny, and charming mystery from a true master of the genre!"   —Kate Carlisle

"Charm. Chuckles. Chills. Hannah Dennison's delightful *Death at High Tide* is another sparkling entertainment by Britain's Mistress of Mystery."   —Carolyn Hart

"Hannah Dennison is a master of the cozy mystery. With her charm and humor, she creates characters you want to know forever and stories you won't forget. *Death at High Tide* is a pure delight—the British island scenery will capture your imagination, and sisters Evie and Margot will make you laugh out loud even as they solve a mysterious murder."

—Paige Shelton

"Christie lives! A deliciously Golden-Age setting, a deftly handled cast of shady characters, a beguiling heroine and sidekick, and a beautifully nested plot full of puzzles—the Island Sisters series opens with a bang." —Catriona McPherson

"Equally atmospheric and classic . . . With notes of Agatha Christie's *And Then There Were None* and touches of *The Guernsey Literary and Potato Peel Society* and *The Durrells in Corfu*, I was completely captivated by Dennison's cleverly crafted plot, well-developed characters, and masterful take on England's sub-tropical paradise." —Ellie Alexander

"A fabulous read! Hannah Dennison's *Death at High Tide* will transport you to wild and beautiful Tregarrick Rock, where you'll find eccentric inhabitants, murder, and great fun."

—Marty Wingate

Also by Hannah Dennison

Death *at* High Tide

An Island Sisters

Mystery

Hannah Dennison

St. Martin's Paperbacks

This is a work of fiction. All of the characters, organizations, and events portrayed in this novel are either products of the author's imagination or are used fictitiously.

Published in the United States by St. Martin's Paperbacks, an imprint of St. Martin's Publishing Group.

DEATH AT HIGH TIDE

Copyright © 2020 by Hannah Dennison.
Excerpt from *Danger at the Cove* copyright © 2021 by Hannah Dennison.

For information, address St. Martin's Publishing Group, 120 Broadway, New York, NY 10271.

www.stmartins.com

ISBN: 978-1-250-79812-1

Our books may be purchased in bulk for promotional, educational, or business use. Please contact your local bookseller or the Macmillan Corporate and Premium Sales Department at 1-800-221-7945, ext. 5442, or by email at MacmillanSpecialMarkets@macmillan.com.

Printed in the United States of America

Minotaur Books hardcover edition published 2020
St. Martin's Paperbacks edition published 2021

10 9 8 7 6 5 4 3 2 1

*This book is dedicated with love and affection to
Barbara Ballard, a.k.a. Scout Barbara.*

WINDWARD POINT

SHIPWRECKS

STLE BUOY

RUINED WATCHTOWER

WILLIAM'S BENCH

WILLIAM'S QUAY

CAVE

LAKE

BIRD HIDE

TERRACE

THE DELL

GALLEON
GARDEN

WILLIAM'S WOOD

TREGARRICK ROCK HOTEL

MERMAID LAGOON

SEA TRACTOR

SKIFF

CAUSEWAY

N
W   E
S

TREGARRICK
ROCK

RHYS DAVIES

Chapter One

"I'm sorry, but I don't understand what you mean." Anxiety pooled in the pit of my stomach, and I knew it had to be reflected in my face because my sister, Margot, grabbed my hand and gave it a reassuring squeeze.

Nigel Hearst, my newly deceased husband's accountant, regarded me with sympathy. "I'm sorry to say that over the past five years Robert had encountered some challenges with two of his major streams of revenue—"

"Yes." I nodded. "I knew he was worried about the safari park after the . . . accident."

Margot's eyes widened. "It was *Robert's* safari park? Was that where a guest tried to take a selfie with a baby rhino and the family sued?"

"It was awful," I said.

"Robert refused to fight it and settled out of court," said Nigel. "But I am hoping that you will be able to keep the house and, of course, your car."

"Keep the *house*?" I said, feeling a rising sense of panic. "Why wouldn't I be able to keep the house? We didn't have a mortgage—did we? I know the settlement was huge, but . . . Nigel, what's going on?"

Nigel adjusted his pink tie and straightened the blotter on his immaculately tidy desk. He refused to meet my eye. "Don't worry," he said smoothly. "I promised Robert I'd take care of you—"

"I think what Evie is trying to ask you is what the hell happened to all his money?" Margot flashed a megawatt smile with her startling white veneers that seemed to bring out the emerald green in her eyes. I cringed with embarrassment. I could always rely on my big sister to get straight to the point.

Nigel looked uncomfortable. "He had an expensive divorce."

"That was nine years ago," Margot said. "Anyway, Evie told me he could afford it."

I was mortified. It was true I had said that, but out of context my comment sounded callous. "It's not about the money, Margot," I said. "I'm just surprised because—"

"It's always about the money," Margot went on. "Evie gave up a lucrative career for Robert. He was a quarter of a century her senior—"

"Twenty-two years, actually—"

"Whatever. Anyway, he must have provided for her future."

"I am perfectly capable of getting a job," I said, shooting Margot a furious look.

Margot winked at me. I'd also forgotten about her warped sense of humor. In fact, I'd forgotten about a lot of Margot's qualities, which were now coming back to me at breakneck speed.

"Are we able to look at Robert's finances?" Margot asked. "No offense, Nick—"

"It's Nigel—"

"I mean, this is my sister's life you are talking about here, and I'm not sure how you expect us to just accept what you're telling her."

I saw concern etched on her face, and even though I was embarrassed, I felt so grateful that she had flown five thousand miles, all the way from California, to be with me. I had phoned her at ten in the morning U.K. time—two, West Coast time—and all I had said was, "Robert's dead." Eighteen hours later, she arrived on my doorstep with a hug and her Gucci luggage.

"Of course, you are welcome to look through everything," said Nigel. "Cherie will give you whatever you need."

At fifty-five, Nigel was still a dashingly attractive man, with a shock of salt-and-pepper hair, dark brown eyes and a charisma that came off him in waves. Today, though, I thought his face looked unusually florid, with small beads of perspiration dotted across his high forehead. He retrieved a bottle of pills from a drawer in his desk and knocked back a couple, dry. "Blood pressure," he said. Then he reached for the monogrammed silver cigarette case, but Margot snatched it out of his grasp.

"You just told us you had high blood pressure." She turned to me. "Did you know that smoking is totally illegal in Beverly Hills? Even outside. Don't look at me like that, Evie. The minute I started running, I gave up just like that." She snapped her fingers. "I haven't smoked for years."

"Is it hot in here?" Nigel got up and opened a window. A

blast of freezing cold November air whipped up the papers on his desk.

"Not anymore," said Margot.

He slammed the window shut.

We fell into an uncomfortable silence as he swiftly reorganized his documents. He really seemed on edge today. Margot's iPhone pinged an incoming text.

"Sorry, L.A.," Margot said apologetically. "Won't be a moment. Talent issues."

"She's a film producer in Hollywood," I said.

"I need to handle this immediately. Excuse me." Margot stood up and disappeared through the door into the outer office. She was dressed in a tight, plum-colored leather jacket, skinny jeans and Louboutin ankle boots. I noticed she'd become very thin. I also noticed that it made her boobs seem much bigger and for a moment wondered if she had actually had cosmetic surgery—something she swore she would never do.

"What's the time in Los Angeles?" Nigel mused. "It must be seven in the morning."

"Margot works all the time," I said with pride.

"Ah. The American dream."

"But I must apologize. She can be a bit direct." I took a deep breath and ventured, "Is it true about possibly losing the house?"

"I'll do everything in my power, you know that," said Nigel. "Robert was a law unto himself. He liked to take risks, and you know that once his mind was set on something . . ." He shrugged. "He would listen to my advice but never take it."

Nigel was right. Robert's harebrained moneymaking schemes

had always been unpredictable, but somehow he always came up trumps—until now. Nigel was the only friend from Robert's old life that he'd brought with him to his new life with me. Nigel had been our rock in a year that Robert called his "annus horribilis." It wasn't just the tragedy at the safari park. There was also the catamaran company that was lost to a fire and turned out not to be insured and most recently a property development deal that was doomed when the investors discovered the land was on a Superfund site. And yet Robert had never seemed disconcerted. He always bounced back, saying, "You win some, you lose some." He had been the eternal optimist. As I sat there in Nigel's office, I just couldn't believe that I would never see Robert again. I felt as if this were all a bad dream.

The door opened, but it was Cherie, Nigel's assistant, who poked her head inside.

"Mrs. Chandler wanted privacy," she said in a croaky voice, pulling the red-and-gold woolen scarf tighter around her neck. Married with a ten-year-old son, Cherie was in her early forties and had worked for Nigel for years. Nigel often said that she was the worst assistant he had ever had but that she made him laugh. Robert once told me that she and Nigel had had an affair. I found that hard to believe. With long straight hair draped around her face and large round glasses, Cherie was nothing like the numerous socialites Nigel often brought over to dinner. She was a bit of an enigma.

"How's your cold?" Nigel asked.

"Getting better," she said, and added a dainty cough to prove it. "The hot toddy you made me at lunchtime really helped."

"Is that a *Harry Potter* scarf?" I asked.

"It's Gryffindor."

"Cherie knows everything about *Harry Potter*," Nigel teased.

"Me too," I said. "I'm a huge fan."

As we waited for Margot to finish her phone call, Nigel and Cherie made small talk, but I could see by the way she looked at him that perhaps Robert had been right. She adored him.

I took in Nigel's plush city office, with his magnificent art collection adorning the three walls. The fourth was all glass and afforded a spectacular view of the Gherkin. I'd never been here before, although I'd met Nigel many times. He was a constant visitor at Forster's Oast, our beloved converted oasthouse just outside Tunbridge Wells in Kent.

Robert and Nigel's friendship went back years, but it was only over the last decade that Nigel had started managing Robert's businesses. Framed photographs of their exploits lined one wall in Nigel's office—catamaran racing, bobsledding, alpine skiing. Anything with speed. But these escapades came to an abrupt halt with Robert's rotator cuff surgery shortly after he and I married nine years ago.

I knew very little about Robert's life before we met and was happy not to ask about it. Margot called me an ostrich, with my head in the sand, and couldn't understand why I showed so little interest in his first wife. But I had my reasons—ones I would never share with her.

The door opened and Margot came back. She pushed her blond hair off her face. Last time I'd seen her, it had been a rich chestnut brown—her natural color. I patted my own hair self-consciously. Margot was right. It could do with a good cut. But when she sat down, I noticed that her hands were shaking.

"Is everything okay?" I asked.

"Didn't Robert have any life insurance policies?" she said, pointedly ignoring my question.

"Margot—," I protested.

"Why don't I make everyone some tea?" Cherie ventured.

"Or something stronger?" Nigel said hopefully.

"Definitely not," said Margot.

This was a first. When Margot had lived in England, boozy lunches were the norm. We were always meeting in the pub when we both worked in London—Margot in publicity for a PR firm and I as an archivist at the Red Fox art gallery in Soho. That was before she met Brian and was whisked off to Hollywood.

"I don't drink at lunchtime anymore," said Margot by way of explanation. "It's not cool in L.A. You'd immediately be checked into rehab. I'll have green tea."

Cherie paused and seemed confused. "Green? You mean peppermint?"

"She'll drink whatever you bring in, thanks, Cherie," I said.

"There may be a small policy of about seventy-five thousand pounds that I'm afraid won't go very far. Robert's estate is a little complicated and it will take time to sort everything out. I want to assure you that I am always here for you, Evie."

"Thank you," I said. "Have you heard from Michael yet?"

"Who is Michael?" Margot demanded.

"He lives in Australia," I said. "He's Robert's son from his first marriage. Obviously he needs to be here for the funeral—"

"I can handle all the funeral arrangements," said Nigel. "The sooner the better, I feel."

"Thank you," I said again. "I'm still waiting to hear from Dr. Barnaby. There was some question about having an autopsy."

"Yes, I heard that too," said Nigel.

"I wonder why," Margot said. "I mean a heart attack is a heart attack."

Nigel seemed taken aback. "Well, it was a little more complicated than that."

"We know," I said quickly, and glared at Margot for being so insensitive not just to Nigel—who had found Robert's body—but to me as well. For as long as I lived, I would always wonder if I could have saved him. If only I hadn't left that morning. If only I hadn't said those awful words. Suddenly the room seemed stifling.

"I need some water," I said.

"I'll ask Cherie—"

"No. It's fine." I jumped up and hurried out of Nigel's office into Cherie's work space, where she was setting out a tray of bone china tea mugs on a utility counter by the far wall.

Suddenly, I heard Margot's voice boom, "Evie won't ask, so that's why I'm here." We were on speakerphone.

Cherie gave a guilty start. She'd been eavesdropping next door! It was then that I saw her iPhone propped against the telephone console and Apple's built-in audio recorder running.

"Nigel likes me to record all of his meetings," she said quickly.

I was surprised. "Even for his friends?"

"Especially for his friends," said Cherie. "Just in case he forgets something."

"And what about his awful first wife?" I heard Margot go on. "Why should my sister—"

I hit the intercom button. "None of your business."

Cherie stuck out her chin. "I'm just doing my job." She handed me a bottle of Perrier water. "If you want flat, you'll have to drink tap."

"Perrier is fine, thank you," I said.

"Oh, hold on a minute—I've been doing some filing . . . I have something for you."

I waited patiently while Cherie hunted through a mound of documents on her desk. "It's here somewhere . . . ah!" She pulled out a cream vellum envelope. "I forgot to give this to Nigel, although actually it's addressed to you."

I took the sealed envelope and my stomach turned over as I recognized Robert's spidery handwriting with his trademark Mont Blanc pen—"For My Darling Wife: In the Event of My Death."

I returned to Nigel's office with the Perrier and the envelope, anxious to know what it contained but at the same time not sure if I could read its contents without crying.

"What have you got there?" Margot demanded.

"Cherie just gave this to me," I said. "It's from Robert."

"Let me see that," Nigel said sharply.

I showed him the envelope. His eyes widened in surprise. He immediately hit the intercom button. "Cherie! That envelope—where did you find it?"

"In my to-file box under my desk," we all heard her say. "Sorry. It must have been sent over with Robert's documents ages ago. I was looking for something else and there it was! I don't know how it ended up in—"

"Never mind," Nigel said curtly, and shut off the intercom, silencing whatever Cherie was about to say next. "Filing has never been Cherie's forte. Well . . . shall we see what the letter says?"

"I'd like to read this in private if you don't mind," I said. "Margot, you can stay."

"Oh." Nigel seemed taken aback. "Yes. Of course." He got up and left the room.

"Go on. Open it," Margot said. "It's probably some bizarre burial request or something."

"I *am* going to open it," I said. "But from now on, please let me handle Nigel. You've been rude to him. He's a good friend."

"Someone has to ask the difficult questions." She regarded me with incredulity. "I still find it hard to believe you didn't notice that Robert was running out of money. I know I would have. Brian and I share everything."

"Robert handled the money," I said. "And I was happy for him to do so. He was always very generous to me."

"Generous!" Margot exclaimed. "I should hope so! It's not the 1950s!" She took my hand again. "What happened to my independent little sister who wouldn't allow a man to even open her car door?"

"Got old."

"You're thirty-six!" Margot exclaimed. "Granted that's old for California, but *here*?"

"Alright, I grew up."

"*Bullchits!*"

I smiled at our childish made-up swear word.

"You were always the rebel," Margot went on. "You were always the one getting into trouble at school. You even lost your virginity before me! And then the minute you met Robert you changed. You became the demure little stay-at-home wife. I mean . . . what about your photography? You just let it all go!"

I didn't answer. Margot had struck a nerve. It was true. I had put my photography dreams on hold while we focused on having a family. A family! I felt sick as I remembered Michael's damning comments the night before his father died.

"Well . . . if you're not going to open it, I will." Margot snatched the envelope out of my grasp and picked up the silver letter opener on Nigel's desk.

"Go ahead," I said. "I don't think I can handle any more emotion right now. You read it."

So Margot did, her eyes swiftly darting across the paper. She went very quiet, then broke into a huge grin. "Well, this is excellent news!"

"No jokes, please," I said.

"I'm not joking. 'If you are reading this letter,'" she read, "'it means you are the proud owner of Tregarrick Rock.'"

"A painting? Who is the artist?"

"Not a painting! You'll never believe what it is—" She handed me the letter. "It's actually a *hotel*."

Chapter Two

"A hotel?" I was puzzled. "Robert never talked to me about buying a hotel. Where is it?"

"Brace yourself," said Margot. "It's on an island off the southwest peninsula."

"In the Caribbean?"

"England, you dumbo. The Scilly Isles. Take a look." Margot handed me the letter.

It was written on Robert's personal headed paper with his old address in Calverley Park, Tunbridge Wells. There were no pleasantries or endearments. It was a straightforward record of a business transaction.

"This makes no sense," I said. "What does 'collateral' mean?"

"It seems that years ago Robert loaned—" She frowned. "His writing is appalling. I can't make out the name—a certain Jay Ferret? Not sure. Anyway, he loaned this Ferret some money—the amount of which is hard to read but it looks like one hundred thousand pounds to me."

"That must have been before me," I said. "What's the date?"

"Uh . . . it's 2000."

"That was well before me." I felt a stab of jealousy. "This letter must be meant for Joanna."

"The first wife?" Margot shrugged. "Of course it isn't. Cherie said it was sent with all Robert's other stuff when Nigel took over his business affairs. No. It's obvious. The loan was never repaid. Anyway, you're his wife now. Joanna was paid off. But if you really want to know, we can call and ask her."

"Are you insane?" I exclaimed. "There is no way I am calling her."

"I thought you said you got along well."

"I'm not calling her." Joanna despised me, but I'd never tell Margot that. "Nigel can sort it out. That's what he does."

"There was also a witness to the loan," Margot mused. "A Millicent Small. At least that's what it looks like. How greedy to hog all those letter *l*'s."

Margot gave me the letter back for me to read. "This seems too good to be true," I said, but I did feel a twinge of excitement. A hotel! I wouldn't be homeless! "Let's see what Nigel thinks. I'll ask him to come back in."

Moments later, Nigel put the letter down with a look of bewilderment on his face. "This is news to me. I didn't start handling Robert's finances until 2010, but let me make some enquiries."

"You've never heard of Jay Ferret?" I said.

Nigel shook his head. "Robert knew a lot of people."

Margot cocked an eyebrow. "People he casually loaned a hundred thousand pounds to?"

"As I said, let me look into it."

"Since this is a formal letter," I said slowly, "wouldn't there be a formal receipt to say the money had been repaid?"

"I'll handle it," Nigel said again. He raked his fingers through his hair. "Really. There's a lot to sort out."

"Yes. Yes, of course. I know you will. Thank you." I had another thought. "Maybe there is some way we could save Forster's?"

"Evie," Nigel said wearily, "I told you. I'll take care of it, but I'm leaving for Paris tonight. Give me a few days, okay? I'll keep this letter, if you don't mind."

It was on our drive back to Kent, when we were sitting in bumper-to-bumper traffic on the A21 in the driving rain, that I said, "Can I come back with you to Los Angeles for a bit?"

"What? Why? You said you hated L.A."

"I know I did. It's just that everything feels so unsettled."

"Of course it does!" Margot said. "You've just lost your husband. It's going to take time, Evie. That's why I'm here."

"What if you asked Brian if he could hire me as the official photographer for Chandler Productions? I could photograph the film stars."

"They're not called film stars," said Margot. "They're called talent. And besides, photographing the talent is completely different from photographing birds."

"Ah . . . I disagree. I'd say the *talent* is all puffed up like peacocks. At least the birds have their original feathers—and eyes."

"You can be such a bitch," said Margot with a laugh. "But at least I see a glimmer of my sister's razor-sharp wit under all that grief. And to answer your question, yes, these are tinted contacts."

"You look like Linda Blair from *The Exorcist*."

"That's the spirit—no pun intended." Margot cuffed my shoulder affectionately. "I've missed you, sis."

"I've missed you, too."

"Which is why I thought I'd stay with *you* for a few weeks."

"With *me*? That would be amazing!" I exclaimed. "How did you pull that off? How will Brian manage without you?"

"I can work remotely as long as I have Wi-Fi," said Margot. "And with the eight-hour time difference, I will have all day to play."

"Is that why you brought so much luggage?" I had been surprised at the two enormous suitcases that the taxi driver had deposited in the hall a few days ago.

"I never travel light."

"You used to travel very light," I reminded her. "In fact, you used to boast about how many days you could wear the same pair of knickers."

"I was nine!" she protested. "What is it with you? Why is it that you love to drag out the most embarrassing memories?"

"Said the pot calling the kettle black," I teased.

We laughed again and I felt a tiny bit better.

"Anyway, you need my help since it seems that all your friends have abandoned you," said Margot.

"Ouch," I said. "Thanks."

"What happened to Rachel?" Margot went on. "And Sarah? And . . . what was the other one called . . . the girl with the big ears—Paula? Pam?" She rummaged in her handbag for an emery board and started filing her perfect nails. "You used to live in each other's pockets."

I kept my eyes fixed on the road, but Margot had hit a nerve. "Robert and I had a very busy life together," I said. "There wasn't a lot of room for other people."

The truth was that my friends became caught up in having families of their own, and since Robert and I didn't, the old gang and I just drifted apart. I'd never been bothered about having kids until about a year ago, and then suddenly, it was all I could think about.

"Didn't you get bored?" said Margot. "I know I would have done."

"Robert was anything but boring," I said, more sharply than I intended. "He was my best friend, Margot. We did everything together, and now . . ."

"Oh God, Evie, I'm sorry," Margot said. "I can't begin to imagine what you are going through."

"It's okay," I said. "Really."

"And that's why I'm here," Margot said briskly. "I thought you'd need some moral support packing up Robert's possessions. You don't want to do that alone."

We fell silent and I wondered if, like me, she was remembering the last time we'd sat together doing the same thing, after Mum passed away so suddenly following Dad's death.

Tears welled up, but I brushed them away.

"I'm sorry," Margot said again. "I didn't mean to upset you, but"—she glanced over at me—"I have an idea."

My heart sank. "Oh."

She laughed. "Don't sound so horrified."

"I am horrified. I know your ideas."

"Remember the promise we made to each other when we both left home?"

"Which one?" I said warily.

"Every year we'd make sure to spend a weekend together somewhere? But we never did. Not once."

"I suppose life just got in the way."

"And then Mum made us promise to always look after each other, remember that too?"

I nodded.

"So . . . let's start right now!" Margot exclaimed.

"Um. Okay."

"I think we should go for a little girls-on-tour weekend to the Scilly Isles."

"You mean, Tregarrick Rock."

"Exactly." Margot grinned. "We don't have to tell them anything. If it turns out you still own the hotel, you can decide whether you want to sell it. If it turns out you don't, then at least we'll have had a great weekend."

"In November? In the Atlantic Ocean?"

"No. The Scilly Isles are between the Celtic Sea *and* the Atlantic Ocean," she said. "Apparently Scilly enjoys a semi-tropical climate that's similar to the South of France."

"How do you know?"

"I looked on Google when you were in the restroom. And you know what?"

"What?"

"Google informs me that the islands are known as a bird-watcher's paradise for migrating birds. People come from all over the world to look at the yellow-browed warbler or the common yellowthroat and the . . . yellow-browed bunting. A lot of yellow birds anyway."

"Did you just memorize all that?"

"You forget—I have a photographic memory. Which reminds me," Margot chattered on. "You could take your camera. I bet it hasn't seen daylight for years."

Margot was right. It hadn't. "How far is it exactly?"

"About twenty-eight miles off the southwestern tip of the Cornish peninsula."

"I don't know . . . it's too soon."

"Au contraire! It could be the perfect place to get your head straight."

"I'm not good company at the moment, Margot. Besides, now that I'm penniless I can hardly go swanning off for a weekend on an island."

"I'll pay," said Margot. "It's my idea, so my treat. Look at it as a healing weekend where you can rediscover your inner child."

I pulled a face. "Inner child?"

"Ha ha! Got you there," said Margot. "You should have seen your face. Seriously, sis, a weekend away would be a good thing. Get some distance. We can brainstorm and plan your next chapter . . . and meet the Ferret—if he's still alive."

"Yes. I can just imagine having that conversation. 'Excuse me, but did you pay back my dead husband's loan?'"

"Aren't you just a little bit curious about Tregarrick Rock?" Margot asked. "It might be amazing! We can have massages, facials and lots of room service."

"A bit of a change from Mum and Dad's guesthouse on the seafront in Hove," I said wryly.

"It always smelled of cabbage," Margot mused. "I never could figure out why, because Mum was always cleaning. I couldn't wait to leave home."

"I loved living there. The Sandpiper Guest House—"

"With not a single sandpiper in sight. Just seagulls."

"There were always interesting people passing through—"

"Who you loved to catch unawares with your camera even then," Margot reminded me.

"Dad confiscated my camera for a week because he thought I was charging that couple for their pictures—but they offered *me* money—"

"Because they were having an affair." Margot rolled her eyes.

"Oh. I didn't know that."

"You were twelve," said Margot. "Industrious but so naïve."

"And you were fourteen," I said. "And boy mad."

I turned off at the signpost marked PENSHURST and we barreled along the country lanes slick with mud from the endless rain that had continued to fall these past few weeks. Wind rushed through the trees that still clung to autumn with leaves of burnt orange, rust, brown and golden yellow.

"I miss the seasons," Margot said wistfully. "Although in California we have four seasons too. Fire, mud, drought and . . . earthquakes."

"And you love it there," I reminded her.

"Sometimes," she said quietly.

I stole a look and caught an expression that surprised me. Margot looked sad. "Are you sure you are okay?"

"Yes. Of course," she said. "I'm living the American dream, remember?"

We turned into a farm entrance marked with a bleached wooden plaque reading FORSTER'S FARM AND FORSTER'S OAST and rumbled over the cattle grid. Winding our way down the potted driveway, I felt the thrill I always did when I caught the first glimpse of the twin cowls atop the conical roofs of the converted hop kiln that was home. Robert had let me have free rein in designing the interior and I'd loved every minute of it.

"It's such a peculiar building," Margot remarked. "But I admit it has charm. I think it would be a great setting for a movie—a horror movie."

I admit that when I first saw the abandoned and near-derelict building, I thought it was creepy. But Robert had been brimming with enthusiasm, and as always it was contagious. He had told me how the hops were raked in from the fields and spread out on the thin, perforated floors to be dried by hot air rising from a wood or charcoal fire below in the kiln.

"But why are there such strange chimneys?" Margot went on.

"The hot air escaped through the cowl in the roof, which turned with the wind," I said. "Then the hops were raked out to cool and sent to the brewery."

"And presto, we have beer."

"It's mostly industrialized now," I said. "But back in the day it was estimated that two hundred and fifty thousand hop pickers from London were traveling to Kent for work. You see, it's not just you who has a photographic memory."

As we turned the final corner into the cobbled forecourt, we saw a black BMW parked outside.

"Were you expecting anyone?" Margot asked.

I shook my head just as a woman got out of the driver's seat. Her hair was tied back in a ponytail and she wore a tailored black coat and heels. I guessed she was in her early forties.

She offered a hand in greeting. "Good afternoon, I'm Tina Leyland from Sotheby's Real Estate. Are you Mrs. Mead?"

I regarded her with dismay. "Yes. That's me, but I'm not sure why you're here."

Tina looked confused. "You didn't get the message?"

"No."

"I spoke to"—she glanced at her iPhone—"Cherie about a preliminary meeting today."

"There must be a misunderstanding," Margot stepped in. "The house isn't for sale."

Tina seemed nonplussed. "I apologize. I'll call my office and let them know."

"Good idea," said Margot.

"Wait," I said. "Do you know when Cherie arranged this?"

"I'm not sure. Last week, I assume. But here is my card in case you change your mind. . . ."

"She won't," Margot said firmly, and hustled me inside.

"I'll phone Nigel." I moved straight to the phone as shock gave way to annoyance. "Why didn't he mention it today?"

Cherie picked up on the first ring. She didn't give me a chance to ask her. "Sotheby's just called a few minutes ago," she said. "Sorry. The appointment was set for next Monday." She laughed. "I must have got my dates muddled up."

I didn't think it remotely funny. "I need to talk to Nigel."

"He's already left for the airport," said Cherie. "You could try his mobile."

Margot excused herself to make some calls of her own while I tried to reach Nigel. His line was busy, but finally I got through. He apologized profusely. "Cherie's not the brightest tool in the shed," he said. "I don't know why she took it upon herself to do this, but it would be useful to have an idea of the value."

"You said we might be able to save Forster's," I reminded him.

"I said we'd try, Evie." He hesitated. "Things aren't looking good on the house. I don't want to give you false hope. I have to go. I need to go through security now." I could hear flights being announced in the background. "I'll see you when I get back. We'll have dinner!"

When I went up to relay my conversation with Margot, she was still on the phone. I peeped into her bedroom, but she gave a quick wave and hurried into the bathroom-en-suite and shut the door.

Despite my grief, fear of the future and the dread that had been my constant companion in the pit of my stomach these last few days, I felt a tiny bit of hope. Having Margot here was like a breath of fresh air.

I'd forgotten how much I missed her energetic and optimistic nature. Even though she could be exhausting, she never let anything get her down—although I had detected an edge to her today that hadn't been there before.

The next three days were spent packing up Robert's personal possessions. I'd wanted to put it off, but Margot was insistent we get it over and done with.

I was glad to have her with me. She was ruthless in the way she sorted out Robert's clothing into different piles for different charities. I kept a few things back—a cream cashmere scarf, Robert's Rolex watch collection and a beautiful Givenchy ankle-length black leather trench coat that Margot had argued had to go. "Too Third Reich and not politically correct," she'd said.

Going through boxes of old photographs was particularly difficult, since they were of a life before me—many taken of him with a stunning, long-haired woman in exotic locations. Joanna. Others were the formal schoolboy panoramic photographs taken every year.

Robert had attended Tonbridge and from there Cambridge University, where he rowed for the Blue Boats. His passion for sailing and all things nautical continued until he was forced to retire shortly after his surgery and he turned his attention to other forms of speed—such as taking up a share in a racehorse.

I remembered him packing away his sailing trophies and storing them in the attic, keeping out just one black-and-white photograph that he put on a bookshelf in his office. It showed two teenagers—one being Robert—tanned and happy standing in front of a six-oared wooden rowing boat. It looked as though it had been taken on vacation in the Mediterranean.

"Did he ever take you out rowing?" Margot asked.

"Not rowing. But sailing, yes."

"I thought boats made you seasick," said Margot.

"They do," I said. "I only tried twice. I was throwing up the moment we left the harbor and hit open water." I remembered how disappointed Robert had seemed when I told him that not only did I get seasick, I was deathly afraid of water—this was after he had purchased and named a new catamaran after me as a birthday surprise.

"I bet he was upset about that," Margot said.

"If he was, he didn't show it. Robert just said that was why God had invented airplanes."

I gestured to six cardboard boxes filled with Robert's personal mementos that he had collected before I came along. "I don't know what to do with all these."

"You said he had a son? Give all this stuff to him," Margot suggested. "What's he like?"

"Michael? Thirty. Entitled. Hates me. What else do you want to know?" The moment I said it, I regretted it. Margot's opinion of how I met Robert had not shifted in all the years he and I had been together. For someone so liberal in so many things, her view of the old-fashioned marriage vows for better or for worse was unshakable. I'd never told her the true version of events because I knew what she would say, and today was definitely not the day to start.

"So when shall we head to Tregarrick Rock?" I said brightly as we paused for our afternoon cup of tea.

"Tomorrow. I have organized everything." Margot handed me a blue plastic transparent folder and withdrew a wad of pages that had been stapled together. "Our itinerary."

"I wondered where all my paper went."

"I like to print things out." Margot spread the sheets over the kitchen table. She'd highlighted half a dozen sections in different-colored fluorescent pens.

"I look at you and wonder if we had the same mother sometimes," I said.

"I'm just detail oriented, that's all. Okay, listen to this. The Isles of Scilly—or Scilly, but *never* called the Scilly Isles—are famed for their Soleil d'Or narcissus, gorgeously scented daffodils. Along with seasonal tourism, these flowers have been the main source of income for more than a century."

"You sound like a guidebook."

"It's from Wikipedia, actually. I copied and pasted. Listen . . . the locals are called Scillonians blah blah blah subtropical climate with winter temperatures comparable to—told you—the South of France."

"Go on."

"With a combined population of two thousand two hundred, policing the one hundred and forty-two islands is quite a challenge. The police force is based on the largest island of St. Mary's and consists of one sergeant, two constables, one police community support officer and one volunteer. Policing is . . . get this . . . by *bicycle*!"

"What? All one hundred and forty-two islands?"

"Obviously most are uninhabited. Some are just little islets. Tregarrick is very small—a mere two and a half miles long by one mile wide. There is one general store, one post office and a pub called the Salty Boatman. There is no hospital or doctor on the island and in case of a medical emergency, a hospital launch is sent from St. Mary's—"

"You might be hard-pressed to find your luxury spa," I said. "It sounds like the Dark Ages."

"All part of the charm, especially this bit . . . there are no cars or streetlights on Tregarrick."

"How do we get there?" I asked.

"Train, then a quick two-and-a-half-hour crossing from Penzance on the ferry—"

"Ferry!" I pulled a face. "No thanks. Can't we fly? Surely there is an airport?"

"Yes, but it's not worth the risk of flights getting delayed or canceled because of the weather at this time of year." Margot gave a heavy sigh. "We're only going for the weekend."

"I'd rather take my chances," I said firmly.

"Don't be so pathetic," Margot exclaimed. "It's a big boat, Evie. You'll be fine."

Chapter Three

"I'm never ever getting on a ferry again," I whispered. "I honestly would have rather died."

"Agreed," said Margot, who looked pale, too. "And I never suffer from seasickness."

"You'll get used to it," said a young woman with a baby in her arms. "First time coming to Scilly?"

"And last—at least on *that*." Margot pointed to the *Scillonian III*, a 170-foot four-deck passenger ship that was moored alongside the stone quay. "I don't understand it. I like boats."

"It's a flat-bottom boat, dear. No stabilizers and there's always a bit of a swell on this crossing. We locals call it the Great White Stomach Pump," she said with a chuckle. "The key is not to eat anything at all—that way there's nothing to come up, is there?"

I turned away and dry-heaved into one of the planters that lined the stone quay of the pretty harbor.

"Where are you staying?" the young woman asked.

"We're going on to Tregarrick," said Margot.

"You'll be lucky," said the woman. "You won't get a boat now. Fog's coming in."

"Oh yes we will," said Margot with a tone I remembered all too well. If someone ever told Margot that something was impossible, she would go out of her way to prove them wrong. "It's only a fifteen-minute crossing, and according to TripAdvisor, there are plenty of locals willing to earn some extra money to ferry tourists across."

"As I said, the fog's coming in. It can be treacherous out there."

"I'm happy to pay whatever it costs," Margot persisted. "You must know *someone* who could do with the cash."

"No, I do not." The woman turned to her partner, a man sporting an impressive beard. I heard her say "Bloody cheek."

"She's from America," I said as if to excuse Margot's behavior.

"You could ask Sandra at the ticket office. She might still be open." Her partner pointed to a small square stone building farther down the quay. "Her husband has a boat." He nudged the young woman and the two shared a conspiratorial laugh.

"Thank you," I said, and set off with my overnight case and camera bag, not bothering to see if Margot was following.

Within minutes, I realized the woman was right about the fog. It rolled in like a sandstorm, and when I turned to see if Margot was behind me, she was just a hazy blob.

Sadly, it looked as if Sandra had already gone home for the day. The door's venetian blind was down despite the sign stating that the office was open from nine a.m. to five p.m.

Margot checked her watch. "It's not even five. It's four-fifty. This would never happen in L.A. What kind of business closes at five?"

"Normal ones."

"There's a light on." Margot rapped on the door. "Someone has to be in there. *Hello!*"

"Read that." I gestured to a small notice in the bottom right-hand corner of the glass door just below the drop-down blind. "It tells us to go to Calico Jack's if this office is closed."

"How very *Pirates of the Caribbean*," Margot said slowly. "Hmm . . . I have an idea."

"And I have a bad feeling," I said. "I don't think we're going anywhere tonight, and to be honest, I just can't face getting onto another boat anyway. Let's find a B&B."

"No. I made reservations at Tregarrick Rock and that's where we are going. Wait. I saw a light. Someone is in there." She hammered on the door. "*Hello!* I know you're in there. It's four fifty-three. You've got seven minutes before—"

The door opened to reveal a woman in her fifties dressed in a navy-blue outdoor coat and holding a plastic shopping bag. Her eyes were flashing with fury. "What's all this caterwauling? I'm closed. Can't you read the sign?"

"Oh, I'm so sorry. I didn't see it," said Margot, switching on the charm. "You must be Sandra. Your friend on the ferry told us you could arrange transportation to Tregarrick."

"No boats are running tonight," Sandra declared. "Too dangerous to navigate the Tregarrick Straits."

"Don't boats have radar or something?" Margot persisted. "Apparently your husband has a boat."

Sandra seemed taken aback. "It's a Topper. I'd never let him go out in this weather."

"What's a Topper?" Margot said to me.

"It's a very small racing boat. With sails."

Margot was not amused. "No wonder that couple on the ferry laughed."

"Good evening, ladies," came a female voice.

We turned to see a petite woman in her early forties with a pixie cut that showed off hoop earrings so large I feared they could get caught on a door handle. She was dressed in fitted leather trousers and a black polo neck beneath a deep red wool jacket. She was perfectly made-up and strikingly pretty.

"Oh, Patty! Am I glad to see you," said Sandra, suddenly all smiles.

"What seems to be the problem, Sandra?"

"This woman is insisting on getting to Tregarrick tonight. Even asked about my Ron taking them over on his Topper—"

"Excuse me," said Margot. "Are you her supervisor?"

"You could say that," said Patty.

"I am not impressed with customer service," Margot said. "We've traveled a long way—from Los Angeles, actually—and this woman was rude."

"There's no need to get upset, ma'am," said Patty. "I'm afraid you'll have to stay here this evening. No boats will be leaving tonight—"

"That's what I told her," Sandra chimed in.

Margot shook her head. "I'm afraid that's totally unacceptable—"

"Margot!" I hissed. "Please—"

"What's the hurry?" said Patty. "Have you got the Mafia on your tail—"

"I told you," Sandra cut in. "They're determined. I mean, who wants to go to Tregarrick in November? That's what I want to know."

"Well, let me enlighten you," said Margot. "I am a producer for the . . . for the next *Pirates of the Caribbean* movie—"

"With Johnny Depp?" Sandra was goggle-eyed.

"Yep," said Margot. "I know Johnny well—and Orlando. Nice guys."

This was news to me, but nothing would surprise me. Margot had always been excellent at networking.

"I've seen them all," Patty enthused. *"The Curse of the Black Pearl, Dead Man's Chest, At World's End*—"

"On Stranger Tides," Sandra put in. "And *Dead Men Tell No Tales*. That's number five. So you're producing number six! Oh my heavens!"

"That's right." Margot gestured to me. "And this is Evie. She is my location scout. That's why she has brought her camera equipment."

My delight turned to dismay. So this was Margot's "idea." It was so typical of my sister to invent such a story. She was always doing this kind of thing when we were children. Once we went to our local park and pretended we were Russian—Galia and Irina. We spoke with fake accents, and soon, quite a crowd of kids were captivated by Margot's wild stories that our parents had defected from the Soviet Union. Needless to say, we were humiliated when our mother came to pick us up and set them straight.

"Well, how fascinating." Patty took in Margot's designer clothing—her Louboutin ankle boots, black Wolford tights and buttoned-up Stella McCartney herringbone coat that she told me cost thousands of dollars. By contrast, I was wearing jeans, a Barbour jacket, bucket hat and sturdy Dansko ankle rubber boots. We couldn't have looked more different. No one would guess we were sisters in a million years.

"I am here from Los Angeles for literally three days and I do not have the time to hang about," Margot said haughtily. "Every day costs my production company money. It's critical we get to Tregarrick tonight."

I stood there wishing the ground would swallow me up. I was right. She was not going to let this matter go.

"And you?" Patty turned to me. "You're the location scout and you didn't know about our November fog?"

"I . . . I . . ."

"The film will be set in the winter," Margot said smoothly. "I needed to get a sense of the weather and atmosphere for authenticity."

"Well," Patty said slowly, "I must say that Tregarrick has more than its fair share of shipwrecks dotted about the ocean floor . . ." She paused. "But this location is not exactly *Pirates in the Caribbean*."

"It's a spin-off," said Margot. "It's called . . . *Scilly Pirates*."

Scilly Pirates? I swore I caught a flash of amusement cross Patty's face.

"Is Johnny Depp still going to be in it?" Sandra demanded.

"Of course," Margot said.

"I can't believe Johnny Depp is coming to Scilly!"

"And Orlando Bloom," said Patty, watching Margot carefully. "Let's not forget him."

"I bet you meet stars all the time," Sandra went on, clearly starstruck by being so close to Hollywood, albeit vicariously.

Margot gave a polite smile and turned her charm full-on to the woman with the pixie cut. "Obviously you are from around these parts. You probably know where we can blackmail or bribe someone to take us across the water without ending up beneath it."

"I'm sorry," said Patty. "Did I not introduce myself? You are right. We are rude! We Scillonians pride ourselves on giving our visitors a warm welcome."

I heard a snigger and saw Sandra giggling nervously behind her hand like a teenager.

"I'm Detective Sergeant Patricia Williamson of the Devon and Cornwall Constabulary."

Chapter Four

My stomach dropped like a stone, and even Margot's usual sangfroid seemed rattled as a tide of red raced up her neck and flooded her face.

"But everyone just calls me Patty." She smiled.

"Oh," Margot said weakly. "Um. Sorry. You threw me a little bit with—I like your trousers."

"Yes, I'm out of uniform," said Patty. "I have a date, actually."

"Oh," Sandra enthused. "Third time, isn't it? Not bad for you."

Patty laughed. "As you may gather, there are no secrets on Scilly. So now we're all going to be friends, perhaps you'd like to tell me your names?" She retrieved a little police notebook and pencil from inside her jacket. "I always keep this on me."

"Margot Chandler and Evie Mead," I said, feeling increasingly nervous.

"I usually make sure I'm there on the quay when the ferry arrives, or at the airport. Owen—Police Constable Owen King—and I take turns," Patty said as she scribbled in her pad.

"We like to greet our visitors just to make sure we don't allow any serial killers onto the islands."

Margot and I exchanged worried glances.

"Just kidding," said Patty. "Crime is nonexistent here. Now you two . . . papers, please. *Now!* Chop-chop." She snapped her fingers with impatience.

I panicked and searched my pockets. "I think I have my driver's license—"

Margot fumbled in her tote bag. "I—oh, I have a business card. I left my passport—"

"Quickly, quickly," Patty demanded. *"Papers, please . . .* otherwise you're both under arrest."

"What?" Margot gasped.

"Just kidding again." Patty grinned. "Isn't that what happens in the movies?"

Margot nodded and showed too many teeth. We all laughed—Sandra brayed—but to be honest, I didn't think it was very funny.

"Don't worry. I don't really need your credentials. I get the passenger manifests," Patty went on. "I must say it's going to be very exciting to have a film crew here from Hollywood."

"We're just scouting for the location at the moment," Margot said quickly. "We'll be going to other places like—"

"The Isle of Man," I put in. "And maybe the Outer Hebrides. Any island that is not in the Caribbean."

"Forecast is good for tomorrow morning, but the weekend weather is rubbish," said Patty. "Oh. Can I be an extra? I've always wanted to be in a movie. I did a lot of amateur dramatics at school."

"Maybe we can all be in it," Sandra said hopefully. "I'll hold Orlando's sword anytime."

Patty hooted with laughter. "You'll have to fight me for that!"

Margot shot me an anguished plea for help. I just shrugged. Hadn't our mother drilled into us that honesty was always the best policy?

"So how long will you both be staying?" Patty asked.

"Until Monday," I said. "Just for the weekend."

"Got to get back to L.A.," said Margot.

"Of course you do," said Patty. "And you'll be staying at the Salty Boatman on Tregarrick?"

"No. My assistant made reservations at Tregarrick Rock," said Margot.

"I doubt that," Sandra chimed in. "They're closed for the winter. Redecorating."

"No, I have reservations," said Margot. "My assistant spoke to the front desk, although the woman who took my—I mean my *assistant's* phone call seemed a little deaf."

"That'll be Lily Travis," Sandra said to Patty. "She often answers if no one else is in reception."

"Oh," said Margot.

"Lily delivered all my babies," Sandra said wistfully.

"And mine," said Patty, adding, "Lily is a bit of a legend. She was the local midwife for decades. Even delivered me, according to my mum."

"She's retired now, though," Sandra said. "Lives at the hotel like a queen, which I just don't understand. I mean—"

"Well, I'm sure Hollywood isn't interested in all our island gossip," Patty cut in. "Although I think Lily is going to love talking to you two. She knows everything about Hollywood—"

"And about everyone on Scilly," Sandra added darkly.

"I bet she'd love to be your consultant," said Patty.

"Mind if I leave now?" said Sandra. "It's gone five."

"Go ahead," said Patty.

"And good luck with Henry tonight!"

"I don't hold out much hope, but you've got to put yourself out there. As for you two—stay right here. I'll see what I can do about finding you a boat."

And with that, Sandra and Patty were swallowed up in the fog, leaving Margot and me standing on the quay with our luggage.

"Don't you *dare* say a word," Margot said in a low voice.

"What were you thinking?" I whispered back. "Seriously. *Scilly Pirates?*" But as I said it, I started to giggle.

Margot began to giggle, too. "It'll be a comedy."

"It would have to be," I said. "And I'm supposed to be a location scout?"

She shrugged. "It's a good cover."

"Why would we need a cover? We're just two sisters going away for a weekend."

"No," Margot said. "We're scoping out your hotel."

"It's not my hotel!"

"Of course it is. I have a good feeling about this," said Margot. "And anyway, do I look like someone who goes anywhere out of season? I mean—*regardez!*" She pointed to her designer luggage and then her Louboutin ankle boots. "No, trust me. This is much better. Plus I can guarantee that we'll get really good service at the hotel if they think Johnny Depp and Orlando Bloom are going to come here."

I gave an exasperated sigh. "But they're not."

"You're so negative!" Margot exclaimed. "Say the hotel is yours . . . I bet we could lure some Hollywood celebrities here."

"But not Johnny Depp," I said. "And *do* we have reservations?"

"I jolly well hope so. The main thing is that for a moment, admit it, you forgot about Robert, didn't you."

Just hearing his name brought me back to reality with a jolt.

"Ah, ladies!" came a voice. "Have we missed the last boat to Tregarrick?"

Margot and I turned to see a man who had also been traveling on the ferry. Between the young couple with the baby and a dozen schoolchildren who must have been on a school trip, he'd stuck out like a sore thumb. He also looked vaguely familiar.

Late fifties, tall and lanky, with ice-blue eyes framed by titanium eyeglasses and a beard that was almost white, he wore a Canada Goose parka and carried a professional-looking camera bag and a walking stick.

"Ah, it's you," he said with a smile. "Are you feeling any better now that you are on dry land?" I noticed that he spoke with a clipped accent.

"A little," I said. "Thank you."

"You're in luck." Patty materialized through the fog. "I've found you a boat. Oh . . . and who are you? Were you on the ferry as well?"

"Alex Karlsson," he said. "Good evening. All the way from Stockholm."

The name definitely rang a bell. I tried to remember where I had heard it before.

"Goodness, how global we are this evening," said Patty with a hint of sarcasm. "These ladies traveled all the way from Hollywood. Who would have thought that Tregarrick in November would be such a popular destination?"

Alex Karlsson smiled. "Who indeed."

Patty gestured to his camera equipment. "Are you shooting a film on Scilly as well?"

"I'm sorry?" The newcomer looked confused.

"We're not actually shooting—," Margot began.

"Well, I *am* a photojournalist." He withdrew a press card from his breast coat pocket and handed it to Patty.

"Alex Karlsson!" I exclaimed. "I thought you seemed familiar! I love your work." I turned excitedly to my sister. "The gallery held one of his exhibitions years ago. Mr. Karlsson is one of the main contributors to *National Geographic* magazine. He travels to all sorts of dangerous locations. His wildlife photography is utterly spellbinding."

Alex graciously inclined his head.

"Your earlier work focused on nudes in nature," I gabbled on. "I'm such a fan!"

Alex seemed delighted. "I'm impressed!"

"I worked at the Red Fox art gallery in Soho for a long time—"

"Before she became a location scout," Margot put in to my extreme annoyance. "I'm Margot Chandler. Hello—and—"

"Evie Mead," I said.

"Are you a photographer, Evie?" Alex said.

"Just an amateur—"

"She's so modest," Margot declared. "She's very good. She'll be doing all our publicity stills for the movie."

I glared at Margot, but she just smirked.

"Ah!" He nodded. "A movie."

"*Scilly Pirates,*" said Patty, who was trying to keep a straight face. "But sadly, you're out of luck if you are expecting to photograph our birds. The season officially ended last month, although you may catch a few stragglers."

"I'm not here to photograph the birds," said Alex. "I'll be photographing the old lighthouse."

"A *lighthouse?*" I said.

Patty seemed as surprised as I was. "Our little old lighthouse on Windward Point? Really? Why? I can think of a million better lighthouses to photograph, and besides, it's off-limits. The footbridge was swept away last winter—Ah, here comes your plucky skipper, willing to risk life and limb to ferry you all across to Tregarrick. Ladies and gentleman, may I introduce the wonderful Cador Ferris."

The first thing I noticed about our skipper was that he was probably one of the most handsome men I had ever met, despite his scruffy attire of guernsey sweater, jeans and Timberland boots.

I guessed that Cador was probably a little older than us, but not by much. He had high cheekbones, astonishing blue eyes and white-blond hair that peeped beneath a knitted black beanie.

Cador gave us a lazy smile. Margot self-consciously flicked back her hair, a gesture I hadn't seen her do since she was a teenager. I felt dowdy in my Barbour and bucket hat and suddenly very old.

"Hel-lo, sailor," Margot whispered in my ear.

"Shut up," I whispered. "You're a married woman."

"No harm in window-shopping," Margot whispered back. "God. I hope he doesn't want to be an actor."

I had thought the exact same thing.

"No, Cador is not an aspiring actor," said Patty, who seemed to have ears like a bat.

Margot mumbled something incoherent.

"Not my thing," Cador said pleasantly. "Although I did watch *Titanic*."

"Cador has agreed to take you to Tregarrick because he lives there and needs to get home. If you play your cards right, he won't charge you either." Patty gestured to the Swede. "Cador, meet the legendary photographer Alex Karlsson, who is here to photograph Windward Point Lighthouse."

Cador laughed. "Whatever for?"

"And two location scouts all the way from Hollywood—"

"I'm the producer," Margot put in. "*She's* the location scout."

"Cador Ferris runs his own marine salvage operation here on St. Mary's. If anyone is an expert on shipwrecks it's him—a perfect consultant for, er . . . *Scilly Pirates*."

"Ferris?" Margot said suddenly. "Not Ferret?"

"Excuse me?" Cador said.

"Your last name is Ferris or Ferret?"

"Why?" he said mildly. "Who wants to know?"

"I was reading up on Tregarrick and its history," said Margot. "Are you any relation to Jay?"

"You must mean Jago," said Cador. "He's my father."

Margot shot me a triumphant look, then added, "What an unusual name."

"It's Cornish," said Cador. "Although now Scilly has its own flag . . . we're enjoying feeling independent."

"You'll find we Scillonians are fiercely patriotic," said Patty. "The flag is orange and blue—orange represents fire-glow sunsets and the blue represents the sea."

"A fog-free flag," said Margot. "Nice."

"The Ferris family have owned Tregarrick since the Dark Ages," Patty continued. "It's one of the few privately owned islands that does not belong to the Duchy of Cornwall."

"Yes, we know," said Margot. "We did our research."

"Cador is the son and heir to the Tregarrick kingdom, but just for tonight he is your captain, so be nice to him otherwise he'll throw you overboard. Right, Cador?" She checked her watch. "I have to go."

"Good luck," said Cador with a wink. "And be gentle with Henry."

"Don't worry. I left my handcuffs behind this time." Patty grinned. "And good luck talking to your dad tomorrow. Don't let him bully you." And with that she disappeared into the fog.

"Not your normal policewoman, is she?" Margot remarked.

"You can say that again," said Cador. "Are we ready?"

Suddenly Alex cried out and doubled over, clutching his stomach. His face was contorted with pain.

"Are you alright?" I asked anxiously.

"Fine. Fine." He nodded, gasping and fumbling in his pocket. "Will. Be. Okay." He withdrew a foil but dropped it.

Quickly I bent down and picked it up. My stomach lurched. It was Zomorph. I knew all about Zomorph—a morphine pain-killer and one that Robert had been prescribed after his surgery.

"How many?" I said.

Alex held up two fingers, so I popped out two pink, clear pills from the blister of six—30 mg each: 60 mg of morphine. Alex must have been a sick man.

"Water?" I asked as Margot and Cador looked on, their faces etched with concern.

Alex shook his head and knocked the capsules back dry— just as Nigel had done days before. "I'm fine. Fine. Really. Thank you." But he looked far from fine to me. His face was a sickly gray and his hands still clutched his stomach.

"Are you sure you want to go?" Cador asked.

Alex nodded and pointed to Margot's enormous suitcase—I had insisted that she leave its mate at home. "Although I'm afraid I won't be able to lift that for you."

"Just how long *are* you staying on Tregarrick?" Cador teased.

"Most of it is camera equipment," Margot lied cheerfully. "And a handful of scripts for weekend read."

"Margot is always reading scripts," I said.

Moments later we had boarded a state-of-the-art vessel called *Isadora* and headed slowly into the Tregarrick Straits. Cador had a full range of marine lighting—fog, search and spotlight—that carried us along in an eerie yellow cloud. Every so often I could hear a strange, haunting whistle.

"It's a whistle buoy," said Cador. "They're dotted all over these parts."

"I've never heard of them," I said.

"They've been around since medieval times," Alex said. "The whistle is caused by air trapped and compressed in the open-bottom chamber. The natural rise and fall of the water level caused by the wave action emits a whistle. Very clever invention."

Margot shivered. "It's creepy."

Isadora was decked out in all the latest salvage technology. I had never seen so many whip aerials, radar screens and all manner of expensive-looking gadgets.

"Wow—all this equipment is amazing," I heard Margot say. "So . . . you really do hunt for treasure?"

"It's a passion of mine," said Cador. "Over the past four or five hundred years, at least eighty vessels have gone down in these waters. The one I have been searching for since I was a kid is the *Isadora*."

"Hence the name of this boat," Margot said.

"Down below there is a map of the islands showing the co-ordinates of the wrecks that have already been located," said Cador. "Go and take a look. It might give you inspiration for your movie. What was the title again?"

"Scilly Pirates," said Margot.

"Ah yes." Cador grinned.

"Coming, Evie?"

"I can't," I said as the first wave of seasickness hit me. "Don't leave me up—" But Margot had already disappeared. I just prayed that Cador wouldn't engage me in conversation about anything to do with movies. I knew nothing about them at all. In fact, the last film I went to see was a James Bond movie with some friends from work a decade ago. Robert and I had preferred the theater, concerts and museums.

Cador pointed to one of the banquettes. "Sit down there and keep your eyes fixed on the horizon," he said. "I know all you can see is thick fog, but just keep your focus steady. You'll soon get your sea legs."

"Thank you," I said, and went and sat down.

Cador presented me with a rubber wristband. "It's an anti-nausea band," he said. "Should help. We'll be docking in Tregarrick in about twenty-five minutes. Usually it doesn't take this long."

"Don't you think you should watch where you are going?" I said nervously as Cador seemed to be looking at me more than he should.

"Don't worry." Cador grinned. "I have been navigating these straits since I first learned to sail when I was five years old."

Alex struck up an easy conversation with Cador as the boat chugged on slowly through the water. The painkillers must have kicked in.

My thoughts drifted to Robert again and that last terrible morning in our kitchen. He had refused to answer my questions and just sat there eating his cornflakes. I was so angry. I just had to get away and think. Would he still be alive if I hadn't walked out?

"Here—drink this." Alex broke into my thoughts and handed me a plastic cup. "It's Coca-Cola, courtesy of the captain and with his apologies that it's not rum."

I looked up into kind eyes. "Thank you."

Alex offered me his elbow. "Come and stand up front with us." So I did.

As Cador navigated solely by radar, he told stories of sunken ships that lay hundreds of feet beneath our own and of his boyhood dream to find the *Isadora*.

"You sound passionate about your quest," Alex said.

"I have always been fascinated by the secrets beneath the sea," said Cador. "I begged my father to allow me to go to uni to study marine engineering, but—it was not meant to be."

"It's never too late," said Alex.

"In this case, it is," Cador said ruefully.

There was an awkward silence. I remembered Patty's parting comment, wishing Cador luck with his father. It took on a new meaning.

"Tell me about the *Isadora*," I said.

"She was a Spanish galleon that sank off Tregarrick in 1659."

"Figureheads of galleons were supposed to embody the spirit of the ship," Alex put in. "They were believed to placate the gods of the sea."

"There's a collection of figureheads in the Galleon Garden in the hotel grounds," said Cador. "You should ask Father if he would allow you to film there."

"Thank you." I felt uncomfortable keeping the stupid lie going and resolved to tell Margot that the sooner we both came clean the better.

"And I assume the wreck still hasn't been found?" Alex asked.

"Nor was her gold, but I'm not giving up," said Cador. "In another time I would have been a pirate."

Alex and I laughed. I realized—by some miracle—I was feeling better.

"The *Isadora* figurehead was dredged up in 1980," Alex said. "Out beyond Windward Point."

Cador seemed delighted. "You know about that?"

"I spent a summer there as a teenager. In fact, I was there when they found her—"

"Then . . . you must know my mother, Tegan Chynoweth—as she was known back then?"

"Does she still live on Tregarrick?" Alex asked casually.

"Never lived anywhere else," said Cador. "She's kept captive in the castle, but she keeps herself busy with her painting."

"Does she—," Alex began, then seemed to change his mind. "No matter."

I regarded him with curiosity. Alex's photography— especially in the last twenty years—had always entailed great personal risk, whether it was shooting polar bears in Antarctica or lions in the Maasai Mara. I wondered what he was really doing here on Scilly.

"The forecast isn't good tomorrow," said Cador. "But I could take you out to Windward Point on Sunday so you can get a look at the lighthouse offshore from the Atlantic side. Ribs from the submerged hull of the five-hundred-ton *Athena* can sometimes be visible when the tide turns. I'd invite you, Evie, but I fear you would say no."

"You're right about that," I said. "But I don't feel too bad. This anti-nausea thing really works—even if it is psychosomatic."

"Thank you, Cador," said Alex. "Of course I will pay for your time."

"A pint of beer at the Salty Boatman will be enough. I'm easily bought." Cador smiled again and winked at me. In that moment, I saw something I hadn't seen in a very long time. A spark of attraction for *me*! I was embarrassed and immediately looked away.

"Well, I'm happy to buy you a pint at the Salty Boatman," said Alex.

"It's a deal. Ah, we're here," he said as a large light in a yellow halo of fog loomed out of nowhere. "Welcome to Tregarrick."

Chapter Five

"This is the perfect location for our movie," Margot said as she joined me on the stone quay. "The atmosphere is sinister and super-creepy."

"I thought *Scilly Pirates* was supposed to be a comedy," I said.

"It is. Think . . . *Wedding Crashers* crossed with *Scream* meets—"

"*Pirates of the Caribbean?*" Cador suggested as he stepped up alongside.

"Exactly!" said Margot.

"I assume this is for Walt Disney?" Alex asked.

"Not this time," Margot said quickly. "Gosh, when the guidebook said there weren't any streetlights, they weren't exaggerating."

"There are forty-seven streetlights on St. Mary's," said Cador. "But none here and that's how we like it."

"Oh, you will want this back," I said, pointing to my anti-nausea wristband.

"Keep it," he said. "Souvenir. Just give me a moment and we'll go to the pub together." Cador turned his attention back to securing the *Isadora*.

"I think you have an admirer," Margot said in a low voice. "Did you tell him you are a widow?"

"No," I said. "But I will."

"Don't do that yet," Margot said. "It might blow our cover."

"We're going to get found out, Margot," I said. "Everyone knows everyone around here. I wish I'd never come."

Margot's face fell. "I'm sorry," she said, serious for once. "I just thought it would distract you. Maybe even make you laugh. I don't know what to do. You're so unhappy I . . . I just don't know what to do," she said again.

I couldn't help but relent a little. "It's okay," I said. "I know that you mean well."

"I'm just rubbish at the whole sympathy thing. I always have been."

"I know."

She reached out and patted my shoulder. It was awkward. Public displays of affection had never been her strong point. "Don't you feel as if we have landed on one of the kingdoms in *Game of Thrones*?" she said, abruptly changing the subject.

Margot's iPhone rang. She glanced down and I noticed her jaw harden. She slipped the mobile into her pocket.

"Aren't you going to answer that?" I said, adding, "It could be Johnny Depp!"

"It's Brian, actually," said Margot. "I'll call him when we get to the hotel."

But her iPhone rang again—and again.

"I thought I turned it off," Margot mumbled.

"It must be important for Brian to keep trying to reach you. What's the time in Los Angeles? Ten in the morning?"

Margot ignored me and called out, "Excuse me, Cador? Can you show us how far away the Tregarrick Rock hotel is?"

Cador pointed behind us into the murky darkness. "Somewhere over there."

"Is it very far to walk?" said Margot.

Cador looked amused. "You can't stay there."

"Why not? We've got a reservation," said Margot.

"I don't think so." Cador grinned. "The hotel closes for redecorating in November."

"Yes, so we've been told," Margot said impatiently. "But I spoke to the front desk and made a reservation. We are expected this evening."

"Do you remember the name of the person you spoke to?" he asked.

"Lily Travis," said Margot. "She sounded a bit deaf."

Cador grinned again. "That's because Lily always answers on speakerphone."

"So? Do we have a reservation or don't we?" Margot demanded.

"Last October Lily booked in sixty-five Japanese tourists and there are only fifteen bedrooms in the entire hotel," Cador went on. "My father was not a happy man."

"Well, as you said, it's out of season so I doubt there will be sixty-five Japanese tourists fighting for a bed," Margot declared. "We'll take our chances."

"Not tonight you won't," said Cador. Seeing our confusion, he added, "You won't be able to get there. It's tidal."

"But . . . the hotel is on Tregarrick," I protested. "Isn't that why it's called the Tregarrick Rock hotel?"

"Well . . . the name *Rock* should give you a clue." Cador didn't bother to hide his amusement. "The hotel is on its own little island and only accessible at low tide on foot across the causeway or by sea tractor. There is William's Quay—a deep-water quay—but it's on the other side of the Rock that's rarely used now. It's too difficult to make the climb up the side of the cliff. It used to be used for trade ships stopping on their way to America."

"Evie!" Margot scolded. "As my location scout, how on earth could you have made such a mistake?"

I refused to comment.

"The sea tractor will run tomorrow," said Cador. "Unfortunately you've picked a bad weekend. It's a neap tide, which means the windows to get on and off the Rock are smaller than usual since the tide doesn't go out as far."

"How infuriating!" Margot exclaimed. "How on earth can you run a hotel business?"

"Your best bet is to stay at the Salty Boatman with Alex, here," said Cador. "Care to join us for a drink this evening?"

Margot muttered something unprintable. "I suppose we don't have a choice," she said crossly. "Where is this Salty Boatman?"

"Right behind you."

Moments later the four of us entered the bar. There was only one other person in there.

"Cor! Nice!" came a deafening screech from the corner, where a grizzled seafaring man in a threadbare jacket, clerical shirt and dog collar sat in a Windsor chair nursing a brandy balloon. The bird was sitting on his shoulder.

"Good grief," Margot said, wide-eyed. "Is that a *parrot*?"

"It's an *Ara ararauna*—a blue-and-gold macaw," I said.

"Another entity that's greedy with a certain letter of the alphabet," she grumbled. "And by the looks of things, his companion is a member of the clergy."

"That's right. Vicar Bill and Roger the macaw," said Cador. "We call the vicar 'Doctor Dolittle' because he can talk to the animals."

"Seriously?" I said.

"Seriously," Cador agreed. "I could put in a good word if you like—assuming you'll need a parrot in *Scilly Pirates*."

"But sadly, Roger is a macaw," said Margot. "Thanks anyway."

The old man raised his glass in a toast. We waved back. The macaw called out, "Cor! Nice!" again.

The pub was quaint but at the same time disappointingly commercial. It embodied everything and anything nautical and smacking of pirates, including an abundance of Jolly Roger flags. Nooks and crannies were staged with anchors, ship's lanterns, life belts and empty lobster pots. Rope netting was draped around the cornices. Shells and ship paraphernalia dangled from wooden ceiling beams overhead. Black-and-white photographs of galleons and other ships from a range of different centuries covered the walls. It was obviously a tourist attraction.

It was only when I went to freshen up and headed for the toilets that I spotted a sign for an art exhibition by local artist Tegan Ferris hanging in the Snug—a small anteroom off the narrow passageway.

Intrigued, I stepped inside to find a series of haunting watercolors of a ruined stone watchtower perched on the bluff of a cliff, with a lighthouse beyond offshore. The pair was painted with a variety of backdrops—at sunrise and at sunset, in silhouette under a full moon and starry sky and under a burning-hot sun. They were painted on a misty morning and a stormy afternoon. I really liked them and hoped I would have a chance to talk to Cador's mother about her work. A sign said her paintings were available for purchase online from her website and also at the Tregarrick Rock hotel.

Upon returning to the bar, I found Margot engaged in a tense conversation with a young woman in her mid-twenties behind the bar. She was wearing black skinny jeans and a black sweater with a plunging V-neckline. Her long straight auburn hair was swept into a messy updo. A row of silver studs ran down one ear rim.

Margot waved me over. "This is Vanessa," she said to me in a weary tone. "Vanessa informs me that there is just one room available so we will have to share, and"—she paused dramatically—"there is no bathroom en suite."

"The bathroom is only at the end of the hall," said Vanessa, who seemed nervous and preoccupied. Her eyes kept sliding over to the booth where Cador and Alex were engaged in animated conversation.

"I'm afraid that's unacceptable," said Margot.

"The foreign gentleman already booked the en suite, you see, and we're out of season and short-staffed—"

"It's not a problem," I said, and tried to put the girl at ease with a warm smile.

Margot slapped her American Express card down on the counter. "Fine."

"Sorry. Our machine isn't working," said Vanessa. "But we don't take Amex anyway."

"I have cash." I retrieved my purse from my handbag.

"It's sixty pounds including breakfast."

As I gave Vanessa the money, I couldn't help noticing her hands. The exterior of her two index fingers appeared to be stained with black ink until I realized they were tattoos with actual words.

"We'll be ordering food," Margot said. "I'm lactose and gluten intolerant and I have a potential nut allergy. I'm still eliminating certain nuts, but I don't want to risk it."

"I didn't know that, Margot," I said. "Robert had a severe nut allergy to peanuts. He always carried an EpiPen in his pocket. You should keep one in your handbag just in case."

"Please make sure you tell the chef, Vanessa," said Margot.

Vanessa handed her a menu from a stack tucked between a wooden beam and a pirate Toby Jug on the bar. "This is all we have tonight."

Margot skimmed the list. "I can only eat salad on this."

Cador joined us at the bar. "Are you ordering food?"

"Trying to," said Margot.

Vanessa turned an ugly shade of red that unfortunately clashed with her auburn hair. I felt sorry for her. She looked at Cador with rapt adoration. He acknowledged her presence with a grunt.

"We can make you whatever you want." A burly, attractive man in his early fifties slipped beside Vanessa and put his arm around her shoulders. With hair cut short, he looked ex-military. "Evening, Cador."

"You'll have the steak and ale pie, of course," Vanessa said to Cador.

"Make it two. One for my new friend over there." Cador pointed to Alex, who raised a hand in greeting. "And whatever these ladies want. Put it on my tab, Dennis." Cador returned to the booth.

Vanessa's jaw dropped. Her complexion deepened. "You're all *together*?" It was then that she noticed the anti-nausea band on my wrist. "Did Cador give you that?"

"Yes," I said. "I suffer from seasickness."

"When?" Vanessa demanded. "When did he give you that?"

"Off you go, luv." Dennis gently turned Vanessa to face the door at the end of the bar that presumably led to the kitchen. He whispered something in her ear and she turned around to give me a look of such dislike that I was completely taken aback.

Margot noticed because she mouthed *What's her problem?*

"Dennis Simmonds," said the man, and thrust his hand across the counter for each of us to shake. "I'll take your bags to your room. By the time you've settled in, dinner will be served."

"Where is everyone?" I said. "It's a Friday night."

"The fog tends to keep people at home," said Dennis.

"Is there Wi-Fi in the room?" Margot demanded.

"Only in the Snug, I'm afraid. Password is 'Salty.' Follow me."

So we did.

Dennis left us to unpack.

The room was charming but basic—and damp, with just one storage heater. Decorated in Laura Ashley wallpaper and matching curtains, it contained two single beds, a pine chest of drawers and a freestanding wardrobe that smelled of mothballs. An old marble washstand stood against one wall with an antique bowl and pitcher painted with violet and pink flowers.

I watched my sister carefully unpack her clothes. She had placed tissue paper in between each garment. None of them seemed suitable for a weekend trip to the Isles of Scilly. There were designer shoes, cute little tops paired with fitted jackets—Californian attire, nothing for the British winter.

"You know, we're only at the Salty Boatman for one night," I pointed out.

"I always unpack immediately," said Margot. "It helps me feel grounded. Do you know that Vivien Leigh used to take her favorite pictures when she and Larry—that's Laurence Olivier—were on tour? She'd hang them up in her hotel room."

"I'm glad you decided against that," I said.

"I left in a hurry, otherwise I might have." She regarded the empty wardrobe. "Do you mind if I hog all four of the wire hangers?"

"Be my guest." I flung myself onto the bed, noting that the mattress had definitely seen better days but at least the pink candlewick bedspread was clean. "What's all this gluten-free thing?"

"I went to see a nutritionist," said Margot. "You should go and see a nutritionist. It might take care of your constipation."

"I do not get constipated," I protested.

"You did when we went camping. Remember?"

"Margot, I was twelve," I said. "It was with the Girl Guides and the food was inedible."

She gave a mischievous grin. "You should have eaten the baked beans."

"I don't like baked beans."

Margot's iPhone vibrated on the nightstand. I spied the caller I.D. Brian.

"He keeps calling you," I said.

She snatched it up and turned the phone off with an expression I had never seen before. "I can't talk to him at the moment. I'm busy."

"Is everything okay between you and the lovely Brian?"

"Of course," said Margot. "Why?"

"It's just that . . . speaking of baked beans . . . in the past if the saintly Brian so much as farted you would move heaven and earth to find out why."

"That was in the early days," said Margot. "You know, when people are in love and things like dainty farts are endearing."

"He's texted and tried to call you at least three times in the last forty-five minutes—and yes, I'm counting," I said. "Come on, Margie. Talk to me."

"There is nothing wrong," Margot said brightly. "Being slightly bitchy here, I worked out what the tattoo said on Vanessa's fingers."

"When?"

"You were in the restroom and she was making me fill in the registration form—you'll never guess."

"I probably won't."

"It said *Dave and I Until We Die*."

"You're kidding."

"Nope. On one finger it said *Dave and I* and on the other *Until We Die*."

"That throws my theory out the window," I said. "I thought she had a thing for Cador, but hey, nice attempt to change the subject. But I'll wait. I'm patient. You'll tell me what's really going on between you and Brian eventually."

"Oh, for heaven's sake!" Margot snapped. "Why do you keep asking me? Anyway, it's none of your business."

I was stung. "You're right. It's not."

"Sorry," said Margot. "I know you care, but honestly, I'm fine."

As I watched Margot carefully hang and put her clothes away, I wondered if I had changed as much as she had.

When she moved to California, we hardly saw each other anymore. When Mum and Dad died, we just drifted apart. Both parents were only children, and other than one or two distant cousins, Margot was all the family I had.

My mobile rang. Cherie flashed up on the caller I.D. "You're working late," I said.

"Twenty-four seven. I'm just confirming tomorrow night's dinner with Nigel."

"*Dinner?*" I said. "Nigel didn't mention anything about dinner. I thought he was in Paris."

"Um. Well. That's my fault because I forgot to tell you. He flies back tomorrow. You can still make it though, can't you?" The anxiety in her voice was palpable.

"Oh Cherie," I said. "I'm so sorry. We've just got to Tregarrick."

"*Tregarrick*. You're on *Tregarrick*?!" Cherie sounded surprised. "Does Nigel know?"

"It was spur of the moment," I said. "But please thank him for the invitation. We'll be back on Monday. Have a lovely weekend."

As I disconnected the line Margot said, "She really is hopeless isn't she."

We returned to the bar and spent the rest of the evening listening to Cador and Alex try to outdo each other with their tales of dangerous adventures. It was fun, and my sister sparkled and made us all laugh with her anecdotes from Hollywood. It felt like old times when we both lived in London and used to meet up after work for drinks.

We did not see Vanessa again.

On our way to bed, Dennis stopped us in the hallway. "Just to let you know, the sea tractor will leave at nine-thirty sharp tomorrow morning because of the tide."

"Cador mentioned it was a neap tide or something," I said.

"Do *not* be late unless you want to swim," said Dennis.

"We won't," I promised.

Chapter Six

"Margot, we're going to be late." I was anxious. It was already nine twenty-five and Margot was nowhere near ready. "I told you not to bother to unpack."

"I'd forgotten what a nag you can be," said Margot. "I'll be three seconds."

Three seconds?

Her bed still had all her clothes laid out, and as she picked up each garment, she arranged it carefully onto smoothed-out tissue paper and then seemed to spend forever folding it just so. "There is a knack to packing, you know."

I went to the window and gazed out at the beautiful cobalt-blue sky.

Our room had a spectacular view that looked out to Tregarrick Rock in the distance, perched high on a bluff at the end of the long sandy causeway. With the tide out it reminded me of the Yellow Brick Road that led to the Wizard of Oz's castle.

Down below was what I guessed had to be the sea tractor.

It was a peculiar contraption on a tractor-like chassis that was essentially an elevated platform with a canopy painted in red and blue. It looked as though it had been designed to ferry passengers across shallow water.

"You'd better hurry up," I said.

"You go on down," said Margot. "I'm right behind you. Tell them to wait. I mean, what's the hurry?"

"For a start, the tide is coming in."

Margot peeped out of the window. "It's hours before the waters meet. I don't think Christian Bale would have a problem with it."

"What are you talking about?"

"Parting the Red Sea?" Margot rolled her eyes. "Christian Bale played Moses in Ridley Scott's movie *Exodus: Gods and Kings.*"

"Well . . . it's just rude to keep people waiting." I knew I sounded self-righteous, but Margot was notorious for being late and simply didn't care what people thought. So I left her to it.

As I stepped outside the Salty Boatman, Dennis hurried over. He was carrying a small leather holdall bag and a sheaf of newspapers and magazines. He seemed agitated. "Where's your friend?"

"She'll be here any minute."

Dennis checked his watch. "You'd better get on board. We'll have to go without her if she's not here in the next five minutes," he said. "We're already running late."

"She's coming," I insisted. "Does the tide come in that fast?"

"It's not just about the tide," Dennis exclaimed. Not so

friendly this morning, I thought. "Last night I specifically told you that you must not be late."

I was taken aback. I hadn't been scolded since I was a teenager. "What about Alex Karlsson? He's not here yet either."

"I have no idea of Mr. Karlsson's plans," said Dennis. "Can you call her mobile?"

I nodded and dialed. Margot answered on the fourth ring.

"It's so weird," she said cheerfully. "I am packing the exact same things as I unpacked last night, but my case just won't shut. I've got to rearrange it—"

"Margot, please—"

"Do you think that chap Dennis will come and get my suitcase in, say . . . fifteen minutes?"

I could actually feel Dennis's anxiety coming off him in waves as he hovered over me.

"We're leaving, Margot," I said firmly. "The sea tractor will just have to come back and get you in—"

"Six hours," said Dennis.

"Six hours?" Margot shrieked. "Wait! I'm on my way."

"She's ready," I said. "Would you go and help her with her suitcase?"

Dennis clenched his jaw in annoyance. He dropped his holdall bag onto the ground and thrust the newspapers into my hands before heading back inside the Salty Boatman.

The quay was much smaller than I'd realized when we disembarked last night in thick fog. Whitewashed stone cottages with navy-blue painted doors and trim ranged around a charming crescent that hugged the water. A cobbled path fronted by a stone wall followed the boundary line and disappeared around a gentle curve framed with subtropical plants and palm trees.

Cador emerged from a cottage called Watchers and seeing me called out a cheerful good morning. He headed over.

"You're still here? Where's Dennis?" Tapping his watch, he added, "Father's not going to be pleased."

The next thing I knew was that Vanessa seemed to have materialized from thin air. She was carrying a black canvas rucksack. "Hello, Cador," she said shyly.

Cador gave her a nod, but it was cold. Vanessa's face fell. "Your friend's late," she said to me. "She's going to get everyone into trouble."

To my surprise, Cador pulled me aside. "Look, if you want me to show you around Tregarrick and the Rock or have any questions, I'm your man."

"Can I come?" Vanessa said over my shoulder. "You promised to show me around ages ago."

"Of course you can," I said.

"No." A flicker of irritation crossed Cador's handsome features. "Sorry, this is business. Evie is scouting for movie locations."

Vanessa pouted but stood her ground. Margot must have been wrong about Vanessa's tattoos. She was hopelessly infatuated with Cador, who was clearly not interested.

"We're here!" came a shout.

Margot gave a wave as Dennis broke into an ungainly trot, carrying Margot's suitcase aloft and with apparent ease. If he hadn't looked so furious, it would have been funny, particularly as Margot was strolling along behind him as if she had all the time in the world.

Vanessa darted to the sea tractor and climbed the steps onto the platform, to be greeted by Vicar Bill and his macaw, which called out, "Cor! Nice!"

Moments later the contraption lurched forward, with Vicar Bill at the helm and Vanessa and Dennis joining him up front. We descended the ramp in a series of violent jolts. I found myself clinging to the underside of the bench, and yet we couldn't have been traveling at more than two miles per hour!

"Bit like riding a camel," said Margot.

Margot spotted the newspapers that Dennis had put in a wooden cubbyhole. She got up and sifted through them—I saw a *Daily Mail,* the *Financial Times* and *The Daily Telegraph.* There was also *Hello!* magazine and *The Week.* She pulled out *The Daily Telegraph.*

"I love English newspapers." Margot frowned. "How odd. I feel like . . . wait—this is yesterday's." She looked through the others. "Dennis!" she called out. "Don't you have any of today's papers?"

Dennis leapt up as if someone had lit a fire under his rear. "Those are not for you!" he exclaimed. "They are only for Mr. Jago and Lily."

"That's okay." Margot shrugged. "I've already read them."

"We can only get yesterday's news today," Dennis said. "I'll have that, please."

As Margot handed back *The Daily Telegraph,* a sudden gust of wind caught the broadsheet and sent it spinning over the side and into the water.

"Oh my God!" Dennis sounded horrified. Vanessa jumped up and wrenched a boat hook from its clips to try to fish the sodden pulp out of the water, but to no avail. It just floated away.

"Oh boy, Mr. Jago is going to be mad," said Vanessa with what sounded like glee.

"It's a newspaper!" Margot declared. "And yesterday's newspaper at that."

"Well . . . I'm not telling him," I heard Vanessa say to Dennis.

Margot seemed unperturbed by the trouble she had caused, but I was beginning to wonder exactly what this Mr. Jago Ferris was like. He sounded a bit of a tyrant.

"God. It's quicker to walk." Margot peered over the edge as the giant tractor wheels carved a wide track through the shallow water. "It can't be more than six inches deep."

I pointed to her Louboutin ankle boots. "But not in five-hundred-pound shoes."

I then had a brilliant idea.

"Margot," I whispered, "no one knows about me being a location scout at the hotel. You're a producer so it doesn't matter, but I'd rather be honest."

"Weren't you enjoying the charade?" she said.

"Not really."

We didn't speak again as the sea tractor lumbered along the causeway. Margot's iPhone rang yet again, but she turned it off.

"Sales call," she said brightly, which I knew had to be a lie. The iPhone was her American phone, and I knew she didn't have an English mobile. It had to be the middle of the night in Los Angeles, but it was obvious that for whatever reason Margot did not want to talk about it.

"I must say, sis," Margot said eventually, "if Tregarrick Rock does end up belonging to you, we'd need to scrap this mode of transportation. Put in a helipad or something."

"I don't mind it," I said. "It lends an air of novelty, and besides, if the hotel is too easy to get to, it wouldn't be so exclusive."

"That's what I mean. Put in a helipad. It's the only way to attract high-paying clientele. Fly them in and fly them out. A bit like Richard Branson does on Necker."

"I thought Necker was destroyed in a hurricane."

"Nope, he rebuilt it. It runs at around thirty thousand dollars a week and includes all meals."

"All meals? Wow. That sounds like a bargain." I laughed. "You are delusional, Margot. No one is going to pay thirty thousand dollars or whatever the equivalent is to come here."

"Think what you like, but I can see events like . . . mindfulness retreats working very well. I checked and there are no reviews on TripAdvisor. No social media presence."

"Maybe that's the appeal," I said. "Some people like to return to a place that doesn't change. Mum and Dad's guesthouse always had repeat guests."

"Well, they catered to that kind of clientele," said Margot. "I can tell you right now that I can't imagine someone like Angelina Jolie sitting up here on this hay wagon trundling along in a puddle." Margot was like a dog with a bone when she had an idea. "The Americans won't go for it."

"We're not catering to the Americans," said Dennis, making us both jump. He had slid into the bench seat behind ours. "People come to Tregarrick Rock to escape from reality. They like the tranquility and the peace. It's a place to regroup and heal."

"It still could do with a helipad," Margot persisted.

"I heard that you're location scouts for Walt Disney," said Dennis.

"Not Walt Disney," Margot said quickly. "Another big studio whose name I can't reveal at the moment."

"Who told you it was Walt Disney?" I said.

"There are no secrets on Scilly," said Dennis. "What else is there to do on this tiny island except talk about other people?"

"Look for treasure," I said lightly.

"And by the way, a word of advice," said Dennis. "When you talk to Mr. Jago about filming, I shouldn't make any comments about putting in a helipad."

Margot laughed. "You are funny! We were just talking nonsense, weren't we, Evie?"

"We sure were."

"The Ferris family have lived on Tregarrick for centuries," Dennis went on. "They're very private. It's bad enough having hordes of avid bird-watchers descending in the summer and roaming all over the island."

"Tourism is the main source of income, isn't it?" said Margot. "You can't have it both ways."

If Dennis was offended by Margot's bluntness, he didn't show it.

"Are you local?" said Margot.

"A Scillonian? Sadly, no," Dennis said. "That honor takes about forty years. I've been here since 2007 and would never want to live anywhere else."

"Does Mr. Ferris live at the hotel?" I said.

"Ninety-nine percent of the time, yes," he said. "They have a suite of rooms in one of the wings. There has been a Ferris living on Tregarrick since the fifteenth century."

"So Cador will follow in his father's footsteps," said Margot.

"Never!" Vanessa declared as she joined Dennis. She had obviously been eavesdropping. "He'd rather die than be stuck here for the rest of his life."

"Vanessa! Quiet," said Dennis.

"Well, it's true," she said defiantly. "Cador wants to look for shipwrecks."

And even though I had only just met Cador, I thought she had a point.

"Cador won't have a choice," Dennis said grimly. "Excuse me." He got up and gestured for Vanessa to follow him to the rear of the sea tractor. When they sat down, he spoke to her in a low voice. Vanessa shifted along to the end of the bench, folded her arms and stared out at the water.

"Oh my Lord," Margot said suddenly. "Look! What a dump."

She was right. As we came to the end of the causeway, we were finally able to see some of the hotel on the bluff above.

At first glance, the building was in typical Art Deco style, with an assorted array of opal-green rooftops, turrets and huge windows. There was a lot of banded glass.

The exterior that had appeared white and sparkling from afar was mottled with orange discoloration and carried an air of weary neglect.

"I'm sure it's lovely inside," I said hopefully.

The sea tractor trundled into the shadow of the bluff. Vicar Bill cut the engine and we juddered to a stop on the beach.

"Where the hell is my newspaper!" a voice bellowed from a megaphone above us. "You're damn late!"

Chapter Seven

"Good grief! Who on earth is that?" Margot remarked as Dennis and Vanessa all but leapt off the sea tractor and headed for a steep flight of steps that wound up the cliff face.

"That would be Mr. Jago," said Vicar Bill. "He's a stickler for punctuality."

Margot seemed incredulous. "For yesterday's newspapers?"

She regarded her heavy suitcase with dismay. "Why would Dennis race off like that? He could have helped."

Vicar Bill sank down onto a bench and fumbled in his top pocket. He took out a plastic bag of nuts and seeds for Roger. Margot gave Vicar Bill a sweet smile. "Do you think you could help us with our luggage?"

"Bad back," he said. "Did you say you thought you had a reservation?"

Margot rolled her eyes. "Yes. Why?"

"Mr. Jago likes to keep November free for doing a bit of painting and whatnot," Vicar Bill said. "Did you speak to Lily?"

"Yes," said Margot.

"She doesn't work there."

"We gathered that," I said.

"But we're here now and we're staying," Margot declared.

Vicar Bill shrugged. "On your own head be it."

Somehow Margot and I managed to off-load her huge suit-case and manhandle it to the bottom of the steps. It looked a very long way up to the hotel.

Margot seemed puzzled. "Where's the elevator?"

"I hate to say this, but it looks like there isn't one." I looked longingly over to Vicar Bill, who was sitting on the top step of the sea tractor feeding his macaw. "Shall we just go home while we can?"

"Seriously? Of course we're not going home," Margot said stubbornly. "We're girls on tour, remember? Besides, don't you want to see your inheritance? We're here and we're going to stay here and have a lovely weekend."

"Admit this is a mistake and—"

"I don't admit my mistakes, Evie, you should know that by now. Come along. Let's leave our stuff here and find a bellboy."

"Now I know what it's like to be marooned on an island," I said grimly.

And yet as we made the climb up the granite steps, I felt my mood unexpectedly lighten. Bright and dense aeoniums grew out of the wall crevices, and huge banks of daisies in full flower lined the way. I spied lofty California pines and holm oaks tough enough to withstand the saltwater air and wind. What struck me the most was the intense evergreen-ness of the place, even in winter.

As we forged ahead, the sound of the sea became distant and muffled and I began to feel a strange sense of peace.

At the top we passed between two majestic Art Deco cast-iron urns on pedestals and stepped onto a vast flagstone terrace lined with more cast-iron urns. The urns stood empty now, but it was easy to imagine just how stunning the terrace would be awash with flowers in the spring and summer months.

Half a dozen herringbone brick pathways bordered by neatly clipped box hedges ran away from the terrace only to disappear around curious rock formations or vanish into thick walls of evergreen shrubs.

To the far right stood a pergola that was covered in wisteria—a riot of purple blooms in the spring but for now used to store garden furniture that was partially hidden under a tarpaulin that had come loose.

And there, just beyond, stood the main entrance—a pair of green-paned floor-to-ceiling glass doors flanked by Corinthian columns and potted palm trees.

Even though the bronze outdoor lighting was dull and tarnished, and paint flaked from the window frames, cornices and lintels, there was a shabby beauty to the Tregarrick Rock hotel that I found enchanting. I liked it.

For a brief, crazy moment, I had this insane thought that if this hotel did turn out to be mine after all, I could be happy here. But just several minutes later that romantic thought came to an abrupt halt.

"Holy cow," whispered Margot. "My least favorite era."

The interior of the hotel couldn't have been further from Art Deco if it had tried. It was a tribute to the 1970s in every way imaginable. In the lobby and reception area stretched a brown shag pile carpet as far as the eye could see. Opposite the spectacular floor-to-ceiling windows that looked out onto another terrace, the walls were papered in geometric browns, oranges and creams. It seemed that only the fixtures and light fittings that remained were Art Deco.

It was an overall jarring mismatch of eras—as if someone had come along forty-plus years ago and decided to modernize the place and then got bored halfway through.

Margot pointed to an alcove fronted by a wooden counter where an old black dial telephone sat alongside a reception service bell and a pretty Art Deco bronze lady lamp.

On the back wall was a pigeonhole key cabinet. The space behind held two desks—one with an old typewriter and the other with a computer that had definitely seen better days.

"Thank God. It looks like they have Wi-Fi," said Margot.

I hit the service bell.

To my surprise, Dennis appeared. He had changed into a formal black jacket and donned a jaunty red polka-dot bow tie.

"But—what are you doing here?" I said.

Dennis grinned. "You'll find everyone on Tregarrick has at least two jobs. I am the hotel manager here as well as helping out at the Salty Boatman whenever needed. That's why we had to dash off and leave you down at the jetty."

"Oh, so you mean Vanessa works here too?" I said.

"That's right. She'll be out in a moment."

"And Vicar Bill?" Margot said.

"Skippers the sea tractor and tends to his flock at St. Andrew's."

"I suppose you're now going to tell us that the policewoman is also the chambermaid," Margot joked.

"No," Dennis said gravely. "She's a bit too busy for that." He reached down and retrieved a leather-bound reservation book and started flipping through it. "I'm afraid I don't see that you made any reservation. I thought as much."

"Yes. We know all about the redecorating," Margot said, winking at me. "But we did. Or at least we tried to make one."

"I don't think we will be able to accommodate you this time," said Dennis, "but I do hope you can stay for lunch." He checked his watch. "Or morning coffee. The tide is a bit dodgy today, so the window to get back to Tregarrick on the sea tractor is pretty small. The causeway will be closed in about an hour and a half."

Margot's jaw dropped. "You *are* joking, aren't you?"

"No." Dennis pointed to a small black chalkboard.

TODAY'S TIDE
LOW TIDE 8:16 A.M.
HIGH TIDE 4:24 P.M.

"Wait a minute," I said. "Cador knows we made a reservation."

Dennis frowned. "Oh, I see. That's different—"

"Dennis . . . *do* let them stay," came a female voice.

We turned to see an elderly woman step through an archway marked RESIDENTS' LOUNGE and head slowly toward us using a crook-handled chestnut walking cane. "Hello! Hello! Welcome, welcome. I'm Lily Travis." Tucked under her arm was a large leather scrapbook.

I guessed she had to be in her early eighties. Bright, intelligent eyes sparkled behind enormous tortoiseshell-framed glasses. She wore a smart dark maroon wool suit, thick tights, sturdy lace-up shoes and a slash of crimson lipstick. Her iron-gray hair fell in tight curls to her jawline. She was a handsome woman.

"Lily, you know you're not supposed to answer the phone," Dennis scolded. "It makes things very embarrassing for us here. You know we don't take reservations in November."

Lily ignored him. "And what are you two beautiful young ladies doing here in November?"

"They're from Hollywood," said Dennis. "They are going to shoot a film here."

"It's not confirmed," Margot said quickly. "We're just looking."

"All the more reason for you to stay here," said Lily. "I'll talk to Mr. Jago—if you don't have the courage, Dennis."

Dennis's jaw hardened at the insult. "*I* shall talk to Mr. Jago. Thank you, Lily. Excuse me a moment." He disappeared through a side door.

"I love the pictures," Lily said wistfully. "Clark Gable. Jimmy Stewart. Now *they* were real film stars. Not like the celebrity types we have these days. What do you think about Kim Kardashian?"

Margot caught my eye and seemed amused. I was, too.

"Oh yes, I like to keep up with who is who," Lily went on.

"Was the *Hello!* magazine for you?" I had noticed Kim Kardashian on the front cover.

"I love *Hello!* magazine. It's called *Hola!* in Spain." She thought for a moment. "Do you watch *Love Island*?"

"Er. No," said Margot. "What's that?"

"Young girls with plastic surgery are all closeted in a house in Majorca and are supposed to fall in love," Lily went on. "I think you can catch up on Netflix."

"You're amazing," I said, and meant it.

"The secret of staying young is keeping up with the young." Lily turned her attention to Margot. "What do the Americans think of Meghan Markle? Of course I was around when Wallis Simpson stole poor David. Disastrous. How things have changed. Poor Margaret. That would be Princess Margaret. She was such an unhappy woman, and just think, if she had been born twenty years later, she could have had her man. Not that Peter Townsend was right for her. I really enjoyed *The Crown*. Did you see it? That's on Netflix too."

"Excuse me, I have to send a text," Margot said rudely, and retreated behind a potted palm, leaving me with Lily.

"No, I didn't see *The Crown*, but tell me . . . what's in your scrapbook?" I asked politely.

"Secrets," said Lily with a conspiratorial wink. "Lots of secrets."

"Thank you, Lily." Dennis reappeared. "I'll see to our guests. I'm happy to say that we will be able to accommodate you this weekend after all, but unfortunately you will have to share a room."

"We're used to that," I said.

He slid a registration form across the counter, asking for the usual personal information. I noted he'd written today's date and the exact time we were checking in—"10:36 a.m."

"And I appreciate the early check-in," I said. "Thank you."

I glanced over at Margot, who was still engrossed in texting, unsure what to do. "I'll check with Margot which office address she wants to use. I assume you don't take American Express?" I handed him my Visa card. "Just use that, please."

I could sense Lily watching me and wondered if she would ever guess that Margot and I were sisters. Even though we were dressed so differently—Margot in designer black leggings with a camel-colored cashmere tunic and I in my usual jeans and Barbour jacket—we both had the same button nose and almond-shaped eyes.

Dennis handed me two brass keys. They were embossed with the name of our room. "As you see, you'll be in the Margery Allingham—all our rooms are named after novelists from the Golden Age of mystery and detective fiction. Back in the twenties and thirties this hotel was very popular as a writers' retreat. Mr. Jago's grandmother was an avid reader and used to hold salons here."

"It sounds wonderful," I said.

"In the Residents' Lounge we have an excellent collection of first-edition novels from those writers who have passed through our doors," Dennis went on. "I hope you make time to take a look."

"I will," I said, and I meant it.

"If you go out, please leave the keys here at reception. They're original to the hotel—Oh, and Mr. Jago does insist on formal attire for dinner." He regarded mine. "No jeans."

Lily noticed my key. "The Margery Allingham is next to me. I'm in the Agatha Christie suite. Good. Vanessa will knock on your door at four and you will come for tea in my rooms—Where is that naughty girl? *Vanessa!*" she called out. *"VANESSA!"*

Vanessa appeared behind the counter. I hardly recognized her. Dressed in a long-sleeved, high-necked black dress, she wore no makeup or jewelry and had scraped her hair back into a severe knot at the nape of her neck.

"Yes, Mrs. Travis?" she said demurely.

"Tea for three at four. And bake a Victoria sponge. Strawberry jam, not raspberry." She regarded Vanessa with impatience. "And you're not wearing the white gloves I gave you. No one wants to see those ugly tattoos."

Vanessa reddened and quickly slipped her hands under her armpits. Lily's change of tone took me aback.

"Why don't you go and make a pot of coffee, Vanessa," Dennis said smoothly. "I'm sure our guests would appreciate some refreshments after their exhausting trip across the causeway."

I wasn't sure if he was being sarcastic.

Vanessa scuttled away.

"Dennis, you really need to talk to her about those unsightly tattoos," Lily scolded. "And then she wonders why Cador isn't interested when she has another man's name inked on—"

"Yes, thank you, Lily," Dennis cut in just as Margot joined us, brandishing her phone.

"Sorry. I was texting our production designer. She's in Europe at the moment and we've been trying to connect all week."

"Hollywood," gushed Lily. "How absolutely thrilling!"

Once again I regarded my sister with concern. Concealer had failed to camouflage the dark circles under her eyes. I knew her job was stressful, but this was ridiculous. I'd heard her leave our room at the Salty Boatman in the middle of the night to call L.A. at least twice.

"Where is my *Daily Telegraph*?" came a commanding voice.

Dennis stiffened and stood to attention. "Mr. Jago," he exclaimed. "I can explain everything."

Chapter Eight

A tall, arresting figure strode toward us.

Lily promptly turned around, muttering something about getting back to her knitting, and hobbled away.

Dressed in a green tweed jacket and brown corduroys, Jago was in his early sixties. He was still a spectacularly good-looking man, with chiseled features and gray hair smoothed back from his forehead. He carried an air of entitlement and of someone used to being obeyed. I immediately found him intimidating.

"I'm afraid the wind caught it and it went overboard, sir," Dennis said.

"Stop making excuses for Vanessa's clumsiness, Dennis," Jago said coldly. "I told you she had one more chance. I want that girl gone."

"Yes, sir," said Dennis. "Of course."

"Today."

"As you wish, sir."

I nudged Margot to speak out, but she seemed as paralyzed by Jago's tyrannical presence as I was.

"It wasn't Vanessa's fault," I said. "It was . . . it was mine."

Jago Ferris swung his attention to me, feigning surprise. "I see. You're the Americans wanting to film a movie here, is that right?"

Now was the time to come clean, but before I could set him straight Margot cut in.

"Margot Chandler of Chandler Productions." She offered her hand. "Pleased to meet you."

"You don't sound American," said Jago.

"Thank heavens for that," Margot said. "A British accent goes a long way in L.A."

"I have some time at eleven," said Jago. "Come and see me then and we will discuss it."

"Excuse me, Mr. Jago," Dennis said a low voice. "But Cador is on your calendar for eleven this morning."

Jago gave a snort of disdain. "Cancel him."

"Of course, sir." Dennis cleared his throat, clearly uneasy. "Is there another time? He's been quite adamant about wanting to talk to you for the last two weeks."

"I'm aware of what Cador wants to talk to me about and the answer is no." Jago smiled, but I saw that his smile didn't extend to his eyes. They remained cold and supercilious. "Eleven in my office, Chandler Productions, and don't be late."

There was no time for coffee with Lily and just enough time to go to our room and leave our luggage. Fortunately for Margot, Dennis descended the gazillion steps to the quay to retrieve her suitcase in record time.

"You're amazingly fit, Dennis," said Margot in an admiring tone. "Do you go to the gym?"

"I was in the army," he said as if that explained everything.

Margot offered him five pounds.

"A tip is not necessary." Dennis shook his head. "You're in England now. Not America."

"There *is* Wi-Fi here, isn't there?" she asked.

"Mrs. Tegan sells her artwork online," said Dennis. "So yes, there is."

When we reached the Margery Allingham room and were safely inside, Margot said, "Bit of a weird setup here, isn't it?"

"I know what you mean," I agreed. "I don't exactly feel welcome."

"That Jago's unsociable," Margot went on. "Reminds me of von Trapp from *The Sound of Music*."

"I really don't want to meet Jago. I don't know the first thing about being a location scout. You can answer all his questions."

"Don't be silly. I know his type. All bark and no bite, you'll be fine." She pulled a sad face. "Sorry, sis, you'll have to meet him without me."

"*What?*"

"I'm afraid you'll just have to," said Margot. "I'm waiting for another call."

"You mean . . . you're not coming?" I was horrified. "But this is your lie, not mine. I wouldn't know what to say!"

"You'll think of something," said Margot. "God, it's fuggy in here. I'm going to open the door to the balcony and let in some fresh air."

"Just crack it otherwise we'll freeze!" I said. "Los Angeles is eight hours behind us. I'm not stupid. What's really going on?"

"For heaven's sake, *nothing*!" she snapped. "Why do you keep asking me?"

"If you don't come with me, I'm . . . I'm going to tell him."

"If that's what you want to do, I can't stop you."

"Really? You mean it?"

"Honestly, Evie?" Margot exclaimed. "I really don't care. Do what you want."

"What's got into you?"

"Nothing!"

I was annoyed and more than a little hurt. "You started this ridiculous tale about me being a location scout," I said. "And now I have to clear up your mess and do some serious backtracking. Why do you do this? Why do you always have to make things complicated?"

A look of bewilderment mixed with sadness suddenly crossed Margot's features. She sank onto the bed. "I'm sorry I'm such an awful sister," she said quietly. "I just wanted to cheer you up and have a bit of a laugh. It backfired. What else can I say?"

"Oh Margot—" I felt terrible. "So . . . come with me. Please?"

"Look. Can you just . . . just leave me be. Seriously. I'm going to unpack." She stalked to the bathroom, closed the door and locked it.

"Hey! I'd like to use the bathroom so I can freshen up," I shouted, but Margot didn't answer.

As I headed downstairs, I decided I'd tell Jago everything

and thought, To hell with Margot and her lies. We weren't kids in the playground anymore.

I found the powder room located through an archway just off reception, not surprised to see the bathroom suite in a jarring shade of alpine blue with a matching shag pile carpet. Quickly I brushed my dark brown shoulder-length hair and applied some Burt's Bees tinted lip balm. In the rectangular mirror over the sink, I thought I looked tired and pale and not remotely prepared for a meeting with Captain von Trapp.

Dennis showed me into Jago's office at eleven on the dot.

"Just wait here," said Dennis. "Mr. Jago will be along shortly."

The room was even more of an homage to the 1970s than the rest of the hotel. Framed photographs hung on wood-clad walls; green shag pile carpet met hideous tartan wallpaper. Teak bookcases were lined with books, and a matching sideboard held half-a-dozen sailing trophies as well as a collection of stuffed songbirds in glass box display cases. I couldn't look at them. It was too upsetting. It was bad enough seeing birds of prey frozen in midflight, but songbirds? What kind of person does that?

But my attention was soon drawn away to an exquisite portrait hanging above the stone fireplace that housed a fake log fire flickering in the gloom.

It was, in fact, a photograph of a young woman with waist-length black hair leaning against the trunk of a vast beech tree under a canopy of autumn leaves. Her arms stretched seductively above her head, palms crossed, and her eyes were closed. Her beautiful face was looking up to the sky. It was only on closer inspection that I realized she was completely naked.

Her nakedness had been skillfully camouflaged by the traceries of light that filtered through the trees in a vivid mixture of reds, burnt orange, rusts and golden yellows. It was one of the most sensual portraits I had ever seen.

I was curious as to who the photographer could be, but Jago suddenly stepped into the room via an archway hidden by curtains that I initially believed had been drawn across French doors.

"That's my wife, Tegan," he said bluntly. "Taken just before her eighteenth birthday. Wasn't she stunning? She used to be so beautiful."

Used to be?

"Everyone was in love with Tegan," Jago went on. "But I got her in the end. She knew what was good for her."

I regarded him with dismay, wondering if he was actually joking, but he wasn't. There was no trace of humor in his cold eyes. My first impression of Jago Ferris had not been favorable, and now I didn't like him at all. He didn't ask me to sit down, nor did he sit down himself. We just stood there.

"I'm afraid you've had a wasted journey," Jago said. "There is no question of any filming taking place here or on Tregarrick. You aren't the first production company to ask to film here. My answer has always been no."

"I'll tell Margot. Thank you. Sorry to waste your time."

"You're a beautiful woman, there was no time wasted on my part," he said with a smirk. "I'm only surprised that you gave up so easily. All men are open to persuasion."

I was taken aback. Was this awful man paying me a compliment or actually hitting on me? Either way, his comment was totally inappropriate. As I headed for the door, he laughed and said something that I knew had to be derogatory. It sounded like "Amateurs."

I stopped. "I believe you knew my husband."

Jago looked amused. "I can't see how. I don't know anyone from Los Angeles."

"His name is—was—Robert Mead. I'm his wife, Evie."

A flicker of something I couldn't quite fathom crossed Jago's face, but he just shook his head. "No, sorry."

"Robert died suddenly a week ago. He had a heart attack."

Jago didn't move. "I'm sorry for your loss, dear, but I'm not sure why you are telling me this. Did you think it might make me change my mind about your film production?"

"No. I just thought you would want to know. I presume you were friends."

"Never heard of him."

Jago Ferris and Tregarrick Rock were hardly common names. Jago was lying. I could feel it. And if he was lying, it was because he knew that he hadn't repaid that loan.

"What about a Millicent Small?" I said, suddenly recalling the name of the witness on the letter. "Surely you know her?"

Jago shook his head again. "No. There's no one called Millicent Small here."

"It was a long time ago," I persisted. "In 2000?"

"In 2000? Really?" Jago frowned. "Without wishing to be rude, how old would you have been in the year 2000? Fifteen? Sixteen?"

"Excuse me?"

"Still a schoolgirl."

I felt my face flame. "What exactly are you implying?"

"I think it's more a case of what exactly are *you* implying?" he said.

And then I realized. He was enjoying this! He knew exactly who I was. He'd commented about my age because he *did* know Robert and he also knew he had married a much younger woman. It took a lot to make me angry, but I'd bottled up the events of the past week and now I was ready to explode.

"Alright," I said. "When my husband died I was given a letter stating that he had loaned you a substantial sum of money in 2000 and in return, you offered Tregarrick Rock as collateral. Now do you remember?"

Jago began to laugh. "Let me stop you right there, dear—"

"And don't call me dear," I fumed. "I am not your *dear*."

"First of all, I have never heard of Robert Mead. Secondly, I have never needed to . . . as you say . . . *borrow* money, and thirdly, you must be out of your mind. Tregarrick Rock has been in the Ferris family for hundreds of years. Even if I had needed to borrow money or take out a loan, I would never have offered the hotel up as collateral. I would sooner have given my soul."

I *knew* he was lying. Yet there was nothing I could do about it.

"Where is this so-called letter?" Jago demanded. "I'd be interested to have a look."

And then I realized I didn't have it! Nigel had kept it.

"What's going on, darling?" The curtain drew aside again and a petite woman in her late fifties appeared. She had a cloud of black hair with a striking streak of white that tumbled to her shoulders, giving her a Lily Munster–like appearance. Violet eyes looked out from wire-rimmed glasses. Dressed in black leggings, ballet flats and a thigh-length flannel shirt that bore paint splatters, she held a paintbrush in her hand.

"I heard laughter," she remarked. "And that's rare."

"This is Tegan," Jago said almost dismissively. "Hard to believe she's the same person in that portrait, although at least she's now clothed—even if she does look like a bohemian artist."

I was appalled at his rudeness, but Tegan just smiled. "That's because I *am* a bohemian artist."

I scrambled for something to say and seized the opportunity to hopefully defuse the situation. "I saw your work at the Salty Boatman," I said. "It's wonderful. Somehow you managed to capture the essence of your subject. The neglect and sadness of the lighthouse—"

"Interesting choice of words," Jago mused. "The *sadness* of the lighthouse? I don't think you were ever *sad* in there, were you, darling?"

"Take no notice of him," Tegan said lightly. "It's always refreshing to talk to someone who knows about art." She looked at Jago with ill-disguised contempt. "I often have to tell my husband that art is supposed to be appreciated, not possessed."

"But that's where you are wrong," Jago said smoothly. "Didn't Picasso say that painting is just another way of keeping a diary?"

"Yes," I agreed. "Picasso did say that."

"And you know how much I appreciate *your* diary," said Jago.

I had no idea what was going on between them and didn't want to. Tegan reminded me of one of the stuffed songbirds on the sideboard. She was trapped, just as they were. She headed to a chair and perched on the armrest.

Gesturing to the portrait, she said, "What do you think of that?"

"I like it." And then I knew exactly who the photographer was. "That's one of Alex Karlsson's early works. I'm sure of it."

Far from being impressed, Tegan looked shocked. She glanced at Jago, whose expression was stony.

"I used to work at a gallery in London," I said. "We honored him with a retrospective exhibition about twelve years ago."

"Was this before you became a location scout?" Jago said with a sneer.

"You're mistaken," said Tegan. "I've never heard of Alex— whatever you said he was called."

"Karlsson," Jago said firmly. "Alex Karlsson."

"What a strange coincidence!" I said. "Alex Karlsson is on Tregarrick. He came over with us on the ferry last night."

All the color drained out of Tegan's face.

"What a coincidence indeed," Jago said dryly. "I wonder what brings him to our little kingdom from his native Sweden?"

"Oh, that Alex Karlsson," Tegan said weakly.

"Yes, Tegan. I know *exactly* who he is." Jago's eyes did not leave his wife's face. "I wonder what business this man has on Tregarrick?" he mused. "Presumably he's not wanting to film a movie."

"Apparently, he wants to photograph the lighthouse," I said.

And with that, Tegan toppled off the arm of the chair in a dead faint.

Chapter Nine

"Are you okay?" I said.

Jago had lifted Tegan gently into the armchair. Despite his vile behavior earlier, it was obvious that he cared deeply. "Put your head between your knees, darling. I'll get you some water."

"No need," she whispered. "I'm fine. Just a bit of a dizzy spell. Sorry about that." She reached out to me and squeezed my hand. "Thank you. You're very kind."

When I looked down I saw a distinctive bruise on her wrist. It looked like finger marks. In her eyes I saw something—a cry for understanding—or a cry for help? Whatever it was, it gave me the chills.

Jago must have sensed a connection between us, because whatever concern he had felt was swiftly replaced with obvious dislike—for *me*!

"Tegan, I should have told you that poor Evie here has just lost her husband," he said.

Tegan frowned. "I am sorry. How terrible."

"Yes. His name was Robert—or should I say, *Bobby* Mead."

Tegan went rigid and her pale complexion flooded with color.

"I told her that we've never heard of him," Jago went on.

"No," Tegan said coldly. "We have not."

"You called Robert Bobby," I said quickly.

"Robert. Bobby. Rob. Bob. Call it whatever you want, but no, we did not know the man," said Jago.

I was now more convinced than ever that Jago had not repaid Robert's loan.

"What are you doing here?" Tegan demanded.

"Evie is a location scout from Los Angeles," said Jago.

Tegan glanced over at Jago in genuine confusion. "You live in *Los Angeles*?"

"No," I said. "I live in Kent. The production company is in Los Angeles." Which was true.

"Naturally I said filming on the island was impossible," said Jago.

The door burst open and Cador stormed in, followed by Dennis, who seemed in a total panic.

"I'm sorry, Mr. Jago, but I couldn't stop him. He was most insistent."

"I'm sick of being put off," Cador fumed. He spotted me and hesitated. "I'm sorry? What's—"

"We're finished here," Jago snapped. "Tegan, go to your studio. I will handle this. Thank you, Dennis. Please escort Mrs. Mead out."

"Yes, sir."

I was grateful to make my escape. The entire meeting had

been a complete disaster. How could Robert have known such an awful man, and why would he have loaned him all that money?

Dennis shut Jago's door behind us, gave a polite smile and hurried back in the direction of reception.

I stood in the hallway, which led to a second staircase that had been cordoned off with a chain and a plaque marked PRIVATE. More photographs lined the walls here . . . and then I saw them.

My stomach turned right over.

They were the exact same sequence of formal schoolboy panoramic photographs that I had packed away just days before. I couldn't believe it.

Jago and Robert had been at Cambridge together. In fact, they had rowed together for the Blue Boats.

I stepped up to look more closely and picked out Robert straightaway. I was almost positive that the young man next to him was Jago. I studied the other photographs, and in each one, the two friends stood side by side.

I headed back to the lobby, but suddenly Tegan blocked my path. Gripping my arm, she bundled me into a storage room and slammed the door.

"I don't know how you can *dare* show your face," she hissed. "I know exactly who you are."

I was mortified. "I don't know what you're talking about," I exclaimed. "Let go of my arm."

"Jo is my friend," she spat.

"Jo? *Joanna* . . . Joanna Mead?" My mind was spinning. "Wait a minute, what are you trying to say?"

Tegan was bristling with righteous indignation. She jabbed her finger into my shoulder. "*You* stole her husband—"

I knocked her hand away. "Don't touch me."

"*You* destroyed her and then you show up here? Why? Why are you here? What do you want?"

"I don't have to answer to you," I said.

"Jo and I fantasized about meeting you," Tegan said, sneering. "But I never thought it would actually happen. I can't wait to tell her."

When I didn't comment, Tegan plunged on. "The four of us were firm friends. We went everywhere together until you came along."

I struggled to keep my voice steady, but inside my heart was racing. "That's not what Robert told me," I said. "Joanna left *him*! She wasn't even living in their house anymore."

"Ha!" Tegan exclaimed. "Of course Bobby would say that." Her eyes flashed with malice. "They were going to make a fresh start, but then you came along and got your claws in."

Robert hadn't said anything to me about Joanna wanting to make a "fresh start." If he had, I would have let him go.

"I just don't get it. You're nothing like Jo," Tegan went on. "You're like a little mouse."

"Perhaps that's why he chose me," I said, determined to stand my ground.

"What did you do?" Tegan cocked her head. "Did you trap him? Tell him you were pregnant?"

The irony of that remark was not lost on me. "Please let me leave," I said coldly, but Tegan barred my way.

"I'm not done with you yet," she said. "They were married for nearly thirty years! He left her with nothing. She works in a supermarket now, you know."

The story that Robert had told me had been so very different. Joanna had cheated on him many times and was always threatening to divorce him. The last time she cried wolf he had just met me and told her to go ahead. Nothing physical had happened between us at that point, but Joanna hadn't believed him, and it would seem that Tegan hadn't either.

Robert had given Joanna the house in Calverley Park and a generous alimony and paid for their son Michael's school and university fees, but she had always wanted more. In the end he had settled on a lump sum and Joanna was finally out of our life—up until now.

"I'm sorry about Joanna," I said carefully. "But frankly, I don't see how this can have anything to do with me. Please let me leave."

Tegan didn't budge. "Joanna thought you wanted a sugar daddy so you could have kids. That's the problem with you Millennials. You don't understand the commitment of marriage."

"I don't know what you want me to say," I said. "I was told their marriage was over. I had no reason to believe otherwise, and if I had, I would never have gotten involved with him in the first place. That's not who I am. And for the record, Robert died virtually penniless. Satisfied?"

Tegan frowned. "You know, I think I believe you."

"I don't care if you believe me or not," I exclaimed.

"So why are you really here?" Tegan demanded.

"Why don't you ask your husband?"

Tegan hesitated. "No. I'd rather ask you. I think you'll tell me the truth."

"You flatter me," I said dryly. "Robert loaned your husband

one hundred thousand pounds and was offered Tregarrick Rock as collateral. The loan was never repaid."

Tegan turned ashen. "I don't understand. Are you saying . . . are you saying that Tregarrick Rock is *yours*?"

"Yes."

"No," she whispered. "Jago would never do that. *Ever.*"

"As I said, talk to your husband." I grabbed the door handle.

"Wait—so . . . you are nothing to do with Hollywood?"

"Does it really matter?" I said.

"If you lied about that, you may have lied about everything," Tegan exclaimed.

"Do you really think I would concoct such a ridiculous story?" I demanded. "I loved Robert deeply, Tegan. Weren't you ever in love?"

To my surprise, Tegan went very quiet. "Yes," she whispered. "I was, and I also know that nothing lasts. All men leave."

And with that, she let me go.

I stepped out into the corridor and realized that I was shaking.

I was desperate to talk to Nigel. How could he not have known about Jago? It was true that Nigel started working for Robert just a few months before I came on the scene, and perhaps by then, the merry foursome had already gone their separate ways. Yes, that must have been what had happened. Jago and Tegan had not seemed too shocked at the news of Robert's passing.

It sounded as if Tegan was still in touch with Joanna and must have found out that way. When Robert died, Michael was on a plane, en route home to Sydney. I'd had the awful job of calling him when he landed to give him the news. He had wanted to fly back immediately, but I told him that it would take at least ten days to plan the funeral and just to wait a little. Of course Michael must have told his mother.

I cut through the lobby to get to the staircase and to my surprise saw Alex talking to Dennis in reception. Alex was dressed in black waterproofs, wore hip waders and carried a rucksack. He must have walked across the causeway.

"I'll wait for her in the Residents' Lounge," I heard him say. "Mind if I remove these waders first? I've brought a change of shoes."

Dennis pointed to a sign marked TOILETS. "Through there. We have a cloak cupboard if you'd like to hang up your outdoor garments."

Alex nodded a thank-you and left.

"Oh! Mrs. Mead?" Dennis called out. "I have a message for you." He handed me a note on hotel stationery. It was from Margot.

I read, *Gone to explore the island. Have taken water and a protein bar so don't expect me back for lunch. See you later. M.*

"Mrs. Chandler borrowed one of our hotel waterproof hooded capes that we like to provide for guests who come here unprepared."

I was annoyed. Why couldn't she have waited for me? After that awful scene with Tegan, all I wanted to do was get off the island. "Is the sea tractor still here?"

"Why?" Dennis asked. "Is everything alright?"

"We might have to cut our trip short," I said. "Is there time to catch the tidal window before it turns?"

"I'm sorry," said Dennis. "But that won't be possible. The sea tractor won't be running until tomorrow morning."

So we really were stuck on the Rock. "Do you know which direction Margot went?"

"Unfortunately, no," said Dennis. "By the way, luncheon will be served at twelve-thirty sharp. Mrs. Chandler told us not to expect her. I assume she's looking for locations for your film."

"Yes, I assume so. Thanks, Dennis." I headed upstairs to unpack, thoroughly irritated with my sister.

As I unlocked my door, I could hear someone moving around inside.

Slowly, I pushed it open and stopped in confusion. "What the hell do you think you're doing?"

Chapter Ten

Lily gave a guilty start. She was holding an iPhone and standing over Margot's open suitcase. I was astonished. "How did you get in here?"

"The balcony door was ajar," she said. "I have the Agatha Christie suite next door, as you know. Oh!" Lily clutched at her throat and seemed mortified. "Goodness! Did you think I was snooping?"

I may have been naïve in many areas of my life, but I wasn't stupid. "What are you doing in here?"

"I was just looking for Mister Tig, the cat. He often wanders into other people's hotel rooms."

"And climbs into other people's suitcases?" I said.

Lily smiled. "Do you mind if I look?"

"Yes," I said. "Margot is very particular about her packing and doesn't like anyone touching her clothes."

In fact, it was unusual that Margot had started to unpack and not finished the job. A shirt, dress and jacket had been draped over the back of a chair and her Tumi toiletry bag had been left on the bed. Red flannel shoe bags containing her shoe collection were lined up neatly at the base of a three-drawer dresser.

"Tissue paper, too," Lily remarked. "You don't often see young people bother with that kind of thing. Lovely clothes."

I regarded Lily with suspicion. She seemed completely un-fazed that I'd caught her red-handed—and with an iPhone!

"I love posting on Instagram," said Lily as if reading my mind. "Or should I say that Mister Tig loves to post. He has his own account."

"Seriously?"

"I'm very serious." Lily grinned. "He has over two thousand followers. He knows everything that goes on in the hotel."

Of course he does, I thought to myself. What a perfect ex-cuse to snoop and blame it on the cat.

"Are you on Instagram?" she asked.

"No," I said. "I don't care much for social media, but if I see your cat I'll let you know."

"Oh no," said Lily. "He's not my cat. He's the hotel cat. Mis-ter Tig was here before I retired. No one really knows where he came from. You could say he adopted me. I think it's because I made him famous. Look."

Lily showed me Mister Tig's Instagram account. I looked at a handsome black-and-white cat's profile. "What magnificent whiskers."

"Yes. He's very proud of those," said Lily. "People call him a tuxedo cat because of his markings. Don't you think it looks like he's wearing a bow tie?"

"I do. And if I find him," I said again, "I'll tell him to go home."

"Mister Tig could have gone down to the garden," she said suddenly. "There is a fire escape at the end of the balcony. He often takes that route. Yes. That's probably what happened. I'll have to check."

"Check?" I said. "How?"

"I have a kitty cam so I can keep an eye on him."

"A what?"

"It's like a nanny cam, only it's for pets," said Lily. "You can buy apps for everything these days. Really, I'm surprised you haven't heard of it."

"Well, it sounds very intriguing," I said politely. "Will you excuse me? I really need to unpack."

To my chagrin, Lily sat down onto a tartan love seat as if she intended to stay and chat. "This is such a lovely room," she said. "Beautiful views of the island from here. Nice to be on this side as opposed to the causeway side."

"Yes," I said. "As I was saying, I really need to unpack."

"Don't mind me." Lily nodded but still made no effort to leave. "I hope the lady you work for has a nice walk."

"Yes, she's gone exploring, apparently," I said. "How do you know that?"

"I have a telescope in my room—I enjoy watching the birds. But I hope she wasn't planning on walking very far. Fog is forecast for later on this afternoon and it's easy to get disoriented in the hotel grounds."

I started putting my clothes away.

"And, you're from L.A.?" Lily chattered on. "I went to Los

Angeles on holiday once with Harold. We went to the Chinese Theatre. Walked along Hollywood Boulevard. It was so exciting, but home is where your heart is. I've lived on Scilly all my life."

And then I had a thought. "You must know everything that goes on here."

"Oh yes. I make it my business to do that. I've always been interested in people."

I bit back the snarky remark that in other words, she was just plain nosy.

"I used to help out at the post office in my younger days," said Lily. "That is, when I wasn't delivering babies. I delivered Cador, you know."

"Do you remember a Robert Mead?"

Lily hesitated for a moment. "Give me some more information, dear."

"He may have come here years ago with his"—I forced myself to say it—"wife, Joanna."

Lily just blinked.

"They were great friends with Jago and Tegan Ferris," I said.

"Oh, if they were friends of Mr. Jago, I wouldn't have known them," she said quickly.

"Not even if they stayed here at the hotel?"

"Oh no. I've only been living here since my Harold passed away," Lily said.

"What about a Millicent Small?" I asked.

A flicker of alarm crossed her wrinkled face. "Who? No. I don't know who she is."

"Or . . . Alex Karlsson?"

Lily went very still. "I don't know him."

"He's a photographer—a very well-known photographer," I said. "One of his portraits is hanging in Jago's office. It's of Tegan."

She shook her head vehemently. "No. I don't know him. I've never heard of him. Why are you asking me all these questions? Are you . . . are you a private investigator?"

A private investigator? I was stunned. For a moment I was tempted to say that I was. The fact that she had asked me meant that something strange was going on. Lily was holding something back.

"Alex Karlsson is actually here at the hotel today," I said. "He's downstairs."

Lily turned ashen. She tried to scramble to her feet but in her haste tripped and fell heavily onto the floor, catching her head on the side of a chair.

"Lily!" I was appalled. "Oh God. Oh no."

I dropped to my knees, praying that she was okay. Thankfully I could hear her moaning.

The fall had not been more than a couple of feet, but I knew how easy it was for the elderly to break a bone. As her moaning became more dramatic, though, I wondered if Lily was in fact faking it.

I managed to get her to her feet, grateful that she seemed to be okay. "Let me help you back to your room."

Lily swayed a little and leaned heavily against me, groaning even more loudly. True, there was a faint red mark on the side of her forehead, but it was obvious to me that she was exaggerating her injury to avoid answering any more of my questions.

We stepped out into the corridor to find Tegan knocking on Lily's door. Although she seemed surprised to see us together, she didn't ask why.

"Lily, we need to have a little chat," Tegan said. *"Now."*

"He's here, isn't he," Lily blurted out. "I didn't tell her anything. I swear I didn't."

"Lily—" Tegan rolled her eyes and forced a smile. "I have no idea what you are talking about. Let's go inside, shall we? Where is your room key?"

Lily looked as if she were going to burst into tears. "I . . . I . . ."

"Lily was looking for the cat," I said. "She thought he was in my room, so she came through the balcony door. She must have forgotten to take her room key with her."

As if on cue, Dennis came hurrying toward us holding a master set of keys. "You wanted the key, Mrs. Tegan?"

"Thank you, yes," said Tegan.

"Is everything alright?" Dennis regarded Lily with dismay. "What happened to your head?"

What had started as a faint mark had rapidly swollen to the size of a small egg.

"Nothing," Lily said, shooting me a look that clearly told me to keep quiet.

"I see it now," Tegan said with a heavy sigh. "You've fallen again, haven't you."

"No," Lily said quickly. Again she looked to me, almost pleading. "I can manage on my own. I don't want to go into a home. Please don't put me in a home."

I was taken aback. I was also puzzled as to why Tegan would

have asked Dennis for a key to Lily's room. Perhaps she'd knocked and wondered if Lily had indeed fallen.

"Oh for heaven's sake!" Tegan groaned. "Don't be so silly. No one is going to do that. I'll take it from here, thank you, Dennis." She took hold of Lily's arm and pulled her close.

Dennis cleared his throat. "A Mr. Alex Karlsson is in the lobby asking to see you."

Tegan froze. "Oh? Who?"

Lily gave a cry of pain. I noticed that Tegan had tightened the grip on her arm. I also noticed that Tegan made no sign of acknowledging the fact that I had already told her Alex had been on the ferry.

"Alex Karlsson," Dennis repeated. "He's come to photograph the lighthouse. He also mentioned that he would like to buy one of your paintings."

"I'll be down shortly." Tegan fumbled with the lock on Lily's door and dropped the key, clearly nervous. "Damn and blast!"

Dennis swiftly picked it up and opened the door for her. Lily darted inside. Tegan hesitated, then said, "Where is Mr. Jago?"

"He told me he was going to chop logs in William's Wood," said Dennis.

Tegan frowned. "And Cador?"

"Also chopping logs in William's Wood," Dennis said blandly. "But at the other end."

Tegan's eyes widened. "Oh dear."

"I fear their meeting did not go well," said Dennis.

Tegan didn't comment and followed Lily into her room.

"I locked myself out. Sorry," I said to Dennis. "I didn't think."

"No problem." Dennis unlocked my door. "Don't forget that luncheon will be served at twelve-thirty."

I slipped back into our room, glad to be alone for a moment to collect my thoughts.

What an extraordinary morning. I couldn't make sense of anything. Everyone was acting so strangely—even Margot. *Especially* Margot. I couldn't believe that she had just gone off exploring on her own without waiting for me.

It was always hard to tell what was going on with my sister. She had never been good at sharing her feelings. I was the one in the family who was said to be "sensitive" and "emotional." Margot was always the practical, sensible, no-nonsense daughter. Dad used to call her the General because she was so sure of herself . . . and bossy.

I flopped onto the bed, feeling sorry for myself. The events of the past hour had shaken me to the core. Jago's denial that he had ever known Robert and then the horrible conversation with Tegan in the storage room.

I lay looking at the ceiling, taking in the cracks and brown rings on the wallpaper that indicated a leaky roof. The room was in dire need of redecorating—the whole hotel was. At least our room wasn't all 1970s horror. Our brass bedheads looked original—single beds again—as well as the matching burl walnut night tables and the lamps with art glass floral balls and silk lampshades.

And then I heard the rustle of tissue paper and a loud meow. A black furry head emerged from inside Margot's suitcase.

It was Mister Tig.

Maybe Lily hadn't been snooping after all.

Chapter Eleven

The cat gave a leisurely stretch and daintily extricated his claws from another of Margot's cashmere sweaters.

His coat was black and glossy except for a white bib and white socks. With a tiny splash of black on his throat, he really did look as if he were wearing a bow tie. He also wore a midnight-blue velvet collar from which dangled a tiny silver key.

"You're so handsome," I said. "What magnificent whiskers you have."

I scooped him up and buried my face into his fur. Mister Tig purred loudly. I felt my spirits lift. My own cat, Rommel, had died shortly after Robert and I got married. Robert had wanted to find another, but at the time I'd been too upset. Rommel was one of a kind and irreplaceable, but now I realized I was ready to offer a new kitty a loving home.

Mister Tig wriggled out of my arms and headed for the balcony door, where to my astonishment he reached up and then, with a little jump, put both paws down on the handle. The glass door popped open and he sauntered outside. I couldn't help but laugh.

Lily had been right about that, too.

I followed him onto the balcony. It was shaped like the letter *S*, with the far end wrapped around a corner turret that was topped with an opal-green cap.

A low dividing wall split the balcony in two at the curve. Empty planters lined the low brick wall. Tarpaulins covered two sets of tables and chairs and a patio swing. Everything had been packed away for the winter.

To my right was a spiral fire escape that led down to the garden.

The view was magnificent. For an island—or "rock"—so very small, the topography couldn't have been more diverse.

On my right, broad terraces of subtropical plants and lofty California pines and holm oaks crept up the hillside to meet evergreen trees that formed a shelterbelt from the north. Another densely planted swath of evergreens ran along the lowest part of the garden—almost at sea level—protecting it from storm battering from the south. At the bottom was a small lake. Several long wooden sheds were partially hidden among the pampas grass and reeds. Given that Tregarrick was a birdwatcher's paradise, I suspected they were bird hides.

The center of the island seemed to be more of a dell. Enclosed by lush plants, the middle was laid to lawn and dotted with topiaries in exotic shapes. I could just about make out the figureheads from the galleons that Cador had told us about yesterday.

On my left stretched a rugged coastline blanketed with

gorse and bracken—a stark contrast to the rich vegetation on the opposite side of the dell. A ruined watchtower perched majestically on a bluff. Beyond that, I could see the top of Windward Point Lighthouse.

With shafts of sunlight breaking through heavy thunderclouds building on the horizon, I felt as if I were looking at one of Tegan's paintings.

I saw no sign of Margot, Cador or Jago in the gardens.

Mister Tig was already meowing outside Lily's balcony door, begging to be let in, but she couldn't have heard him. I waited for a moment, but his meows became more persistent. He attempted to repeat the same circus trick with the door handle, but of course the door opened out onto the balcony, not into the room.

Finally, Lily appeared at the balcony door, wreathed in smiles. "Where was the naughty boy?"

When I told her he had been hiding in Margot's suitcase after all, she insisted I come in and see her rooms.

The Agatha Christie suite was spectacular.

"This is the south side of the hotel," Lily said, beaming. "This is the best suite with the best views—especially from the top of the turret—although I can't get up those stairs anymore. It's horrible getting old."

Floor-to-ceiling windows matched our room next door, but whereas we had one window, Lily had three.

Apart from a flat-screen TV that was broadcasting a reality TV show, it was furnished with exquisite Art Deco furniture—credenzas, armchairs, Tiffany lamps and a walnut-veneer demilune cocktail cabinet that was tucked in one corner. A pair of faceted frosted-glass-paned French doors opened into a bedroom with an enormous king-size bed with a walnut-veneer sunray headboard. It was stunning.

Wall-to-wall bookshelves housed a slew of silver-framed photographs—all of a much younger Lily—certificates, porcelain figurines and cut-glass paperweights.

There was a stack of *Hello!* magazines on a side table.

How could a retired midwife-cum-postmistress from a tiny island afford to live in such luxury? Perhaps she was related to the Ferris family and this was a grace-and-favor apartment. Perhaps I had judged Jago and Tegan too harshly. No wonder she didn't want to go into a retirement home!

"Yes, I've been so fortunate," said Lily as if reading my mind. "Mr. Jago and Mrs. Tegan have been so kind. They treat me like one of the family."

So that answered my question. "It's lovely."

Lily touched her forehead and winced.

"Let me look at that," I said.

The swelling had got bigger. Lily had fallen down very hard, and it was possible that she had suffered a concussion. "Perhaps you should get a doctor to look at that?"

"Don't be silly," Lily scoffed. "Calling out the medical launch from St. Mary's happens only in a real emergency." Lily went on to explain that the hospital was on the main island. Margot had said the same. "That's why Tregarrick was very lucky to have me. I was a midwife, you know."

"So you said."

"I've delivered every single baby on these islands since 1955 until . . . well . . . let me think . . . what year are we now?"

"It's 2020."

"Good heavens. The last baby I delivered was in 2012. I keep records of everything. There are stories I could tell you that would make your hair curl."

I gestured to the scrapbook I'd seen her with earlier and that now sat on a side table. "In there?"

"Goodness, no. My little black book is under lock and key," said Lily. "The scrapbook is just a hobby of mine. I like to collect newspaper clippings of juicy scandals—especially about celebrities. Would you like to see it?"

"Perhaps another time." I pointed to the large cretonne-knitting bag in gaudy shades of blue and orange that sat at the foot of a wingback chair where Mister Tig was industriously washing his paws. "You certainly keep yourself busy. What are you knitting?"

"Those." She pointed to a beautiful Art Deco daybed with a walnut-veneer finish where six hand-knitted cushions with intricately designed crests sat in a row.

"I sell them on Etsy," said Lily. "They're very popular. I've almost finished sewing up Dorne."

I frowned. "Sorry, I don't follow."

"*Game of Thrones*? Come along now, surely you've watched *Game of Thrones*?"

"Oh! No." I shook my head. "Too violent for me."

After admiring the cushions and the almost-finished Dorne with its rather terrifying orange sun-like crest and golden spear, I gestured to the telescope. "You said you saw Margot? Where was she going?"

"She was heading for the coast path. I assume that she

wanted to take a look at the ruined watchtower for your film, but she should be careful. It's quite a drop to the beach."

"I'm sure she'll be careful."

"Before you go, dear, would you get the arnica from my medicine cabinet in the powder room? The door is by the entrance. I can't reach it," said Lily. "I'm not sure if I should be standing on a ladder at the moment."

The powder room was painted in baby pink, with a faceted vanity mirror on one wall and double cupboard doors above a washbasin on the other. Lily's makeup was spread out neatly on a white linen cloth. She certainly took good care of herself. A collapsible two-step ladder was tucked in the corner.

I set it up, opened the cupboard doors and gasped in surprise.

Lily had her own personal pharmacy, with over-the-counter bottles from aspirin to ibuprofen. She had half a dozen or so bottles of prescription pills that, I noticed, had mostly expired— one bottle by fifteen years! There was a variety of homeopathic creams, a handful of EpiPens, syringes in sterilized sleeves, gauzes and bandages all neatly organized in alphabetical order.

I grabbed the tube of arnica and the bottle of aspirin. Lily was sitting in the wingback chair with Mister Tig on her lap, absentmindedly playing with the little key on his collar.

The cat regarded me with one eye open but then settled back and began to purr again as I gently applied the cream to Lily's bruise.

"Thank you, dear," said Lily. "Lunch is in twenty minutes. We can continue our conversation then. So exciting knowing you are going to make a film here!"

Five minutes later I was back in the Margery Allingham room, half hoping that Margot would have changed her mind and returned. I didn't relish having lunch with Lily alone.

I suddenly realized I could call Margot's mobile and ask her how long she planned to be or where I could find her later. To my confusion, I heard her mobile ringing close by, but I couldn't see it on the coffee table, sofa or desk. I rang it again and finally tracked it down to underneath the sofa.

The screen was cracked—as if she had hurled it across the room. There were nine missed calls, but I couldn't access the list because it was password protected.

Margot and her iPhone were joined at the hip. She would never have left the hotel and gone for a walk without it. But then I remembered how many times she had refused to answer it recently. Perhaps she had decided it was better left here. But that didn't explain the cracked screen.

My iPhone rang. Margot! But when I looked at the caller I.D. it was Nigel's office.

"Hi, Evie," I heard Cherie say. "Can you hold for Nigel?"

"Yes, of course." Thank God. I couldn't wait to tell him everything.

I heard a click and a "*Merci beaucoup*," then Nigel was on the line. Immediately he must have sensed something in my voice.

"What's happened?"

"Oh Nigel," I said. "I'm so happy to talk to you. Everything is going wrong. We should never have come here."

Chapter Twelve

"You're *where*?" Nigel sounded shocked.

"Tregarrick Rock," I said. "Didn't Cherie tell you?"

"No, she didn't."

"Margot thought it would be a good idea to have a weekend away, but it's been completely disastrous. I met Jago—"

"Oh Evie!" Nigel groaned. "I told you I would take care of this. What did Jago say?"

"He's such a horrible man." I knew I must sound hysterical, but I didn't care. "And his wife—she's awful and—"

"Wait a minute, calm down," said Nigel. "Start at the beginning. Tell me exactly what happened. You said you talked to Jago Ferris?"

"At first he denied knowing Robert at all, but then I saw some school photographs of him with Robert! I couldn't believe it. They were at Cambridge together and pretty good friends by the looks of things."

"That makes sense as to why he loaned him the money," said

Nigel. "I didn't know Robert back then. You've got to remember that arrangement between them happened well before my time. Robert had such diverse circles of friends and acquaintances when he was . . . well—"

"Married to Joanna," I finished for him.

"He used to call his friends 'horses for courses,'" Nigel said. "He was a bit of a chameleon, changing his friends with his latest hobby."

"You make him out to be so shallow," I said. "I never saw that side of Robert." And I hadn't. It was bizarre. Nigel was talking about a man I didn't know. "He was never like that with me."

"You knew him at a different stage in his life, that's all."

"And then it turns out that Tegan and Joanna were best friends," I said. "They went everywhere in a foursome. It makes me feel—"

"Why don't you just come home?" Nigel cut in.

"We can't until tomorrow!" I wailed, and went on to explain that the hotel could only be accessed at low tide across a causeway. "Oh—and remember there was a witness called Millicent Small?"

"Yes, I remember," said Nigel. "Did you find her?"

"Apparently no one has ever heard of her," I said.

"You're assuming she lived there," said Nigel. "A witness can be anyone at all. It doesn't have to be a family friend or—"

"No," I said firmly. "I'm convinced that the loan was never repaid."

There was a silence on the other end of the line.

"Nigel?" I said. "Are you still there?"

"Yes," said Nigel. "I think you may be overreacting."

I plowed on. "There is an elderly woman here who knows everything and everyone on the island," I said. "She was the midwife and the postmistress for years. Now she lives at the hotel in the Agatha Christie suite—we're in the Margery Allingham—all the rooms are named after detective writers from the Golden Age. Lily's cat has Instagram. Can you believe it?"

"Evie! Slow down! Stop!" Nigel exclaimed with a laugh. "Let me get a word in."

"Yes, yes, of course," I said. "Sorry. You called me. Why did you call me?"

"I wanted to apologize. If Cherie had given me the letter when I first started taking care of Robert's business affairs, we wouldn't be in this situation. So many years have gone by—it's going to take me a little while to unravel the mystery, but—this is really awkward. I don't know quite how to tell you . . ."

And then I knew. "The letter was meant for Joanna, wasn't it." Robert had addressed it to his first "darling wife." Not his current "darling wife."

"Yes," said Nigel. "I traced the money to a joint account that Robert closed following his divorce from Joanna."

I felt an unexpected wave of disappointment. "So the loan *was* repaid," I said. "I see. Well. Never mind. It was a nice idea while it lasted!"

"I'm sorry," Nigel said.

"But why wouldn't Jago tell me?" I said. "I don't understand."

"Best to forget about that now," said Nigel. "However, I have been looking into some options for Forster's Oast."

"Oh good. Thank you. What are they? Will I be able to keep the house?"

"I'll be back in the country on Monday. Tell you what, why don't you and Margot come to dinner on Tuesday evening and we'll talk more. *Excusez-moi! Garçon*—" I heard a smattering of French and then, "Evie? Are you still there?"

"Yes. It sounds like you have to go."

"I must," said Nigel. "I'll see you on Tuesday. Got to eat some snails."

When he rang off, I realized I really was disappointed about the hotel. It was silly, really, since a week ago I hadn't had any idea that it even existed. I couldn't wait to tell Margot and decided that if she wasn't back by the time I had finished lunch, I would go out and look for her.

Lily invited me to join her in the dining room that had thankfully kept its Art Deco roots. We dined alone—no Jago, Tegan, Cador, Alex or Dennis.

With its ornate stained-glass ceiling, peacock motifs and beveled mirrored walls, the dining room was a little shabby, but beautiful. Octagonal tables were set around a small parquet dance floor. A white grand piano sat in one corner, and in another was a stunning Art Deco bar. Floor-to-ceiling windows looked out onto yet another terrace.

When Vanessa led me to Lily's table, Lily put the Dorne cushion back into her cretonne-knitting bag.

"Oh, what a treat!" she declared. "Someone to talk to! Where's your friend?"

"Not back," I said. "But she often skips lunch."

"Those Hollywood types don't eat, do they," said Lily. "They have to keep paper-thin. It's unnatural if you ask me. Makes their heads look far too big for their skinny bodies."

To my surprise, Lily was good company. She entertained me with amusing anecdotes about Mister Tig and his dietary disappointments.

"He had been looking forward to eating the lizard," Lily said. "But when he took a bite, he said it tasted like plastic."

I laughed. "You're making it up!"

"No, I'm not," Lily said gravely. "My brother told me. He is an animal communicator. In fact, he gets along better with animals than people."

"I don't believe in all that rubbish."

"You're doubting the word of a man of the cloth?"

"Wait—Vicar Bill is your *brother*?!" I exclaimed.

"That's right." Lily took a sip of water. "Fortunately that wretched bird gives Mister Tig and me a wide berth. Now—where is that lazy girl with our crumble?" She picked up a spoon and began tapping it on the side of her glass. I was glad to see she was feeling none the worse for her fall.

"I can't stay for pudding," I said.

"Yes you can. Vanessa makes an excellent apple-and-blackberry crumble," Lily declared. "You know, she learned to cook in prison. Got some fancy catering qualification."

"Prison?"

"Oops." Lily clapped her hand over her mouth. "I shouldn't have said that. No one is supposed to know."

Lily cocked her head and waited for me to ask the inevitable question, but I was determined not to.

"It was in all the newspapers," she said slyly.

"As you said, I'm not supposed to know."

Lily leaned over and said in a low voice, "Aren't you curious as to what she did?"

"Not at all." I took a sip of ice water. Of course I was curious! But I definitely didn't want to open up that kind of a conversation with Lily.

"She bought a prosthetic one on Amazon. It would never have fooled me, but apparently the doctors were taken in for quite some time."

"A prosthetic what—"

"Ssh! She's coming!" Lily cried as Vanessa reappeared with a tray containing two bowls of steaming hot crumble and a pot of local clotted cream.

I couldn't help but look at Vanessa in a different light. Suddenly the tattoos on her fingers took on a more sinister air. Were they gang related? A prison sentence was pretty serious. How did she get the job working on Tregarrick? How long had she been out, and did Patty the policewoman know?

Vanessa set the bowls down and left the clotted cream in the middle of the table.

"Not in the container. Put it into a glass bowl," Lily chastised. "Didn't they teach you anything in that *institution*?"

Vanessa reddened.

"I don't mind it in the pot," I said quickly. "Thank you, Vanessa. The crumble looks delicious."

"It's homemade," she said bluntly, and turned to leave.

Lily didn't wait for her to be out of earshot before declaring, "She's going to get her heart broken again, but she won't listen. I tried to tell her that Cador is not interested."

Vanessa stopped in her tracks.

"This is delicious," I said again, hoping to shut the old woman up, and added a third spoonful of cream onto my crumble.

"Now, you're far more his type," Lily went on loudly. "Intelligent, beautiful—and my brother said you got along very well last night at the Salty Boatman. Yes, I can definitely see you two together."

Vanessa stiffened, then marched out of the dining room.

Lily seemed to enjoy tormenting the poor girl. I was rapidly revising my opinion of her. There was a malicious streak that I didn't like at all.

"Actually I've recently lost my husband," I said. "He was the love of my life. I'm not interested."

"You're young, you'll bounce back," Lily said dismissively. "Was he a movie star?"

"He was to me," I said, and took another mouthful of crumble.

"I've had two husbands. Ralph, and then there was Harold—now Ralph was a tiny little man, which of course got him teased mercilessly at school—"

I listened politely and enjoyed my crumble as Lily droned on about poor Ralph's failings. I decided I'd had enough of Lily. I was desperate to interrupt her and go back to my room, but she didn't stop to draw breath.

To my relief, Vanessa returned with a *cafetière* of freshly brewed coffee, so I saw my chance.

"Ah! Coffee! But not for me," I exclaimed. "Sorry, Lily. I'm afraid I have to go back to my room and make a phone call."

"Vanessa! Put it here," Lily commanded, and made a space

on the table. Just as Vanessa was about to set the *cafetière* down, she tripped over Lily's knitting bag, only just managing to keep her balance. But the damage was done. Coffee had spilled onto Lily's precious cushion.

"You stupid, *stupid* girl!" Lily shrieked, and snatched up the cushion, using her white linen napkin in an attempt to soak up the liquid. "This will be stained now!"

"That's not my fault," Vanessa snapped. "How was I to know that your bag was on the floor?"

"I don't know why Jago keeps you on here," Lily grumbled. "If I had my way, I would have shown you the door months ago."

"It was just an accident," I protested, and shot Vanessa a look of what I hoped showed sympathetic support, but she ignored me.

"We all know why Dennis protects you," Lily ran on. "But he can't protect you forever."

Vanessa spun on her heel and hurried away.

I rose from the table. "I must go. It was nice talking to you."

"Wait, I'll come with you, Evie." We left the *cafetière* untouched. "I always have a nap in the afternoons."

Leaving Lily in her room, I hurried back to mine and was disappointed to find that Margot was still not back. She'd been gone for hours, and the island wasn't that big. I felt a twinge of anxiety. I jotted down a quick note to call my mobile and left it next to hers on the desk. I marked it "URGENT" in large capital letters.

Taking my Barbour, hat and my mobile, I set off for the elevator.

I heard voices at the end of the corridor.

"She'll be in her room. Let me do the talking first, please," and a man's clipped reply:

"We're doing nothing wrong. Just old friends."

It was Tegan . . . and she was with Alex! I had no desire to see Tegan ever again.

"You have no idea who you're dealing with," I heard her say. "That old bitch has made my life hell."

On impulse, I turned tail and fled. I ducked down another corridor on a hunch that it would eventually lead me to the back staircase that I'd noticed next to Jago's office.

I was right. It did. This wing of the hotel had to be the staff quarters and Jago and Tegan's private suite of rooms. I hurried down the staircase feeling like a trespasser and bumped straight into Jago waiting for me at the bottom.

"Good afternoon," he said.

Chapter Thirteen

I felt as if I had been caught stealing. I was also stuck on the wrong side of the cordon marked PRIVATE.

Once again I marveled at how this man could have been one of Robert's closest friends.

Jago was hot and sweaty. His hands were dirty. Dennis had mentioned he'd been chopping logs.

With exaggerated fastidiousness, Jago unhooked the chain to allow me to pass and muttered something. I couldn't be sure, but I thought I heard him say, "Can't even read."

"I heard that," I snapped. "And yes, I can read."

Jago seemed amused. "She speaks."

Finally, I had had enough. "Why did you lie to me? I know you and Robert went to Cambridge together."

Jago sneered. "And what makes you think that?"

"I saw the school photographs in your office," I said. "Robert had the same ones hanging in his. You both rowed for the Cambridge Blue Boats."

"I haven't spoken to *Bobby*—as he preferred to be called—for more than a decade," said Jago. "It was typical of him. When he grew tired of a friendship, he just moved on. When he met you, he discarded us—"

"Or he was forced to choose?" I suggested. "I know that Tegan and Joanna were close friends. She told me."

"What? When?" For the first time Jago seemed unnerved. "Did you . . . did you tell her about the loan?"

"Yes," I said. "She didn't believe me."

He gave a snort of contempt. "She wouldn't."

I felt foolish but still angry. "Why didn't you just tell me at the beginning?"

"Why?" He sounded incredulous. "I was curious to see just how much of a gold digger you are—"

"I'm flattered you would think so," I said sarcastically.

"I don't think you've got it in you. You're nothing like Joanna, are you," he said. "Now Joanna, she was a pistol. Fiery. Smart. Kept Bobby on his toes all the time. Funny as hell, but a real handful."

"Why are you telling me this?" I had given Joanna very little thought when Robert and I got together, but now . . . now . . . it was as if she were actually standing in the room.

"He liked the fact that you were boring and would never fool around," Jago went on.

Boring? I couldn't believe that Robert would say that about me. "I've done nothing to you, Jago," I said. "Why are you being so incredibly cruel?"

"Am I?" A flicker of sadness crossed his face. "I forget you're just a kid. In my experience, if you marry a beautiful woman then cruelty goes with the territory."

And then I realized that he had to be talking about Tegan. As if reading my mind, Jago added, "Yes, I turn a blind eye to the affairs my wife has with the tourists. But she'll never leave me as long as she thinks there is money in the bank."

I bit back the comment that if anyone was a gold digger, it sounded like Tegan was. I also wanted to add that it seemed as though she and Joanna were like two peas in a pod.

"Come with me," he said.

"Why?"

"I want to show you something."

"No thanks."

Jago gave a heavy sigh. "Do you want to know or not?"

With great reluctance I followed him into his office. He headed for a four-drawer filing cabinet. It was locked. Frustrated, he returned to his desk and started looking for keys, becoming more and more frantic.

As I watched him, I noticed that the Karlsson portrait had been removed and was standing against the wall with the front hidden from view. Given that Jago had admitted to knowing about Tegan's infidelities, I was surprised that this one seemed to bother him so much.

Exasperated, Jago hit a button on his retro desk phone and shouted, "Dennis, did you take the keys to the lighthouse?"

"Yes, sir," Dennis said. "As a precaution."

"Bring them to me."

"I'll be right there, sir."

Jago retrieved a key to unlock the filing cabinet. He sifted through the drawers until he found what he was looking for. After opening a manila folder, he brought out a letter and handed it to me.

"Here, read this," he said.

With a pang I recognized the headed notepaper and return address—Calverley Park, Tunbridge Wells. It was a receipt stating that the loan for one hundred thousand pounds had been paid back in full on March 21, 2011.

"Satisfied?" he said. "I cashed out a life insurance policy. In case you were tempted to ask where I got the money."

But I was barely listening to him. I stared in dismay at the typewritten receipt and signature.

It was definitely not Robert's signature. It seemed strange that the loan had been handwritten but the receipt had been typed. My stomach was in knots. "This isn't Robert's signature."

Jago's handsome face darkened. "What exactly are you implying?"

I took a step back. "I'm not implying anything," I faltered. "I'm just saying that this is not my husband's signature."

"I suppose now you are going to ask me for proof of payment? Well, that won't happen. I paid in cash."

I opened my mouth to say that was exactly what I wanted him to do, but I just didn't have the courage. Nigel had said the loan had been repaid, and here was the receipt on Robert's headed notepaper to prove it. It must have been Joanna who signed on his behalf. Why did it matter? It didn't affect me, so why should I care?

Dennis entered the room. "Here is the key to the lighthouse,

Mr. Jago—oh—sorry. I didn't realize you were in a meeting."
He must have picked up on the atmosphere, which was frosty,
to say the least. "Is everything alright?"

"Never better. Perhaps you could show Mrs. Mead out." Jago
pointed to the portrait. "And get rid of that, will you, Dennis?"

"Certainly. Where would you like me to put it?"

"You can burn it."

If Dennis seemed surprised, he didn't show it, but I must
have because Jago regarded me with distaste. "What? Are we
offending your artistic sensibilities?"

I didn't answer and left the room.

Tegan and Vanessa were in the lobby. There was no sign of
Alex Karlsson. I felt as if I were running the gauntlet. I just
wanted to sneak past them and dash outside.

"It's got to be in there," Tegan snapped as Vanessa continued
to search the drawers behind the counter.

"Here, let me look," said Tegan. "You're hopeless."

Tegan lifted up the countertop and ducked underneath.
"Stand aside." She started foraging through the drawers.

Vanessa spotted me coming. "If you're going out you have to
leave your room key. It's the rule."

So I left it on the counter, but then I had a thought. Even
though my mobile had not rung when I was being interrogated
by that hateful man, Margot could have come back to the hotel.

"Do you know if Margot—Mrs. Chandler—returned yet?"

Vanessa shrugged. "No idea."

A twinge of anxiety hit me again. Maybe she had actually
gotten lost. Lily had said it was easy to get disoriented. "Do you
have a map of the island?"

"Can you wait a minute?" said Vanessa as Tegan became more frantic in her search.

Dennis entered the lobby carrying the portrait. "Can I help you, Mrs. Tegan?"

"Ah, Dennis." Tegan waved him over. "I'm looking for the key to the lighthouse."

"Mr. Jago has the key," he said. "I'm afraid the lighthouse is out of bounds."

Tegan bristled with indignation. "According to whom?"

"It's just not safe," said Dennis. "As you know, the footbridge was washed away last winter."

"Washed away. That's one way of putting it." Tegan's jaw hardened. "As you know, my friend has come all the way from Sweden specifically to photograph Windward Point Lighthouse."

"I'm sure that he can photograph the lighthouse from the ruined watchtower." Dennis's expression remained neutral. "After all, that was the original lighthouse and must be of far more historical interest—if you don't mind me saying."

"I do mind. Wait . . . what have you got there?" She must have realized what Dennis was carrying because she ducked back into the lobby. "Where are you going with that?"

"Ask Mr. Jago," he said gruffly. "I'm sorry. I just follow orders."

Tegan grabbed his arm in a panic. "Please . . . please give that to me. It's very sentimental."

"I can't, I'm sorry—"

"Please don't destroy it," she begged.

Dennis pulled away and, clutching the portrait, walked out of the main entrance. A blast of wind whirled through the lobby as he left the hotel.

Tegan watched him go, her face white and pinched.

"Excuse me, Mrs. Tegan," I heard Vanessa say. "Would you mind staying in reception so I can take Cador his lunch?"

"Lunch? What?" Tegan seemed distracted. "Why?"

Vanessa reddened. "Cador didn't come in for lunch. So I made him his favorite brioche. Brie and apple chutney." She gestured to a package wrapped in aluminum foil.

"Oh for God's sake!" Tegan said irritably. "He's not interested in you, Vanessa. Stop being so pathetic and running after him the whole time. And get that dreadful tattoo removed. I can't imagine any man giving you a second look when you've got *Dave and I Until We Die* inked on your hand like a drug lord groupie."

I heard Vanessa gasp. I was shocked at Tegan's callous remark. Maybe Jago and Tegan deserved each other.

"Oh, give that to me." Tegan held out her hand for the package. "I'll take my son his lunch."

Vanessa meekly did as she was told.

"No. Wait. Where is Mr. Karlsson now?"

"In the Residents' Lounge," said Vanessa.

Tegan turned to me. "Are you going outside?"

"Yes."

"Give this to Cador," she said rudely. "He's probably still at William's Wood. Cut through the dell and then skirt the lake. You can't miss it. The woods are only on one side of the island." And with that, she headed off to the Residents' Lounge.

"Can I have a map, please, Vanessa?" I said.

She reached under the counter and handed me a folded sheet of paper in silence.

"Thank you." I hesitated, anxious to put the young girl at ease but not really knowing exactly how. "If Margot comes back, please tell her we're going to leave first thing in the morning and to start packing."

Vanessa's eyes widened. "You're leaving?"

"I wish it were sooner. Actually, if you see her, please ask her to call my mobile," I said.

"You'll be lucky," said Vanessa. "There's no signal in the dell." She thought for a moment. "Does Cador know you are leaving?"

"Why would I tell Cador? Oh, surely you don't think there is something between us?"

"Well, isn't there?" Vanessa demanded.

"Of course not!" I exclaimed. "I just lost my husband. Trust me, dating is the last thing on my mind."

"But you would say that, wouldn't you?" she said. "I saw how you looked at each other. I'm not blind."

I realized I was wasting my time trying to convince Vanessa otherwise. "How did Cador get here today?"

Vanessa shrugged.

"Did he dock the *Isadora* in the deepwater quay?" I asked.

"You mean William's Quay?" she said. "I don't know."

It was possible, given that it was neap tide, that Cador wouldn't have wanted to be stranded here overnight. If so, maybe there was a way for him to take Margot and me back with him.

"I will ask him." So, clutching Cador's lunch, I set off to do just that.

Chapter Fourteen

Once outside, I stopped on the terrace to take a look at the map and get my bearings. I recognized Tegan's artwork straightaway.

For a moment it was easy to imagine how beautiful it would be here at the height of the summer, with wicker tables, chairs and sun umbrellas up on the terrace; cocktails being served and perhaps everyone watching the sunset; maybe a game of croquet and a swim in the Mermaid Lagoon—an area of the property that I did not know existed until I saw it on Tegan's map. Cradled in a natural rock formation, the lagoon was several hundred yards from the coastline and accessed down a flight of steps to sea level. I assumed it was the hotel's answer to an outdoor swimming pool.

The map was exquisitely illustrated and provided a bird's-eye view of the extensive grounds. Each landmark was carefully drawn and labeled. Although not to scale, it showed the ruined watchtower on Windward Point, where majestic galleons laden with gold sailed on by to the New World—or sank, judging by the number of tiny anchors that Tegan had drawn in the ocean to mark a shipwreck.

Windward Point Lighthouse was just beyond, having been built on a small islet of rocks. This map showed a wooden footbridge—presumably the very one that had been washed away—linking Windward Point to the lighthouse.

On the coast path was a memorial seat labeled William's Bench. I looked for William's Quay, and sure enough, it was on the other side of the island, accessed by a steep flight of steps.

I set off to find Cador. Everywhere was sumptuously planted with mature banks of blowsy and tender subtropical plants. There were wide avenues of fine gravel lined with emerald-lawn clearings where—to my delight—gangs of Chinese pheasants darted across my path. I should have brought my Canon! If we were indeed stranded, I resolved to come back with it and take some proper photographs.

As I descended another flight of steps to the dell and headed for the Galleon Garden, I could no longer hear the crash of the surf on the rocks. It was eerily quiet.

The Galleon Garden was peppered with figureheads displayed in clipped box hedge alcoves. There had to be dozens, ranging from golden tigers to Neptune from the sea. A light mist had begun to roll in, creating the sinister impression that the figureheads were still riding the prows of their ships. I felt a shiver of foreboding and the distinct feeling that I was being watched.

The *Isadora* figurehead was there. She was bigger than I had expected and reminded me of Sleeping Beauty with her waist-length flaxen hair, fair skin and touch of red on her bow-shaped lips. Her long dress was painted sky blue with a bodice trimmed in gold braid. Isadora had one hand raised as if shielding her eyes from the sun's glare. She was beautiful.

Alex had said he'd been here when the figurehead was raised from the sea. Alex and Tegan had known each other for decades. Judging by everyone's reaction to Alex's reappearance, I found my imagination take a dangerous turn. What was he really doing on Tregarrick Rock?

Tegan was clearly unhappily married. I'd seen the shock on her face when I told her that Alex had been on the same ferry we had and Jago's knee-jerk reaction about destroying Alex's portrait of Tegan. Jago's bitter revelation about his wife's affairs only led me to conclude that she was conducting another one right under his nose. And Tegan had had the nerve to judge me!

Suddenly I was startled by a figure emerging through the mist. "Margot? Is that you?"

There was silence.

"Margot?" I said crossly. "Stop messing around."

Still silence.

The figure did not move. My heart began to thump in my chest. "Who is it?" I demanded. "Show yourself!"

Cador stepped forward, holding an axe. "It's only me."

"Why didn't you say so?" I exclaimed. "You scared me—especially holding *that*!"

He regarded the axe and grinned. "I had to be sure it was you and not Vanessa," he said. "Whenever Father and I have words, we chop logs—better than chopping up each other. What are you doing out here?"

"Looking for Margot—and also for you," I said. "The mist came down so fast."

"It always settles here. The Galleon Garden is in a natural dell."

"Are you going back to Tregarrick this afternoon?"

"Eventually," said Cador. "Depending on the weather."

"Did you dock your boat at William's Quay?"

Cador shook his head. "I use that place as a last resort. It's very difficult to get into. No, I came over on a skiff. It's moored next to the sea tractor. Why? You're not thinking of leaving, are you?"

"We have to," I said.

"So no filming here after all."

"Filming?" I was puzzled.

"The reason for being here?" Cador reminded me. "Scouting for a location?"

"Oh yes," I said. "I don't think . . . don't think it's suitable after all. The difficulty of the tide . . ." Which sounded like a convincing enough reason to me because it was true! But I still wished I hadn't lied to him.

"You know, in the summer months the water is turquoise. Just like the Caribbean. You're not seeing Tregarrick Rock at its best in November."

"I just do what I'm told," I said.

"Or did my father put you off?" Cador persisted. "I feel I must apologize for his rudeness."

"Not at all," I said. "I do need to find Margot, though."

"I saw her at least an hour ago, maybe more," he said.

"Do you know which way she went?"

"I'm sorry, I didn't notice. I was a bit preoccupied with my own problems." He gave an apologetic smile. "If I were you, I'd go back to the hotel and wait for her. The mist is only going to get worse."

"Is there a quicker route?"

Cador jabbed a finger. "Cut through the woods. It will loop you back to the hotel near the kitchens. It'll take you about ten minutes tops." He hesitated before adding, "I'm very disappointed that you are leaving so soon."

"Yes. Well. It's just one of those things," I said lamely. "Would you mind taking us back in your skiff?"

"For someone who says she gets deathly seasick, I wouldn't recommend it," said Cador. "When the tide comes in and meets over the causeway, the swell makes the crossing on the *Scillonian* feel like a millpond. And besides, there wouldn't be room for all that luggage."

"I feel as if I am being held captive on Alcatraz," I said wryly.

Cador laughed. "I hope I can persuade you to come back to Scilly in the summer. Would you consider it?"

There was something in his tone that surprised me. Lily had said I was Cador's "type," and there was no denying he was an attractive man. I felt confused and ashamed that I would even think about him in that way.

I gave a polite smile. I had no idea where I would be next summer. Even the thought of next week filled me with anxiety. Whoever had said that Tregarrick Rock felt like a sanctuary was right. My real life in Kent suddenly seemed so far away.

"Oh, I almost forgot." I withdrew the brioche wrapped in

foil. "For you. It's from Vanessa—Brie and apple chutney. She said it was your favorite."

He made some dismissive comment. There was a rustle in the undergrowth and the sound of a snapping twig. He grabbed my arm. "Ssh!"

There it was again—the crunch of dead leaves and then silence.

"Vanessa!" Cador called out sharply. "I know it's you. I know you're there!" He rolled his eyes before adding in a low voice, "She just doesn't get it. Won't take no for an answer."

"If it is Vanessa, she may have a message for me," I said quietly. "Margot could have tried to call—"

"You won't get a phone signal anywhere in the dell," said Cador. "You'd need to go to higher ground."

"I realize that, but I need to know if Margot is back."

"Alright, but don't say I didn't warn you," said Cador. "I took Vanessa out for one drink . . . and now she just won't leave me alone."

"Vanessa?" I said loudly. "Come and join us."

Cador rolled his eyes again.

Sure enough, Vanessa emerged from the shadows. I noticed that she had applied heavy red lipstick. "Did you like your brioche, Cador?"

Cador barely looked at her. "Excuse me, I've got to go—"

"Where are you going?" Vanessa demanded. "Can I come?"

"I've got to go and feed the cat." And with that, he hurried off. I thought it rude and unnecessarily unkind.

"What did he mean by that?" Vanessa exclaimed. "Feed the cat? Lily feeds the cat."

"I really have no idea."

She regarded me with suspicion. "It's code, isn't it. He wants you to meet him somewhere secret."

"Of course not."

"But you would deny it, wouldn't you?"

Perhaps there was something in Cador's reaction to his admirer after all. "Did Margot get back to the hotel?" I said, changing the subject.

Vanessa hesitated for a moment. "I think I saw her about twenty minutes ago."

"Oh good. Where?"

She smiled and when she smiled, she looked quite pretty.

She pointed in the direction of the lake. "She was going that way. See that path?"

"Toward the ruined watchtower?" I was surprised. It was away from the hotel. "Are you sure?"

Vanessa scowled. "You asked me and that's what I saw. Maybe she's lost. She didn't take a map, and it's easy to get turned around."

"Thank you."

"You should go and find her," Vanessa said suddenly. "Mizzle is coming in, too."

"What on earth is mizzle?"

"It's a misty drizzle," she said. "You'll get soaked through and won't be able to see in front of your hand."

"Then I'd better hurry after her." I hesitated before adding, "What are you doing out here?"

"Just making sure Cador got his lunch."

I left her watching me and headed for the lake. I hadn't been walking for more than ten minutes when I heard the sound of voices heading my way.

"Dennis won't destroy it, he wouldn't dare. He likes me," said Tegan. "He'll have hidden it somewhere."

Impulsively I darted through an opening marked TO THE BIRD HIDE. QUIET, PLEASE. I didn't want to see them. I'd just wait among the bushes for them to pass on by.

Chapter Fifteen

Unfortunately, Tegan and Alex stopped right outside the entrance.

"Can we look at the lake?" Alex asked. "Just for a minute?"

Damn and blast!

I took off along the duckboards that were lined with bulrushes and pampas grass that zigzagged across the wetlands, only to come to an abrupt end at a small rectangular wooden shed on the edge of the lake.

I was completely trapped, but then I had an idea. I opened the door and stepped inside.

A dull light filtered in from one of the open shutters that looked out over the water. A low bench stretched the length of the building, with two rows of shutters above it.

I braced myself for Alex and Tegan's arrival, and sure enough, I felt the vibration of the duckboards as they drew closer and heard Tegan say, "Do you think Jago saw us come this way?"

"I don't care if he did," said Alex. "We're doing nothing wrong."

"You don't understand his temper," Tegan said.

Quickly, I took up my position and brought out my iPhone, hoping I looked as if I were out to photograph the birds.

The door opened and Tegan and Alex entered.

"What are you doing here?" Tegan exclaimed.

"Hello." I brandished my mobile. "I just saw a heron."

Alex just smiled. "You can get a good photograph with an iPhone these days."

I immediately realized my faux pas. What would a so-called professional photographer be doing taking photographs of birds with an iPhone? But before I could answer, Tegan gave a cry of alarm.

A shadow loomed in the doorway. Inexplicably, my heart turned right over.

It was Jago. I couldn't see his expression because the light was behind him.

Alex suddenly bent over double, clutching his stomach and gasping in pain. He collapsed onto the bench.

Tegan uttered a cry and only just managed to stop herself from going to his side.

"Cowards as well." Jago stepped into the hide. "You're coming with me!" He went to grab Tegan's arm, but I stepped quickly in front of her. A flicker of confusion crossed his face.

"Keep your voice down!" I hissed. "You'll scare away the golden plovers."

Jago glanced out of the open shutter, as did I. There—to my relief and astonishment—really was a pair of golden plovers.

"Thank you for showing Alex and me the bird hide," I said to Tegan.

"You're welcome," she said, but I could hear a tremor in her voice. "Really, Jago, do you always have to be so rude to our guests?" She pushed past him, but he grabbed her wrist, whispering something into her ear before releasing her and letting her leave. He followed her out and slammed the door behind them, leaving me alone with Alex.

"Do you need your medication?" I asked him.

Alex shook his head. "I'm already taking too much."

I sat down beside him. "Are you alright?"

Alex hesitated. "I may as well tell you," he said slowly. "I've got terminal cancer. I've been given six months."

"Oh. God. I'm so sorry. I don't know what to say."

"Tegan didn't expect me to come, but I just had to see her one last time."

"Ah." I sat down beside him and felt compelled to take his hand.

"Funny that I can tell a complete stranger my personal life," Alex mused.

"Yes. It happens sometimes." I thought of all the things I wished I could share with Margot but never would.

"I think I have made Tegan's life more complicated now," Alex went on. "We met forty years ago and yet it seems like it was yesterday. I feel the same way about her now as I did then."

And it seemed that Tegan still felt the same way, too. "Forty years is a long time."

"I'm guessing it's more years than you have been on this earth," he said.

"Yes," I said. "When did you and Tegan last see each other?"

"September first, 1980. I spent the summer at the hotel with my parents."

"The year the *Isadora* figurehead was dredged up?"

"Tegan and I were crazy about each other," he said. "But our parents thought it was just a holiday romance." He gave a sad smile. "I never forgot her. She was always at the back of my mind. I lived a nomadic life, as you probably gathered, since you know my work."

I nodded. "You were one of the first exhibitions I helped put on at the gallery. I did a lot of research on you."

I vividly remembered the stories about Alex Karlsson's glamorous life—his constant dance with danger, the fast cars, exotic locations and, always, a beautiful woman on his arm. "You were a bit of an enigma. All my friends had crushes on you. Including me!"

"Karma is a bitch, as they say." Alex gave a sardonic smile. "I would have made a terrible husband. Didn't want to feel trapped. I've always enjoyed my freedom and now I'm just a pathetic lonely old man dying of cancer."

"Who is one of the most talented photographers I have ever met," I enthused. "And whose work will live on forever."

Alex fell quiet for a moment. "When you know your days are numbered you start to look back at your life. Make a reckoning of good and bad. Foolish mistakes as well as wise choices. I knew I had to find out why Tegan stopped replying to my letters. We were soul mates—young, yes—but I knew she was the one. I couldn't understand it. At the beginning, we wrote every day, and then . . . I remember it distinctly, around Christmas the letters just stopped."

"But how did you find her?"

"The Internet. Google alerts. Tegan sells her art online," he said. "I found her website and just followed her work. I didn't contact her, you understand. In fact, I didn't want to. I was shocked that she married Jago Ferris and hurt because it happened so quickly—just months after she stopped writing to me."

"What made you change your mind?"

"When she turned fifty." He smiled again. "I reached out to wish her a happy birthday. We started e-mailing—all innocent enough. Just old friends until . . ."

"Until what?"

"She asked me why I had never replied to her letters. We worked out that hers and mine had been intercepted. Her mother worked at the post office—"

"She was a friend of Lily's?"

"Exactly." Alex nodded. "Of course Tegan's mother died years ago . . . ."

No wonder Lily had panicked when she learned that Alex had come to see Tegan. She must have known that her part in the deception would be discovered.

"What happened to the letters?"

"Lily says they were destroyed, but Tegan doesn't believe her. She says that Lily is a bit of a hoarder." Alex gave a heavy sigh. "Staying in touch was difficult in those days. Back then we relied on letters. Phone calls were out of the question. They were too expensive. When her letters stopped coming I threw myself into my work. I've always been a workaholic. I thought of her every now and then, but it was only a few months ago, when I realized that my time on this earth was running out, that I knew I had to see her again."

I felt a twinge of compassion for Tegan, but also a spark of anger for Alex. How dare he just turn up out of the blue and upset her life—they didn't even have a future together.

"So what are you going to do now?" I asked.

"Try to save my portrait," he said. "I told Tegan that my earlier work was worth quite a bit. It would give her some money of her own. Enough to buy her freedom."

"Don't you think it's made things difficult for Tegan?" I said. "You being here."

"Yes," he admitted. "But I'm a dying man so I think that gives me a pink pass."

"How long are you planning on staying at Tregarrick?" I asked.

He shrugged. "For as long as I'm upright. I've got nothing else to do."

"Except photograph the lighthouse?"

"Ah . . . the lighthouse." He smiled at some past memory.

I had completely forgotten the time and the fact that I was supposed to be looking for Margot. "Did you see Margot, by any chance?"

"Your friend?"

"Actually, she's my sister." I found I wanted to be honest with this man.

I told Alex that I was a widow and that our trip to Scilly was just for a weekend away to placate Margot; that even though she was a Hollywood film producer, I wasn't a location scout. I left the bit out about the loan and Robert's connection to Jago Ferris.

"Oh, I'm sorry for your loss," said Alex, and then, to my dismay, I felt tears well up and spill down my cheeks. I brushed them away.

"Sorry," I whispered.

Alex put his arm around my shoulders and held me for what seemed a long time but was probably just minutes, before finally, I pulled myself away.

"That was embarrassing." I sniffed. "As you said, funny that we can confide in total strangers that we know we'll never see again."

Alex gave a nod of agreement. "You know, I think I did see your sister. Was she wearing one of those hideous black waterproof hooded capes?"

"Yes."

"I saw her going up the fire escape onto a balcony."

"Really?" I exclaimed. "When?"

"A good hour or so ago."

I felt relieved. "Good. At least she found her way back to the hotel safely."

Vanessa must have been wrong.

I checked my watch. "I have to get back. Are you coming?"

"You go. I am going to stay here for a moment."

I left him in the bird hide and jogged back along the duckboards, surprised at the fading winter daylight. It got dark so much earlier here.

I took an animal track through a wooded glade but stopped

in surprise when I came to a clearing. This was not the way I had come earlier—or was it? I stood facing a wall of shoulder-high bracken.

I pulled out the map to check my bearings and realized I must have taken a wrong turn when I exited the bird hide, but if I cut down this path, it should lead me back to the Galleon Garden.

Fifteen minutes later I was hopelessly lost.

Chapter Sixteen

The mist had come down quickly and I soon realized why the locals called it mizzle. My hair hung in damp clumps around my face. My woolen gloves were soaked through. I also realized that the squiggles that symbolized the maze on the map were just that, squiggles. They were not paths at all.

The bracken came above my shoulders and the grassy path was narrow and covered with moss that muffled my footsteps. I tried using the flashlight on my iPhone, but it was useless. All it did was cast a yellow light and make my surroundings fuzzy.

I stared at the compass feature on my iPhone and it made no sense to me at all. I was all turned around.

The needle said I was facing east, but wouldn't that put me walking toward the coast path? I stood in the clearing and stared at the two paths in front of me. I couldn't hear the waves, and given the thick mist and lack of phone signal, I assumed I had to be nearing the Galleon Garden again.

Soon I reached another clearing with a choice of *three* different paths. I fought down the first twinge of panic. All the paths looked the same! Tegan's map was useless.

I consulted my compass again. Now it showed I was facing south. South was the hotel, wasn't it? I plunged down the left track, walking quickly. To my relief, the path began to rise steadily upward.

Yes, I was certain I was on the right path, but then, abruptly, it steepened and I found myself stumbling over a mound of lichen-covered boulders. Suddenly the bracken fell away and farther up the mist gave way to dark clouds.

I could hear the sound of the surf crashing below now. I had to be on the northern tip of the island after all, but at least I would be able to get my bearings when I got to the top—and use my phone.

I struggled uphill for a while, passing by a wooden bench with a plaque—William's Bench. Out of the mist loomed an enormous rock formation that completely blocked the path. There was no other choice but to turn back.

Then . . . a rattle of stones and out of the corner of my eye I caught a flicker of movement. Someone was there.

"Vanessa?" I said. "Is that you?"

But instead came a harsh cry as a bird took flight. The whole place was giving me the creeps.

I became aware of a familiar smell drifting on the vagrant breeze. It was cigarette smoke. It hadn't been my imagination after all. I was being followed. But who smoked? Jago? Vicar Bill? Margot—even though she claimed to have given it up?

And there was something else—a peculiar whistling sound,

haunting and eerie. Surely it couldn't be the whistle buoy off-shore? If it was, then I had to be nearing Windward Point. Walking along such a treacherous path in these weather conditions was madness.

Carefully I began to retrace my steps, conscious that on my right had to be the cliff edge. Mist had thickened to fog. I could barely see one foot in front of the other.

I switched my iPhone on again, but it was hopeless. There was a signal—albeit weak. I tried calling Margot, but her phone went straight to voice mail.

I took another step forward, but to my horror the ground abruptly fell away. Time just slowed down. I felt myself tip forward, arms wheeling, trying to keep my balance—I could hear screaming. It was coming from me.

Then, strong fingers clamped on to my shoulders and hauled me backwards, spinning me around. I lost my balance and fell heavily onto the rocky ground. I cried out as a searing pain shot through my shoulder.

"You stupid girl!" came an angry voice. "You could have been killed!"

It was Dennis. I was shocked and so shaken I could only blurt out, "I nearly . . . I nearly went over the edge."

"Are you hurt?" Dennis demanded as he helped me to my feet.

I shook my head.

"What the hell are you doing out here?"

"I was looking for Margot," I faltered. "I got lost."

"Have you seen Mr. Jago?"

"Yes. A little earlier," I said. "At the bird hide and possibly a few moments ago—I smelled cigarette smoke. He smokes, doesn't he?"

"Yes."

Jago must have escorted Tegan back to the hotel and then come out again.

"You're still shaking," he said.

"You scared me." And he was still scaring me. There was something distinctly menacing about Dennis suddenly materializing out of thin air, dressed in his hotel black waterproof hooded cape and Wellington boots.

"I'm sorry," he said. "I didn't mean to, but . . . I want to show you something."

I hesitated.

He took my arm.

I stiffened.

"I'm not going to hurt you!" Dennis said, exasperated, and gently guided me back to the slab of rock where I had been standing just moments before. He switched on an LED flashlight.

"Why are you only just turning this on now?" I said. "I would have seen you coming."

"I'm afraid I can't tell you why," said Dennis. "You just have to trust me that there was a reason. Here—see this?"

I stood back and dug my heels in. "I really don't want to."

"*Look!*" He trained the LED beam along the ground and then . . . to my acute distress . . . to the lip of the cliff. "The path has crumbled away. You were very lucky."

"I know," I whispered.

Dennis moved closer to the edge. "Do you want to see just how far down it is?"

"Please," I begged. "Just let me go back to the hotel. I believe you."

"It's a sheer drop of about seventy-five feet. All the way down to the—" He suddenly froze. "Oh no. Oh God."

His voice sounded strange. It was high-pitched and stilted.

My stomach turned over. Panic rose in my chest. "What's the matter?" I exclaimed. "What's wrong? What is it?"

"Stand back," Dennis said harshly, but this time I didn't. I took his flashlight and gingerly stepped forward to look into the abyss.

He didn't even try to stop me.

Heart in mouth, I swung the beam down and saw what looked like a pile of rags on the beach at the bottom of the cliff. "Oh God," I whispered. "Who *is* it?"

For a moment I thought, petrified, of Margot. But no, Alex had seen her going up the fire escape. Was it Alex? I knew he had planned to walk this way.

"Who *is* it?" I said again.

Dennis's voice cracked with alarm. "It's-it's-Mr. Jago."

Chapter Seventeen

I was horrified. "He must have fallen."

"No," said Dennis. "Mr. Jago knew this path like the back of his hand. He did not fall."

He turned to me, his face a mask of shock. "What were you really doing up here?"

"I told you, I was looking for Margot."

Dennis regarded me with suspicion. "Did you see Vanessa?"

"Yes. She . . . she followed me to the Galleon Garden," I stammered. "I don't know where she went after that."

Dennis's jaw hardened. "Why would she follow you?"

I felt uncomfortable. "Because Tegan asked me to take Cador his lunch."

"So Cador was still out here? When? What time was this?"

"I don't know," I exclaimed. "Hours ago! Surely . . . it was just an accident. Perhaps Jago was going to the lighthouse? It's this way, isn't it? Remember? I was in his office when you gave him the keys."

Dennis shook his head. "No, something isn't right." He ran his fingers through his closely cropped hair. "I told him I would handle it."

My stomach flipped over. "What do you mean? Handle what?" I thought of Jago's fury in the bird hide and of Alex's determination to see the lighthouse one more time.

Dennis looked at me with an expression that I couldn't quite fathom.

"Why are you looking at me like that?" I whispered, but then I was struck by an alarming thought. "Is the beach tidal?"

"Good grief!" Dennis exclaimed. "Yes. The tide does come in right up to the cliff base! Quickly, we have to go and move his body onto higher ground."

"I should go for help," I said.

"You're not going anywhere," he said coldly. "You're staying right here with me."

But then he stopped. "Listen."

"I can't hear anything." My ears strained, but all I heard was the crash of the surf below and the siren song of the whistle buoy.

"Listen!" Dennis swung the LED flashlight out to sea, but there seemed to be nothing there except the dark, black water.

He grabbed my hand.

"What are you doing?" I dug my toes in. "I want to go back to the hotel."

"I can't leave you here. I . . . I need you to come with me."

My heart skipped a beat. "Why?"

"You need to come with me," Dennis said harshly. "The path down to the cove is treacherous. If I fall, no one will know where I am."

I relented. "Alright. But I don't need to hold your hand."

Dennis took off with me trailing behind. By the light of his torch, I realized just how narrow the path really was. It clung to the cliff face and in many places was no wider than a two-foot ledge. Yes, I'd been very lucky.

When we reached the rock formation, Dennis pointed to a narrow fissure. "We can get through there. I'll go first."

It was a squeeze, but out on the other side we emerged at the top of a steep flight of steps hewn into the rock face. It zigzagged down out of sight. A rope handhold was secured by a series of rusty iron rings bolted into the cliff.

I was struck by the obvious—how on earth would we be able to bring Jago's body back up here?

Then suddenly, the fog lifted as quickly as it had come down. A three-quarter moon shone brightly among a carpet of stars to light our way.

We were halfway down the steps when another path veered off to the right and forked. A bleached wooden signpost indicated that to the left were steps up to the ruined watchtower and to the right, a muddy track down to Windward Point Lighthouse.

"Dennis!" I called out. "Perhaps Jago didn't fall from the top. The path to the lighthouse is just there—see?"

But Dennis didn't answer. He seemed set on getting to Jago's body as quickly as possible and hurried on down, jumping the final ten feet or so. He tore across the beach.

I scrambled to the bottom and followed, but not before I noticed a deep V-shaped trough in the sand from the shoreline at the base of the cliff.

It looked like the hull of a boat. Someone had dragged a boat up here, and the fact that the mark was still evident meant that it had been recent. It wouldn't be long before the tide would wash that trough away. It was already coming in very quickly. If Dennis hadn't spotted him, Jago's body would have been washed out to sea and no one would ever have known what happened to him.

"Evie!" Dennis waved me over. "Quickly!"

I took off at a run. Perhaps Jago was still alive, I thought, but as I drew closer I realized it was impossible.

"See?" Dennis exclaimed. "Do you *see*?"

Jago was lying facedown in the sand with the back of his head smashed to a pulp. "Oh God," I whispered. "Oh no!"

"These are not the wounds of someone who took an accidental fall," Dennis said shakily.

"No, no, they're not," I whispered. "What should we do?"

"The force must have come from behind. This was deliberate."

I felt sick and just stood there, feeling helpless.

"Who would want to do this?" Dennis cried. "Who *could* do this?"

I shook my head. "I just don't know."

Dennis stood up and took off his waterproof hooded cape. He laid it over Jago's face. "Help me drag him up to the ledge. The incoming tide won't get him there."

I nodded agreement. "We're not supposed to move him, though—but—"

"Have you a better idea?"

Moving Jago was difficult. Dennis did the best he could by

wrapping Jago's head in the cape, but he still got blood on his clothes. Somehow we managed to haul Jago onto a ledge just half a dozen feet up from the sand. I was physically and emotionally exhausted. Dennis looked shattered.

"What now?" I said.

"Go to the top. Call for help. Then tell Cador. If anyone can get a boat to this beach it's him. Otherwise we'll have to wait for the medical launch—no, the coast guard would be better. They'll be able to airlift Jago's body out."

"You can't possibly stay here all night," I said. "At least come back and get some warm clothes."

Dennis muttered, "Leave no man behind."

I hesitated, unsure whether to tell him about the trough I'd noticed on the sand, but my face must have given me away.

"What's the matter?" he said.

"I want to show you something. The tide is coming in, but the marks might still be there."

We hurried back down to the beach. Dennis crouched to study all that remained of the V-shaped trough. But it was enough.

"It's the hull of a boat, isn't it," I said finally.

"Looks like it," he said gruffly.

"And in another thirty minutes it would have been washed away."

And then I was struck by a terrible thought.

Cador was the only person capable of navigating these waters. He'd fought with his father earlier in the day. Could their argument have turned violent?

We left the beach.

"That still doesn't explain why Jago was walking on the coast path," Dennis said again. "Or why you were walking there, too."

"But I've already told you. Surely you don't think—" I was appalled.

"I know you and Jago argued," said Dennis. "What were you arguing about?"

I was stunned. "It's none of your business!"

"Is that why you were in such a hurry to get off the island this afternoon?" Dennis frowned. "And why didn't your friend come down for luncheon? Where is she? You said yourself you've been out looking for her—"

"You're being ridiculous," I said hotly.

Dennis grabbed my arm. His face was an ugly mask of accusation.

"Take your hands off me!"

"Your plan backfired because you got lost." Dennis was getting more and more agitated. "You and your friend are in this together. I heard you on the sea tractor making plans to take over the hotel—"

"You couldn't be more wrong!" I exclaimed. "You're not being logical! Where would I begin to get a boat?"

But then all of a sudden, Dennis sank down onto a step and put his head in his hands. He seemed devastated. "It can't be Cador. I won't believe it—he'd never do that. He and Mr. Jago may not see eye to eye, but Cador's not a violent man. He'd never do that to his father."

"I'm sure you're right." But what did I know? My own safe world had been turned upside down in the last twenty-four hours. Did anyone really know anybody?

"Mr. Jago was a good man," Dennis went on quietly. "Yes, he was rude, arrogant and entitled, but he saved me from a life on the streets. I'd have done anything for him."

I didn't know what to say, so I just listened.

"After I got back from my last tour in Afghanistan I was in a pretty bad way. Mr. Jago found me outside the railway station. I was homeless. He offered me a job working in the garden here. That was thirteen years ago." Dennis shook his head, clearly distressed. "Mr. Jago didn't deserve this . . . he . . ."

"Let's go for help," I said gently. "Together."

Dennis got to his feet and suddenly his expression hardened. "When I find out who did this, I will kill them."

Chapter Eighteen

Dennis stood in front of the reception counter, hands clenched. "Mrs. Tegan—"

"One moment, I'm almost finished." Tegan continued tapping away on one of the computer workstations, cursing under her breath as she hurriedly entered some information. Her coat was tossed across the back of the chair and I could see she was still wearing her hiking shoes.

"Really, we need new computers," she grumbled. "These are archaic!"

Dennis began to shiver. He had been silent on our walk back to the hotel after insisting that he would be the one to break the news to Tegan first and let her call the police. I thought that was a little odd, but when I protested he told me to keep out of it. But now I wondered if shock was starting to set in.

Dennis struggled to clear his throat. "Mrs.—"

"What?" Tegan looked up, irritated. "What can be so important?"

"There's been . . . there's been . . ." Dennis couldn't finish the sentence, so I did it for him.

"An accident," I said.

Tegan sat very still. Her face showed no emotion. "He's alright, though, isn't he?"

Dennis shook his head.

"No," Tegan whispered. *"No!"* She leapt up from the chair. "Where is he?"

"We left him on a ledge above the beach. Safe from the incoming tide," I said.

"He was on his way to the lighthouse, wasn't he?" Tegan asked.

"I don't know," I said. "But it looked like it."

"He was determined to go," she exclaimed. "*Determined.* You didn't leave him alone out there, did you?"

"Just for now. He's safe from the tide," I said again. "Dennis has come to get warm clothes and then he is going back."

"Is anything broken? Can he walk?" Tegan demanded.

"Dennis," I said quickly, "why don't you go into the office and phone the coast guard or the police or whatever you need to do." He nodded and left us.

I turned to Tegan. "Let's go and sit down."

To my surprise, she allowed me to guide her into the Residents' Lounge. I'd not been in there before, but it was hard to miss the seventies décor. We sat down on a garish modular sofa in brown leatherette.

Strain was etched in lines on Tegan's face that had not been there yesterday. She looked a decade older than her years.

"I should thank you for saving me from my husband's wrath

this afternoon in the bird hide," Tegan said in a dull voice. "So . . . thank you. And now . . . I'm being punished. Yes. I'm being punished."

I squeezed her hand. "I'm sorry."

"He's dead, isn't he."

"Yes."

She nodded as if she had been expecting it. "What happened?"

"It looked like it happened on the coast path on the way to the lighthouse. He . . ." I didn't want to give the details. I would leave that to the police.

"The path . . . it's dangerous," Tegan said slowly. "I told Alex we couldn't get to the lighthouse, but he must have walked back after all. I *told* him the path was dangerous." She gave a wistful smile. "He never cared about danger. He was determined to see the lighthouse again before he . . . well . . . perhaps this is the best for all of us. Alex was a very sick man."

With a jolt, I realized that Tegan believed it was Alex who had fallen, which meant that she hadn't been with him since the incident in the bird hide. Alex couldn't have returned to the hotel.

"Tegan, I—It wasn't Alex. It was . . ." I took a deep breath. "It was your husband."

Tegan's jaw dropped. *"Jago?"* She shook her head vehemently. "No. That's not possible. Jago would never go there. Never." She turned to me, wide-eyed. "What really happened, Evie? What aren't you telling me?"

I took a deep breath. I hadn't wanted to say anything, but she would find out soon enough. "It may not have been an accident," I said slowly. "It looked as if your husband was . . ." I thought of Jago's bloodied head and found I just couldn't finish the sentence. But I didn't need to.

"You're saying that someone deliberately hurt him."

"It would seem so," I said carefully.

Tegan went very quiet. We sat there for what seemed like minutes until she said, "Where is Cador?"

"I saw him out by William's Wood earlier, but that was hours ago." Of course Cador had to be told. "Do you want me to find him? Alex? Call someone?"

"I don't know where Alex is." Tegan bit her lip. "We argued." She mumbled something incoherent that sounded like "Cador can't have known." I thought of the V-shaped trough in the sand.

On a teak sideboard was a silver tray with cut crystal decanters and a selection of glasses. I got up and poured us each a balloon of brandy.

"Here," I said.

The liquid burned my throat, but I was grateful because it seemed to clear my head.

"Can I have a cigarette, please?" She gestured to the sideboard. "There is a packet of Benson Lights in the drawer at the back. Lily orders them for me on the Internet and hides them from Jago. I don't suppose I need to worry about that anymore."

I did what she asked. Tegan lit up and inhaled deeply. I remembered the smell of the cigarette smoke earlier on the coast path. "Does Alex smoke too?"

"Of course," she said. "Anything that puts him in danger."

Tegan took a gulp of brandy. "They always fought, you know. They were so different. Jago thought Cador's dreams of hunting for shipwrecks childish. He was adamant that Cador take over the running of the Tregarrick estate. But he *did* love him. I know he did." She looked at me with a sad smile.

"What's happened?" Vanessa appeared in the archway. "Why is Dennis so upset?"

Tegan's behavior changed immediately. "Thank you, Evie," she said imperiously. "I will take things from here."

I had been dismissed. I got to my feet, downed the rest of the brandy and put the balloon back on the silver tray.

"You're supposed to be on duty, Vanessa," Tegan said. "Where have you been?"

Vanessa didn't answer.

"Have you seen Cador?" Tegan demanded.

"No. Why is Dennis so upset?" Vanessa said again.

I slipped out of the Residents' Lounge, anxious to get back to my room, and ducked under the counter to retrieve my key from the hotel pigeonhole cabinet.

As I popped it into my pocket, I couldn't help but notice the computer screen. It was open to a travel page. I stepped closer, knowing I was being nosy, but I just had a strange premonition that I knew what would be up there.

I was right. It was a confirmation for a one-way air ticket from Heathrow Airport to Stockholm. The date was for Monday morning. Of course, I thought. Tegan must have been helping Alex with his return travel plans. But then I noticed that there were two passengers listed as traveling, and the second one was Tegan Ferris. A closer look showed me that the ticket had not been purchased yet. She had to have stopped when Dennis and I turned up.

I felt sick. So they had been planning to run off together. Maybe Jago and Alex had bumped into each other on the coast path and there had been a struggle.

I wished I hadn't seen the reservation. Now I didn't know what to do—or whom to tell. The police?

I only hoped that Alex was right and that Margot had returned to the hotel. I desperately needed to talk to her. She would know what to do.

And then I was struck by the most terrible thought. What if Margot had something to do with this? It seemed so outlandish, but then nothing had been normal since the moment we got here. It couldn't be, could it?

I hurried back to our room.

Chapter Nineteen

Margot opened the door wearing a fluffy white robe, her hair wrapped up in a towel. She looked terrible. Her eyes were puffy and red.

"What's wrong?" I asked.

"I should ask the same of you." Margot stepped back to let me inside. "You look as if you have seen a ghost."

She unwrapped her hair and started drying it. "It's just as well I brought my hair dryer and my robe," she grumbled. "They don't have any hospitality items here at all—What? Why are you looking at me like that?"

"Where have you been? Why were you gone for so long?" I demanded. "And you left your mobile. You never leave your phone behind!"

"I could say the same of you," Margot retorted. "I've been back for hours. Whatever is the matter with you?"

"Jago's dead!" I said. And promptly burst into tears.

Margot looked shocked. "What are you talking about?"

And so I told her everything.

There is one thing I will say about my big sister. She may come across as blasé most of the time, but when it really matters, she always comes through.

"You seriously thought I had something to do with it?" Margot was incredulous. "Jeez, Evie."

"Of course not," I protested. "It's just . . . you were wandering around out there—I hate it here. I want to go home. But we can't. We're stuck!"

"We'll talk action plan later," she said briskly. "For now, clothes off and a hot bath. You're going to love the bathroom."

"Don't tell me, there's an avocado corner bath like Mum and Dad had at the guesthouse?"

"It *was* hideous, wasn't it?" Margot grinned. "But no, you are in for a treat."

For a moment, I forgot all about Jago as I admired an Art Deco bathroom in onyx and marble. There were floor-to-ceiling beveled mirrors and ocean-inspired taps and handles that adorned the original vanity units and, naturally, a rolltop bathtub.

"Not a shag pile carpet to be seen," said Margot. "Although the green linoleum is pretty disgusting."

Margot ran me a bath, adding in lashings of her aromatherapy bubble bath that apparently she got for a "steal" at Barneys, a store in Beverly Hills.

As I luxuriated in chin-deep bubbles, Margot perched on the loo seat and asked me to tell her everything all over again.

"Holy cow," she said. "You're talking murder, Evie."

"I know," I said. "It was horrific. I'll never get that image out of my mind."

"*Cui bono?*" Margot whispered. "Who benefits?"

"Alex and Tegan." I went on to tell her about the cigarette smoke on the coast path and the airline reservations I'd seen on Tegan's computer. "They met when they were teenagers," I said finally.

"How very *On Golden Pond*."

"They're not that old," I said.

"In Hollywood you're in the grave at thirty," Margot said. "At the sign of the first wrinkle women are shipped out to Death Valley on a one-way ticket. But that's irrelevant. Tegan is—was—married."

Margot pursed her lips in disapproval. She had very strong opinions when it came to fidelity, so of course I left out the unpleasant altercation I'd had with Tegan in the storage room.

I'd never really told Margot all the circumstances of how Robert and I first met. Even though Joanna had moved out and I was not the cause of his divorce, he had still been legally married.

"Evie?" Margot broke into my thoughts. "I said what about Cador?"

"The only way he'd benefit was by not having to answer to his father," I said.

"And then of course, there's you."

"What do you mean?" I said slowly.

"You!" Margot rolled her eyes. "You would benefit."

"How come?"

"You just told me that the receipt Jago showed you was not signed by Robert. Therefore there is no proof that the money was ever actually received by Robert. Ergo . . . it is feasible that you are laying a claim—however weak—to ownership of the hotel."

"But . . . that's ridiculous!" I exclaimed.

Margot shrugged. "I'm not saying that's true, I'm just saying that when the police start asking questions, you should have a good answer prepared."

"You're delusional," I said.

"Who saw you outside?"

"Vanessa, Dennis, Cador . . . Tegan, Alex and Jago. Everyone."

"And then you disappeared." Margot smirked. "So what were you doing on the coast path?"

"I got disoriented and lost looking for you." I was getting annoyed. "Why are you asking me this?"

"Because you don't have an alibi."

"I don't need an alibi! You watch too much television, seriously." But something in Margot's reasoning was unnerving. She had a point. "And anyway, since we are talking alibis, what about you?"

Margot paused. "Good point."

"You were seen in a black waterproof cape and Wellingtons by at least one person," I said.

Margot looked at me as if I'd just accused her of shopping at the pound store. "Are you out of your mind? Do I look as if I would wear . . . I can't even say the word—"

"Dennis told me you borrowed one. And Alex saw you go up the fire escape."

"He needs his eyes tested," said Margot.

"Why didn't you take your mobile?"

Margot looked me straight in the eye. "I had a frustrating call with one of the talent. He was being difficult and I was over it."

"Who? Johnny Depp?" I laughed, but Margot did not.

"Will you just stop bugging me!"

"I'm not!" I exclaimed.

She stood up and flounced out of the bathroom, slamming the door behind her. I was hurt and confused. What on earth was wrong with her?

When I returned to our bedroom, Margot had changed into skinny jeans and a deep chestnut thigh-length roll-neck sweater. She was working on her laptop.

Margot didn't look up, but she did say, "Oh, there's an envelope for you. It's on the side table. It's probably a welcome letter. I didn't open it." It was as if her outburst had never happened.

The envelope had the Tregarrick Rock logo in the top left-hand corner.

"They'd better not charge me for lunch," Margot grumbled.

"It won't be on the bill yet," I said. "We just got here!"

When I opened it, my stomach turned right over. I stared at the contents in disbelief, then mounting horror. "Who gave you this?"

"It was under the door when I woke up from my nap," Margot said, continuing to tap away on her keyboard. "Why? Is there a problem?"

I thrust the letter under her nose.

Margot gasped and looked at me in shock. "Holy cow. Oh hell."

Meet me by William's Bench at 4:00 p.m. to discuss hotel. Come alone. J. Ferris.

Chapter Twenty

"When did this arrive?" I tried to keep my voice steady, but I was shaken to the core.

Margot was wide-eyed. "No idea. I told you. It was on the floor when I woke up from my nap."

"What *time* was that?" It was critical that I work out the time the letter arrived and when I physically walked out of the hotel with Cador's lunch.

"I don't know! I only noticed it when I woke up."

I was furious. "You didn't see my note? I left it on the table. You should have called me."

"Not everything is about you, Evie. If you must know I was tired—jet lag—so if the note was there, I didn't see it." She stuck out her jaw. I knew that stubborn look.

"I can't believe no one in reception thought to tell me you were back," I said. "Vanessa is useless."

Margot hesitated. "If you must know, you are right. I did go up the fire escape."

"Why on earth didn't you say so?"

"I just did."

"Go on."

"I spied that awful Lily in reception arguing with Vanessa and just knew she'd corner me. I wasn't in the mood for small talk, so I darted back outside and went around to the terrace at the back. Our balcony door was unlocked—by the way, Dennis was lighting a bonfire and burning something and I saw Tegan standing at a window watching. It was very weird."

"Oh, he did burn her portrait after all. I thought I saw smoke." I was deeply disappointed at the loss of one of Alex's early works.

When I told Margot she said, "There you have it. Motive. Alex and Tegan must have pushed Jago off the cliff." She gave a yawn. "This place is full of mad people. It's like Los Angeles."

"There's something else." I reminded Margot about the receipt that Jago showed me, whose signature I was positive wasn't Robert's.

Margot nodded. "So maybe Jago was going to admit that he still owed you the hundred thousand pounds but didn't want his wife to know about it. If the signature on the receipt was not Robert's, whose was it?"

"It has to be Joanna's," I suggested. "After all, this happened when they were married—and no, I already told you that I am not calling Joanna to ask her, thank you very much."

"There is a third possibility," said Margot. "You told me that Jago knew how treacherous that coast path was. What if he deliberately threw himself off the cliff? I mean . . . he realizes that he owes you all that money, he finds out that his wife is going to run off with a Swede and he knows that his son would prefer to be a pirate and go hunting for treasure—"

"So he knocks himself on the back of the head?" I said.

"Oh, good point."

"It still doesn't explain the note to me," I pointed out.

Margot frowned. "Did you ask Jago how he paid the money back?"

"He cashed in a life insurance policy."

"No, I mean *how,* as in . . . did he hand deliver the cash?"

"I'm more worried about why he didn't ask me to meet him in his office."

"Because he didn't want to be overheard, that's why," Margot declared. "You are definitely going to need an alibi."

I felt sick. "You're right."

"Of course I'm right!"

"It looks as if I deliberately arranged to meet Jago and . . . yes, I had every reason to push him off the cliff! Oh my God! Who will believe me?"

"Now let's all calm down," said Margot. "You're beginning to get hysterical."

"Yes! I am getting hysterical!" I said hysterically. "And with good reason!"

"Wait . . . what if *Jago* lured you to the cliffs because he intended to push *you* over the edge, but someone got to him first."

"Not helpful."

"I think we should just throw this note away," Margot declared. "What's the point of it now? Obviously Jago slipped it under the door. Only you and I know about it. It's not as if you have done anything wrong." She tore the note up into pieces and tossed it into the wastepaper basket. "See how easy that was?"

"But . . . what if Dennis slipped it under the door?" I exclaimed. "He told me he'd do anything for Jago. So maybe Dennis knows that I was supposed to meet him. How could I possibly prove it was just a coincidence? What should we do?"

"Call Nigel. Get him to phone Joanna just to confirm that she received the money."

"I already spoke to him." I filled Margot in on the conversation I'd had earlier. "We're going to meet him for dinner on Tuesday."

"I still think we should ask Joanna."

"Over my dead body."

"You should be careful saying that," said Margot. "Shall I order room service? I'm starving."

But of course there was no room service, and Vanessa reminded us that we should dress for dinner. Cocktails would be served at six-thirty in the Residents' Lounge, followed by dinner at seven-thirty. It seemed strange that after what had happened it was business as usual, but Vanessa said that was what Tegan had insisted on.

It turned out to be just the two of us eating in the dining room. Jazz music played softly in the background.

Outside was black as pitch; the wind howled and rain pounded on the windowpanes. I thought of Dennis sitting with Jago's body and wondered what had been decided. Had Tegan called the coast guard? The police?

When I asked Vanessa—who was decked out in a 1920s maid outfit—where everyone was, she told me that Lily had prescribed Tegan a sedative and that she had gone to bed. Lily was too upset to come down for dinner and would be eating in her room. She added that Cador and Dennis had gone to bring back Jago's body.

There was no sign of Alex.

Margot seemed in a strange mood, almost euphoric. She had taken the Tregarrick Rock dress code seriously and donned a tight black dress with a plunging neckline. She'd piled her hair up on top of her head and bragged about the glittering diamond drop earrings that she told me had been a tenth wedding anniversary present and cost five thousand pounds.

I had to borrow one of her cashmere tunics but couldn't squeeze myself into any of her trousers. In the end I wore a pair of her Wolford leggings and, since we almost took the same-size shoe, managed to force my feet into her Louboutin ankle boots.

My stomach was in knots. I had no appetite at all.

I couldn't stop thinking about Jago's note asking me to meet him, nor could I get the image of Jago's bloodied head out of my mind. He had been struck hard, but with what? A rock? An axe? Cador had an axe.

Vanessa set down a pitcher of cold water.

"No ice?" said Margot.

"The machine has broken," Vanessa said.

"So what happens next?" Margot asked as she topped up her wineglass. "Surely they can't leave Jago's body on the cliffs."

"If they can't get the coast guard out tonight," said Vanessa, "the medical launch will come tomorrow."

"So just think, if Evie and Dennis hadn't found your employer on the beach," Margot went on, "he could have been washed out to sea and no one would have been any the wiser. Mr. Jago Ferris would have just vanished—still, at least you get to keep your job."

"Margot!" I could have throttled my sister. Why would she say that? I'd told her what I'd learned from Lily about Vanessa's dubious past and hadn't thought for one moment that she'd repeat it. But then, with a sinking feeling, I remembered that Margot never could keep a secret.

"Yes," Margot went on, "it must have been very difficult to find a job with a prison—Ouch!" she yelped. "Evie! What the hell? That hurt!"

"Sorry, I thought it was the table leg." I glowered at my sister, hoping she would get the hint and shut up, but to no avail.

"I can't believe Jago and Cador are actually going to move the body," Margot said incredulously as she slathered butter onto her second bread roll. "That would never happen in America. I mean—that's tampering with a crime scene."

"The tide was coming in, if you recall," I reminded her.

Vanessa went very still. "What do you mean, *crime* scene?" she said. "I thought Mr. Jago fell."

Margot feigned amazement. "Dennis didn't tell you? I thought you and he were joined at the hip."

I had thought the same, too.

Confusion flooded Vanessa's face. "Does that mean that the police will be asking questions?"

"Of course they will," said Margot through a mouthful of bread. "You'd better have an alibi."

Vanessa reddened. "Why would you say that?"

Margot gave a magnanimous sweep of the empty dining room. "Well . . . how many people are there on this island? One of us has to have clobbered him. Didn't you ever read *And Then There Were None*?"

Vanessa just stared.

Margot laughed. "It's one of Agatha Christie's best-known novels. It was made into a miniseries starring Aidan Turner. It seems all very apt if you ask me."

Vanessa looked bewildered. "Aidan Turner? I don't understand."

Margot took another gulp of wine. "I thought that Aidan Turner made a delicious villain. And *Poldark*. Let's not forget him in that show. Is there any more bread?"

Vanessa nodded and darted out of the dining room.

There was something reckless about Margot's behavior this evening that I hadn't seen since we used to go clubbing together in our early twenties.

"What's the matter with you?" I hissed. "And what's with the wine? I thought you didn't drink."

"I changed my mind," she said, and reached for the bottle again. "This rioja is quite good, actually."

"And you do realize that there is gluten in that bread."

"I'll take my chances." Margot upended the empty wine bottle with dismay. "Should we get another bottle?"

"No," I said firmly. "You've had more than enough."

Margot regarded my untouched steak and kidney pie. Waving her fork, she said, "Don't you want that?"

I shook my head. "I'm just not hungry."

"Pass it over. I'll eat it."

"It's got pastry on the top."

"I know, but look—" She pointed her fork at the remains of an unappetizing vegetable casserole that Vanessa had made.

"You asked for vegetarian," I said. "Vanessa told you she had limited ingredients."

With a defiant look, Margot tucked into the pie. "You don't understand. I live on salads, poached chicken and fish. Brian told me I was fat. Everyone in Los Angeles is a size zero."

I was appalled. "You've never been fat."

"They're all like sticks over there," Margot went on wildly. "Sticks with big tits—tits that aren't their own tits. They buy them as if they are shopping at Macy's—that's a big department store in case you haven't heard of it. See these?" She pointed to her chest. "Brian bought them for my thirty-fifth birthday."

"Yes. I did notice," I said. "But keep your voice down."

"Why? There's no one here!"

Vanessa returned with the bread. She had an odd expression on her face as she saw Margot polish off my steak and kidney pie.

"I'm sorry," I said. "There was nothing wrong with it, I just don't feel hungry."

"There is still some apple-and-blackberry crumble left from lunch."

"Lovely!" Margot said. "Bring it on!"

Margot then ate a large serving of apple-and-blackberry crumble, custard and Cornish clotted cream.

"You're going to be ill," I warned her. "Come on, let's go upstairs."

"You're no fun anymore," she grumbled.

Later, as we stood outside our hotel room door, Margot suddenly froze and grabbed my arm. "Quickly! I have to get to the loo."

"Okay."

"Now, Evie! *Now!*" She snatched the key and unlocked the door, then raced straight to the bathroom.

From outside, I heard the rather unattractive sounds of explosive diarrhea and a lot of groaning. I was not remotely surprised. I took off my clothes and makeup and put on my pajamas.

After fifteen minutes when Margot still hadn't come out, I tapped gingerly on the door. "Are you okay?"

"No," came the reply. "And don't say I told you so. This is not normal. I've been poisoned."

"Don't be dramatic," I said. "You drank almost an entire bottle of wine all by yourself and ate food you don't usually eat. You'll be fine in the morning."

Then, to my surprise, I heard her begin to cry. Margot never cried.

"Let me in, Margot," I said.

"No. You'll die in here," she said miserably, and cried out in pain. "I feel awful. Oh. It's my stomach."

"Open the door," I demanded.

Margot was deathly white. She was lying in a fetal position, clutching her stomach and clearly in pain.

"This isn't normal," she muttered again. "I know the difference. I purge. You have to believe me. This is all wrong."

"I'll call for the doctor." And then I realized that was not an option.

Margot must have had the same thought. She managed a weak smile. "They couldn't get a doctor out with a dead body on the beach, so I doubt they'll come out for me."

She was right. There was no doctor on the island—but then I remembered Lily. She was a nurse. She'd know what to do, plus she had an arsenal of drugs in her cupboard.

"Stay right here, I'm going to ask Lily."

Chapter Twenty-one

Lily did not answer, and of course her door was locked, yet I could hear the television blaring. She had to still be up.

I trooped back to our bedroom. Margot had managed to pull herself into a sitting position, but she still looked like death warmed up.

"I'm going via the balcony," I said. "Lily keeps the door unlocked for the cat. Don't move."

"I'm hardly going dancing," she whispered.

I slipped on my Dansko rubber boots, grabbed my coat and drew back the curtains. It was pouring with rain. Outside on the balcony, I almost tripped over a very wet Mister Tig. He immediately darted into our room and under the bed. Despite calling him, I just couldn't get him to come out. He seemed frightened.

I'd have to deal with him later.

The door to Lily's balcony was—as I expected—unlocked. I was soaked—just in the two minutes it had taken me to make the crossing.

"Lily?" I called out, but her sitting room was empty, even though the TV was on full blast, broadcasting *I'm a Celebrity . . . Get Me Out of Here!*

I stepped inside along with a rush of wind that swept the magazines off the coffee table and onto the floor.

Lily's doors to her bedroom were closed.

"Lily?" I called out again. "It's Evie. Are you here? Are you awake?"

But there was still no answer. I was in a dilemma, but awake or not, Lily had what I needed to help poor Margot, who was writhing about in agony.

I opened Lily's bedroom door a crack. All was in darkness, apart from the shaft of light from the open door. Lily was fast asleep, tucked up under the duvet.

I'd leave her a note.

In the powder room I searched among Lily's bottles and packets of medications before settling on some Imodium. There was a small red leather box tucked at the back, but it was locked.

As I headed to Lily's desk to scribble a note, I tripped over her cretonne-knitting bag, spilling the contents onto the floor.

Suddenly, there was a rap on the door. "Lily? It's Vanessa! I've brought you some supper."

Without waiting for Lily's reply, she unlocked the door and saw me gathering up the contents of Lily's knitting bag. "Lily has already gone to bed," I said.

Vanessa regarded me with surprise. "What are you doing in here? How did you get in?"

"Through the balcony door," I said. "Margot isn't very well." I brandished the Imodium. "I'm hoping this will help."

Vanessa set the tray of sandwiches and hot chocolate on Lily's desk. "What's the matter with her?"

"I think she ate something that upset her stomach."

Vanessa scowled. "I hope you're not saying that it was my cooking."

"I have Lily's cat in our room," I said. "I'll bring him back in a moment."

Vanessa frowned. "What is Lily's cat doing in your room?"

"He was locked out on the balcony."

"In the rain?" Vanessa seemed genuinely puzzled. "He hates the rain. Lily would never go to bed without checking he was snuggled in his igloo. He always sleeps in her room."

"I'll go and get him." At least I wouldn't need to go out in the rain again. "Do you have the set of master keys?"

Vanessa gestured to the side table in the vestibule and carried on laying up the TV tray table for Lily, even though I had told her that Lily was asleep. "I'll bring them right back."

After giving Margot a glass of water and two Imodium, I helped her onto the bed and took off her shoes.

"Let's get you comfy and settled," I said.

Margot was still pale, but I was relieved to see a faint tinge of color on her cheeks. "I think it was the pie," she whispered.

"Or maybe the bread rolls?" I teased. "The apple-and-blackberry crumble? The wine?"

She gave a weak smile and snuggled under the covers. "Did you check the expiry date on the Imodium?"

"Yes, of course." But I hadn't.

Suddenly Mister Tig began to meow by the balcony door. He was thrashing his tail back and forth and kept jumping up, trying to work the door handle.

"What's wrong with the cat?" Margot asked.

"He wants to go home." But as I scooped him up, he lashed out, spitting and hissing and taking a swipe at my face. He actually scratched me. I touched my cheek and there were faint traces of blood.

I was shocked. "He's scared of me."

"No, he's possessed. He's a demon cat." Margot managed to lift her head from the pillow. "This is like one of those horror films. Two girls are stuck on an island. There is a dead body. Then a storm—"

A deafening clap of thunder and bolt of lightning exploded on cue. We were plunged into darkness.

Margot gave a yelp. "I was joking."

The lights flickered back on and suddenly there was a blood-curdling scream.

Margot sat bolt upright.

The next moment, someone was hammering on our bedroom door.

"Lily's dead!" shrieked Vanessa. "She's dead!"

Chapter Twenty-two

Vanessa was a wreck. Her hands were shaking and her face was as white as a sheet. My first thought was that Lily's tumble earlier in the morning had been more serious than I'd realized. Perhaps she had been concussed after all.

Leaving Margot behind—much to her indignation—I followed Vanessa back to Lily's bedroom, where she had turned on the bedside lamp.

Lily looked peaceful lying in the bridal bed. She was on her back with the covers pulled up under her chin. Her eyes were closed, and were it not for the nasty bump on her forehead, it would appear that she'd just taken an afternoon nap and drifted off to sleep forever.

Vanessa seemed frozen. "Will the police have to come in here too?"

"I would think so," I said. "Why don't you go and find Tegan? I'll stay here."

She nodded and left.

I sank onto the little upholstered chair next to the night table to wait. Didn't bad things always come in threes? Robert, Jago and now Lily.

It was then that I noticed the knitted cushion that Lily had been at great pains to finish. It had fallen onto the floor just feet away from Mister Tig's cat igloo. I realized now that I hadn't noticed it missing in her cretonne-knitting bag.

Something didn't feel right. Why had Lily brought the cushion into her bedroom but left her knitting bag in the sitting room?

I bent down to pick it up and stopped. Lily's tortoiseshell glasses lay under the cushion on the carpet. The lenses were cracked.

And then I spied a lace-up shoe peeping out from underneath the bed.

Gingerly, I lifted Lily's duvet and gasped. She was still wearing the other shoe. Lifting the duvet higher, I realized she was fully dressed!

I dropped the duvet and fled the room, headed straight to the telephone on Lily's desk and called the police.

Patty picked up on the third ring. She seemed to be finishing a conversation because I heard her laugh and a man's voice saying, "You are a naughty girl." Sultry music was playing in the background.

"If this is about Jago Ferris," Patty said somewhat breathlessly, "I believe that Cornwall Air Ambulance have already retrieved his body from Windward Point. I already told Dennis that we'd be out there first thing tomorrow morning. Can't do anything tonight."

"I'm not calling about Jago Ferris," I said, and told her about Lily, specifically discovering the fact that she was fully clothed.

"She was an eccentric old bat," said Patty. "Nothing would surprise me."

"But . . . what about the knitted cushion?" I insisted. "And her broken glasses?"

"Listen, you've had a horrible day. I told you there is no crime on Scilly. There will be a perfectly reasonable explanation in both cases. I am sure of it."

"I hope so." Was she drunk? Hadn't she been told about Jago's head injury?

"Your best bet is to get a good night's sleep." Patty sounded completely unconcerned. "Just don't touch anything," she added. "Oh Henry, *stop* doing that. Sorry, got to go." And with that, Detective Sergeant Patricia Williamson disconnected the line.

I put the phone down, feeling annoyance mixed with relief. Obviously Patty had made it to the fourth date with Henry, and maybe I was overthinking everything. Patty had said there was no crime on Scilly and she should know. Regardless, I decided to wait until Vanessa returned with Tegan so I could tell them that I'd spoken to the police and also that Cornwall Air Ambulance had been able to move Jago's body—presumably to the morgue.

I hoped they wouldn't be long because I was worried about Margot. As I waited, I noticed Lily's scrapbook on the desk and took a quick peep. It was just as Lily had implied—press clippings of celebrities and salacious stories from the tabloids. I also noticed a jumble of silver-framed photographs displayed along a walnut dresser.

The photographs were all of a much younger Lily—one

of her wearing a blue-and-white nurse's uniform with an old-fashioned cape astride a bicycle with a pannier basket on the handlebars. Another showed her on her wedding day outside an ancient church. Then I looked closer at the back row of photographs and my heart almost stopped. I couldn't believe it!

Clutching the photograph, I raced back to our room via the balcony, not caring how wet it was.

"What's the matter?" Margot exclaimed. "You look as if you have seen a ghost."

"I'm glad to see you aren't one."

"I'm feeling much better, thank you," she said.

I handed her the photograph.

"What am I looking at?" she said. "Who are these people?"

"Who do you think?"

It was a photograph of two men and two women dressed in team colors of turquoise blue and white. Judging by the big-hair hairstyles of the two women, I guessed it had been taken in the late eighties.

A silver trophy stood on a small table between each couple. In the background was a partial shot of a catamaran with the name of the vessel clear as day—*Joanna*.

I jabbed a finger at the tall man on the left with the white hair. "That's Robert, Margot."

"He had white hair even then," she mused. "Handsome guy—and the woman beside him . . . wow . . . she's stunning."

"Thanks, Margot, yes she is. That's Joanna."

"She looks like a young Elizabeth Taylor. Robert even christened his boat *Joanna*," Margot went on, but catching sight of my face, she reached out to squeeze my hand. "I'm sorry. Not good to see how happy they all look in this photograph. I always assumed she'd be a frump."

"That's not why I'm showing you this," I snapped. "Don't you see? This was in Lily's room. She must have known Robert. I think that's her standing next to him, but Lily doesn't have a mole and this woman does."

"Those are easy to remove," said Margot. "Maybe there is something written on the back of the photograph?"

"Don't—"

But Margot had already unsnapped the clasps and removed the backing. "Holy cow. You won't believe this."

She passed the photograph back to me. It was clearly marked: *Anderson Cup July 1987*. Underneath were four names: Bobby, Joanna, Jago and . . . Millicent.

"Lily is Millicent Small?" I was stunned. "What idiots we are. Of course Lily must be short for Millicent."

"And Small could have been a married name," Margot declared.

"She told me she'd been married twice."

"That should be pretty easy to confirm."

"But what's the point now?" I said, exasperated. "I *asked* Jago if he knew a Millicent Small. I even asked *her*. Why would they lie?"

"Maybe Jago asked her to lie?" Margot suddenly froze. "No. Wait. Sorry. Got to run to the loo—" And she dashed back to the bathroom.

"I'm going to put this back," I called out, and was about to leave by the bedroom door when I had a thought. What if I bumped into Tegan and Vanessa in the corridor?

I decided to take the balcony route, thinking that this whole ordeal was becoming like a farce.

And just as I passed Lily's window, I stopped. I could see Vanessa through the gap in the curtains leafing through Lily's enormous leather scrapbook. It looked as if she were alone.

Then, to my astonishment, Vanessa tore out several pages, crumpling them up and thrusting them into the pocket of her maid's outfit. A moment later, the door opened and Tegan came in with Vicar Bill and Roger the macaw.

Unfortunately, the bird must have sensed I was out on the balcony because he started to flap his wings, shrieking, *"Fire in the hold! Fire in the hold!"*

I was about to beat a hasty retreat when the balcony door opened and Tegan looked out. "What the hell are you doing out there lurking in the rain?"

"Getting wet?"

"Come inside," she commanded.

Swiftly, I dropped the photograph into the planter. It was impulsive, but I didn't know what else to do with it.

I stepped back into Lily's room, feeling horribly self-conscious in my pajamas and Dansko boots. Roger the macaw yelled, "Cor! Nice!" Vicar Bill retreated into Lily's bedroom with his bird and closed the door behind them. Mister Tig immediately jumped off the wingback chair and went to sit outside the door, meowing plaintively to be let inside.

Tegan regarded me with suspicion. "How did you get that scratch on your face?"

I explained that Margot had got food poisoning and that I'd gone to ask Lily for her advice but she wasn't answering my knock. I knew that Lily kept the balcony door open for the cat, so I decided to try my luck that way. Mister Tig had been outside in the rain, and when I opened my door, he ran into my room.

"The cat darted under the bed," I said. "When I tried to get him out he scratched me."

Tegan frowned. "Why was the cat outside in the first place? You're quite certain you didn't let the cat out when you entered Lily's room?"

"Positive."

"Well, we'll know the truth soon enough." She frowned. "You say your friend had food poisoning?"

"Yes. It was severe enough for me to go for help."

Tegan turned on Vanessa angrily. "This just *has* to stop! I won't have it!"

Vanessa reddened and mumbled something incoherent.

"Do you think I'm stupid?" Tegan fumed. "Every time an attractive woman stays that Cador shows the *slightest* interest in, you poison them with your cooking."

I looked at Vanessa in astonishment. She spun around and ran out of the room. There was an awkward silence.

"I'm sorry," I said. "I know how you must be feeling."

She looked up sharply. "*Do* you? Do you really?"

"Yes. Losing a husband is devastating," I said. "And now Lily—"

Lily's bedroom door opened and Vicar Bill looked out. "Is Lily's iPhone around?"

"What on earth do you need that for?" Tegan demanded.

"She always left it on her nightstand," said Vicar Bill. "It's not there now. That's unusual."

To me, that was further evidence that Lily's death was suspicious, but I decided to keep my theories to myself.

Back in our room, Margot was fast asleep. She'd left a lamp on for me. I slipped out of my coat and boots as quietly as I could and crawled into bed, absolutely exhausted. Yet even though I was tired, my mind was spinning. I couldn't stop thinking of Robert and Joanna and how happy they must have been all those years ago.

And then there was Alex.

Alex had been on the island this afternoon. He could easily have seen Jago waiting for me on the coast path. It would have provided a perfect opportunity to get rid of his rival, especially given the foggy conditions. The destruction of Tegan's portrait could have been the last straw. And yet, as I thought of our conversation in the bird hide, he seemed to be a man resigned to his fate, not a man moved to violence.

But where did Lily fit into all this? I was convinced she'd been murdered regardless of what Patty said on the phone. What was Vanessa tearing out of Lily's scrapbook and hiding in her pocket?

And then there was Jago's note. Why had he wanted to meet me at William's Bench on the coast path instead of in his office?

As I lay in bed wide-awake, it slowly dawned on me that perhaps the wrong person had been thrown over the edge. Margot had made a good point. Maybe it was supposed to have been me.

Chapter Twenty-three

"I won't be sorry to leave," I said to Margot as I zipped up my overnight bag. "Come on, we can't afford to miss the sea tractor this time. I don't want to stay here another minute."

"I'm nearly packed," said Margot, who was nowhere near packed. "But I could do with some coffee."

"There is no room service here as well you know," I said. "But if I have to make you one so you'll be ready on time, I will."

"Black. No, put in a splash of milk and three heaped tea-spoons of sugar and don't you *dare* say a word."

When I stepped out into the corridor, I was surprised to see a young police officer standing sentinel outside Lily's bedroom door.

Fresh faced with a sprinkling of freckles, he couldn't have been more than twenty-two or -three. He gave a nod of greeting and squared his shoulders. I knew that Scilly was a world unto itself, but since when had one of the four police officers that roamed all 142 islands managed to spare an officer to stand guard outside an elderly woman's door?

A gnawing sense of unease settled in the pit of my stomach. Maybe Policewoman Patty had taken me seriously after all.

I was glad to see Dennis in reception. "What's going on? There's a policeman outside Lily's bedroom."

"I honestly don't know." He looked shattered. Dark shadows bloomed under red-rimmed eyes. He needed a shave and his clothing looked crumpled.

"Can I order a coffee for Margot?" I said. "Actually, don't worry. I'll ask Vanessa."

"I'm afraid you'll have to make your own," he said. "Have you seen her this morning, by any chance?"

"No. Just last night." I decided against repeating Tegan's comment about her poisoning attractive women guests.

"She was in a terrible state. But . . ." He hesitated. "She wasn't in her room. In fact, her bed wasn't slept in last night."

I thought for a moment. "Perhaps she was consoling Cador?"

Dennis shook his head. "No. I was with Cador for most of the night. We had to wait for the air ambulance."

Alex Karlsson joined us at the counter.

I was surprised to see him at the hotel already but then realized he had to have stayed over. My suspicion of his part in Jago's death deepened.

"Tegan said Vanessa has not brought her morning cup of coffee. If you point me in the direction of the kitchen, I am happy to make it."

"Then I shall show both of you the kitchen. My apologies

for its state," Dennis said as he led the way. "As you can see, Vanessa was too upset last night to wash up."

The kitchen looked as if a bomb had hit it. Though Margot and I had been the only dinner guests, Vanessa had managed to use every available counter space.

Alex and I barely exchanged two words while waiting for the kettle to boil to make the coffee. He seemed preoccupied and I sensed he did not want to talk to me.

For once, Margot was as good as her word. When I returned to our room with two coffees and two croissants that I had found and zapped in the microwave, she was ready to go.

"You see," I exclaimed. "You can do it when you really try."

"I just don't want to get the blame if we miss the hay wagon." She took the mug of coffee and wolfed down the croissant, adding a huge dollop of raspberry jam.

"What?" she said defiantly.

"I'm glad to see you've got your appetite back."

I noticed that she had applied only mascara and a slick of lipstick. It looked as if my super-glamorous sister had shed her Hollywood veneer for just a moment. She was even wearing jeans—albeit with a designer label.

"Is Dennis coming to take my suitcase?"

"No," I said, and told him that Vanessa was missing.

"Did the old bat die in her sleep?"

I cringed at Margot's callousness. "Unlikely," I said, and told her about the young policeman standing guard outside Lily's door.

"Or they've got nothing else to do," Margot said dryly.

Margot used her charm on the police officer, who told us

shyly to call him Owen. He agreed to take Margot's enormous suitcase down to the jetty.

"Go on, Owen," Margot teased. "You can tell us. Did someone do her in?"

"I'm not at liberty to say, ma'am," Owen said stiffly.

"You watch too many movies," Margot declared. "That phrase is overused. I'm in movies, actually. If you tell us what you know—strictly on the QT—I'm pretty sure I can get you a part in my next movie spin-off of *Pirates of the Caribbean*."

I glowered at her, but she just smirked. So I left them to it.

When I passed on through to begin the long descent to the jetty and the waiting sea tractor, there was no sign of Dennis.

Vicar Bill was nowhere to be seen, either. In fact, the jetty seemed deserted.

Margot, with Owen struggling a few feet behind her carrying her suitcase, joined me and said, "Where is everyone?"

"Stop right there," boomed a familiar female voice.

Patty emerged from the shadow of the cliff. She was dressed in uniform. "Going somewhere, ladies?"

"As a matter of fact, yes," said Margot. "We are flying back to Los Angeles tomorrow and need to get to Heathrow this evening."

"I'm afraid that won't be possible," Patty declared. "You'll have to stay another night or two until the police and our forensic medical examiner have had a chance to finish their inspections."

My heart sank. "So . . . you agree that Jago's fall was no accident?"

"I'm not at liberty to say."

"I'm not quite sure how we can help you," said Margot.

"Oh, I think you can," Patty declared. "In fact, I'm certain of it."

"Of course we'll help however we can," I said quickly. "I suspected you might have wanted to ask me some questions since I was with Dennis when we found . . . when—"

"And let's not forget that you were in Lily Travis's suite of rooms when she lay dead in her bed last night." Patty cocked her head. "Hmm?"

"But . . . but I didn't know that she was . . . dead at the time," I protested. "It was Vanessa who found Lily, and if you remember, it was me who called you!"

"True," Patty agreed. "But sadly I was a bit distracted and wasn't really paying much attention." She flashed a smile that didn't reach her eyes. "But now I am, so . . . back to the hotel you go."

"It's really inconvenient," Margot fumed. "I have to be back in L.A.! I have people relying on me! I could lose the funding for—"

"*Scilly Pirates?*" Patty's voice was heavy with sarcasm. "Now as I said . . . back to the hotel. Chop-chop! Luckily the Devon and Cornwall Constabulary will be able to loan Owen out again as your personal bellhop."

Owen blushed. "Sorry, ma'am."

"I suggest you ladies go and unpack and then meet me in the Residents' Lounge in thirty minutes. Then we can all have a little chat."

Chapter Twenty-four

We were the first to arrive.

Owen was waiting by the entrance to the Residents' Lounge, looking grave. "Patty will be here shortly."

The Residents' Lounge took its 1970s décor to a new level. At the far end was a built-in wall unit in teak with a fake fire in the center flanked by large speakers. Above the left side was a turntable eight-track and stereo and above the right, a well-stocked bar with a mirrored back. The upholstery, curtains and cushions were all in red and green. A shag pile carpet that had seen better days gave off a strange musty aroma. If it hadn't been for the floor-to-ceiling windows—a welcome and recurring feature of the hotel—the lounge would have felt claustrophobic. Instead, there was this amazing feeling of light and space.

Various leatherette armchairs were grouped around occasional tables, along with a dark red Chesterfield sofa in front of a long teak coffee table. Two wingback chairs were positioned in an alcove overlooking the terrace. Periodicals, magazines and yesterday's newspapers were arranged in newspaper racks.

Margot drifted over to the window and gazed out, deep in thought. I glanced at the wall of bookshelves. They were jam-packed with collections of detective and mystery fiction from the Golden Age—first editions, judging by the leather and cloth covers. Dennis hadn't been joking. I wondered what Agatha Christie or George Goodchild would say about the characters about to assemble in the Residents' Lounge.

Dennis carried in a tray with a *cafetière* of coffee, milk and sugar, a pot of tea and a plateful of biscuits. He set it down on the teak sideboard, then took out some small plates, cups and saucers from the cupboard underneath along with some paper napkins.

Patty appeared with Tegan and Cador. Tegan looked drained. Cador's expression was hard to read. He led his mother to the Chesterfield and they sat down.

Alex followed and headed for a chair in the far corner. Margot and I took the two teak-framed armchairs (in an alarming shade of mustard) opposite the Chesterfield. Dennis switched on the fake flame, then retired to the back of the room. No one spoke.

Vicar Bill entered, mercifully minus his macaw but surprisingly carrying Mister Tig. The vicar was wearing a black clerical shirt and collar under a threadbare jacket. He took the cat to one of the wingback chairs and settled him on his lap.

"No sign of Vanessa Parsons yet?" Patty asked, pulling out her police notebook.

"Not yet." Dennis forced a smile.

"She's not in her room," said Tegan. "I already looked. Did you see her this morning at all?"

Dennis shook his head. "It's most unlike her."

"We'll find her," said Patty.

"What about you, Cador?" Tegan said. "When was the last time you saw her? She sticks to you like glue."

"Yesterday afternoon," said Cador. "In the dell when I was talking to Evie."

Tegan sneered. "She's probably gone off in a huff."

"She can't have got far," said Cador. "Did anyone try to phone her?"

"Of course," said Dennis. "But her phone was switched off."

"Told you. A huff," muttered Tegan.

"Alrighty, then," said Patty. "Let's help ourselves to coffee—or tea—and what looks like homemade biscuits—or should I say *cookies*, since we have an American in our midst."

"Actually, I'm not American," Margot said. "And no, thank you, I already ate a croissant this morning."

"I thought you had food poisoning," Tegan remarked.

"I'm feeling much better," said Margot. "Thanks for asking."

Patty took up her position in front of the fireplace. She took a sip of tea. "Lovely," she said. "I do enjoy a good cup of tea." She surveyed the room, looking at each of us intensely. "Feels a bit like a scene from *Poirot*, doesn't it. Suspects in the lounge and then we find out the butler did it."

Margot nudged me and mouthed, *What the hell?* Margot might not have been American, but she certainly had taken up some American phrases.

"Suspects?" Tegan's face was pale. "I resent what you are implying."

"I'm not implying anything," said Patty. She took another

sip of tea. "I'm telling you the hard, cold facts. Jago was deliberately struck over the head with a blunt instrument."

There was a collective gasp of horror, but although I wasn't surprised at the news, I was surprised that Tegan didn't know the details. Surely Dennis would have told her.

Tegan's face had taken on a waxy hue. I saw her glance over at Alex, who seemed to be studying his hands on his lap.

"But he j-just fell—didn't he?" Tegan stammered. "I thought he fell."

"My team is combing the entire coast path, particularly the area around William's Bench and the ruined watchtower and Windward Point Lighthouse."

"By team, I assume you mean young Kip?" said Tegan, who seemed to have rallied.

"You are correct," said Patty. "Police Constable Kip Granger has the eyes of an eagle."

I caught a glimmer of alarm cross Tegan's features and saw her shoot Alex another look. He shook his head. It was such a subtle gesture that if I hadn't already known about his feelings for her, I wouldn't have noticed.

"But why the footpath?" Tegan said. "I thought Jago fell from the coast path near William's Bench."

"As I said, we may be a small team, but we pride ourselves on being thorough . . . which is why we need permission to search the bedrooms."

"The *bedrooms*!" Tegan exclaimed. "But . . . whatever for?"

"Now that's a secret," said Patty. "Seriously? Do you really need to ask? Let me give you a clue. Anything that could be incriminating."

"If someone had hit Jago over the head, he—or *she*," said Margot, pointedly looking at Tegan, "would hardly have taken the weapon or *incriminating* object back to their room. Wouldn't they have just thrown it into the sea?"

"Ah! An opinion from Hollywood and one I welcome," said Patty. "Back in the real world you'll find that criminals leave behind all sorts of strange clues. A stray Kleenex tissue, perhaps? Or maybe a cigarette end?"

"Of course you must do what you have to do, Patty," said Cador.

"Surely you can't be accusing us—by that I mean myself, Cador, Dennis and . . . and Alex," said Tegan.

Cador put a restraining arm on his mother's. "Just let the police do their job, Mum."

But Tegan shrugged it off angrily. She turned to glare at Margot and me. "We never had any problems until *they* turned up."

"And Vanessa," Patty put in. "Let's not forget Vanessa—wherever she is. Did she make these biscuits, Dennis? They really are rather good." The policewoman helped herself to a second and took a bite.

Suddenly Tegan got up. "I'll come with you. My room is in rather a muddle."

Patty smiled. "Actually, my team is already searching the bedrooms. What's that phrase? 'Don't ask permission; beg forgiveness.' Sorry!"

Tegan sat down, clearly annoyed.

"But Mrs. Tegan makes a good point," said Patty. "Can I call you Tegan?"

"Cut the crap, Patty," said Cador. "Mum used to babysit for you when you were still in nappies."

"As I was saying," Patty said through a mouthful of crumbs, "we have no crime on Scilly and suddenly we have *two* murders."

"Two?" Dennis said sharply.

"Is this to do with Lily?" Tegan said suddenly. "It is, isn't it. Oh God." She shot another anguished look at Alex, who swiftly looked down at his hands *again*.

Patty went very still. "Why would you think this had something to do with Lily Travis, Tegan?"

Tegan looked like a deer caught in headlights. She blinked and turned red. "I—I don't feel well. I need to go and lie down."

"You can lie down after we're done," said Patty in a tone I'd not heard before. I realized her mild-mannered banter hid a woman of steel. She was able to get people to relax, and then she'd instantly switch to bad cop, taking them off-guard. There was something slightly psychopathic about Patty's personality that was distinctly unnerving.

"I'm ninety-nine percent certain that Lily was suffocated by the Kingdom of Dorne," said Patty. "For those unfamiliar with the television series *Game of Thrones*, it was one of the seven kingdoms."

"She was knitting all seven to sell on Etsy," I said, then wondered why I even thought to mention it.

"What a good idea," said Margot. "Although I was never a fan."

"I'm certain that when we are finished with our investigation, we will find trace wool fibers in her nose—and don't look at me like that, Mrs. Chandler. Just because I police all these islands doesn't mean I'm not up to speed on the latest procedures and discoveries." Patty took another bite of her biscuit. "And, as Evie—can I call you Evie?"

"Yes," I said.

"As Evie told me last night, Lily had been put to bed fully-dressed. Bit of a red flag there."

"But why hurt Lily?" Dennis sounded bewildered. "Unless . . ."

"Unless what?" Patty prompted.

"Nothing," Dennis said quickly.

"Is this something to do with our missing person?" Patty demanded.

"No. Nothing. Nothing at all," said Dennis.

"*She's* got something to do with this!" Tegan pointed an accusing finger at me. "I know it. Dennis found her near William's Bench! And then she was lurking on the balcony last night looking into Lily's room."

"I already told you why I was in Lily's room," I protested. "Margot had food poisoning. I knew that Lily kept all kinds of medicines in her powder room."

"Ask Mrs. Mead the *second* where she was yesterday afternoon," Tegan ran on. "We all saw her creeping around the island."

"I g-got lost in the b-bracken," I stammered. "That's how I ended up by William's Bench." I appealed to Dennis for help. "Dennis pulled me away from the cliff edge. I would have gone over! Dennis saved my life."

"Ask her about the money!" Tegan sounded triumphant. "Ask her *that*!"

"You don't know what you're talking about," Margot jumped in. "If anyone has anything to gain it's Tegan and—" She pointed wildly at Alex. *"Him!"*

Cador looked confused. "What the hell is going on? Have you . . . wait—"

"We're old friends," Tegan whispered.

"Yes, I realize that," said Cador. "I know that Alex came here years ago for the summer and that he helped pull up the *Isadora* figurehead, but—Oh. I see. One of *those* friends."

"Please let me explain," Tegan begged.

"I'd rather not hear, thanks." Cador seemed disgusted. It would appear that his father must have told him about Tegan's infidelities with the tourists.

Patty was watching us all with interest and had helped herself to a third biscuit. It was as if she were allowing the players to settle into their parts.

"Let's all calm down," she said. "I'm afraid I'm going to have to ask you all some very difficult questions—anyone want more tea or coffee, or perhaps a bathroom break?" She looked at Margot. "Isn't that what you Americans say?"

"Is that a question?" said Margot.

"Don't antagonize her," I whispered.

"She's really annoying me," Margot whispered back.

Patty zeroed in on me. "Evie—I understand that you lost your husband on November second."

I was taken aback. "Why . . . yes."

"Your *husband*?" Cador exclaimed. "You never mentioned—"

"So just to clarify," Patty cut in. "If you are working for Mrs. Chandler—is it alright if I call you—"

"Margot. Yes. Yes," Margot snapped.

Patty cleared her throat. "If you are working for Margot on this film called *Scilly Pirates* in Los Angeles and you and your husband live in Penshurst, Kent—I can't remember the postcode offhand—I'm a little confused."

"Excuse me, ma'am. Something you should see." Owen entered the lounge with a handful of Ziploc bags. He handed the first to Patty. I could make out a small plastic bottle with a pointed tip.

Patty's eyes widened. "Where did you find this?"

"Vanessa Parsons's bedroom, ma'am."

Owen leaned over and whispered into Patty's ear. She nodded agreement. "Has she done a runner?"

"I can't say. Her clothes and iPhone are still in her room."

"I'm worried about her," Dennis spoke up.

"Vanessa is a liability," Tegan declared. "Why Jago agreed . . ." She fell silent.

"Mr. Jago was kind enough to give her a second chance," Dennis said coldly. "My niece has had a rough life, but I can promise you that she would never—"

"Vanessa is your niece?" Margot exclaimed. We exchanged looks of surprise. It certainly explained Dennis's patience with the tormented young woman.

"I can assure you that the police are fully aware of Vanessa's rough life," said Patty. "Up until now she has given us no cause for alarm."

"I'm glad to hear it," said Cador in a voice heavy with sarcasm. "She's only been stalking me on a daily basis. I would say that is cause for alarm!"

Owen looked at Dennis. "And I found a small box from Amazon in his room, but it was addressed to Vanessa Parsons."

"A box from *Amazon*," Patty exclaimed. "Fancy that. When was it delivered?"

Dennis's expression didn't change. "It arrived a week ago. She . . . Vanessa doesn't know I have it."

"And do we know what's inside?" Patty asked.

Dennis didn't answer.

Patty turned to Owen and said, "I can hazard a pretty good guess." She pointed to her stomach and made the most peculiar hand gesture, as if she were pregnant. Owen grinned.

"Well, if Miss Parsons doesn't show up in the next twenty-four hours," Patty went on, "I think we should have a little look inside that box."

"And I found this, too." Owen produced the next Ziploc bag. It contained pieces of torn-up paper. "It was in Mrs. Mead's bedroom. I took the liberty of putting it back together."

"Oh no!" I whispered.

I knew exactly what those pieces of paper were.

Chapter Twenty-five

"What note? What are you talking about?" Tegan said. "For God's sake, Patty, stop being so mysterious."

"A note asking that Evie meet your husband at William's Bench on the coast path."

Tegan gave a cry of alarm. "Jago asked *her* to meet him there? *Why?*"

"I'm coming to that," said Patty. "You see, we're very quick at putting the pieces together—literally—although I will say that tearing an incriminating note into four large bits didn't exactly give us a challenge." Patty regarded Margot and me coldly. "Surely one of you would have thought to have eaten it. Don't they do that in Hollywood?"

"Evie didn't see the note until after she got back," Margot said. "It was pure coincidence that she was anywhere near William's Chair or Bench or whatever you want to call it."

"Yes. That's completely true," I said.

"The envelope must have been slipped under our bedroom door when I was taking an afternoon nap," Margot went on.

"How convenient," snapped Tegan.

"What time did you get back to your room after your morning stroll?" Patty asked.

"Me?" Margot looked surprised. "Maybe around two. Two-thirty. I can't remember exactly."

"Apparently you didn't come down for lunch."

"I ate a protein bar. I don't usually eat lunch," said Margot. "And anyway, I got lost in the bracken. It really is a maze, isn't it?"

"As did I," I put in. "Which was why I happened to end up at William's Bench in the first place. I already told you this."

"I've had the most awful jet lag," Margot went on. "So when I got back to good old Margery Allingham I took a nap, and when I woke up, I noticed that an envelope had been slipped under our door. It was addressed to Evie. I just thought it was one of those welcome letters."

"Is there a time on the note?" Tegan said sharply. "A date?"

"I don't think so," I said.

Tegan snapped her fingers at the policewoman. "Give it to me, and no, I won't touch the contents."

Patty handed her the Ziploc bag. Tegan smoothed it over so she could read the note through the plastic. After less than thirty seconds, she laughed. "This is not from Jago."

For the first time, I caught genuine surprise cross Patty's features. "Are you certain?"

"Having been married to him for forty years, I can assure

you that I know my husband. Jago was obsessive about writing the date and the exact time down to the minute on every note he wrote. It was one of his peculiarities."

"Even a note like this?" Patty said.

"Absolutely."

"Mrs. Tegan is right," said Dennis. "Mr. Jago was a stickler for punctuality. If you care to look at the hotel register you'll see that he insists—insisted—on writing down the time a guest would check in and check out. I have a selection of his notes as well if you would care to compare them."

"So if Jago Ferris didn't write it," said Patty, "who did?"

No one answered.

Patty nodded to Owen, who handed her yet another Ziploc bag containing a letter. "We found this in Lily's room."

"Where?" Tegan sounded panicked.

"In her desk," said Owen.

"What else did you find?" Tegan demanded. "The book? Was the book there?"

Patty ignored her. She was too focused on donning disposable gloves and removing the letter from the plastic bag. Suddenly her eyes widened in surprise. "Now this is really fascinating."

"What is it?" Tegan said. "Let me see!"

"It doesn't concern you." Patty turned to me again. "This is a copy of an arrangement concerning a loan to Jago Ferris for one hundred thousand pounds from a certain Robert Mead—presumably your husband, Evie—which was witnessed by Millicent Small—or, as she was also known, Lily Travis."

"What!" Cador seemed shocked. "Why didn't I know about this?"

Tegan didn't react. Her face seemed devoid of emotion.

"The caveat being that if the loan was not paid back, the Tregarrick Rock hotel would become the property of Robert Mead—and . . . therefore—given your husband's demise . . . must now belong to you, Evie. Congratulations."

"Mum?" Cador exclaimed, but when she didn't answer he regarded me with confusion. "Is that why you came here?"

"No," I said. "That's not why we came here. And the loan was paid back."

"That's not true," Tegan fumed. "You insisted that the loan was never paid back—I heard you and Jago arguing!"

"At first, yes," I said. "But then he admitted it had. There was a receipt. Why would I push him off the cliff? I have nothing to gain!"

"But you were angry," said Tegan.

"Why the loan?" Cador persisted. "Why would Dad even need to borrow that much money?"

"I have no idea," Tegan said wearily. "Storm damage repairs? A new roof? Jago never discussed money with me."

Cador seemed bewildered. "But why would he borrow the money from Evie's husband?"

"I don't know," I said. "This all happened before I married him."

"But . . . what's this got to do with filming a movie here?" Cador looked at me. "Evie?"

"Ah," said Patty. "Now that's another story!"

I didn't think my heart could sink any lower, but it did.

"I *am* a filmmaker," Margot shouted. "I live in Los Angeles. I can show you my passport! I have a green card!"

"Ah, that's right. I almost forgot," said Patty. "What you ladies don't seem to understand is that Scilly takes anyone who visits our shores very seriously. We do background checks on all the tourists. We have access to all the passenger manifests. I knew exactly who you were even before we were officially introduced."

Margot gasped, but I was too shocked to utter a sound. I was furious. *Furious with Margot!* If we had been honest in the beginning, none of this would have happened. None of it!

"But . . . why didn't you say so at the time?" Margot demanded.

"Because I was having far too much fun watching the Scilly sisters flounder."

Cador's jaw dropped. "What?"

Tegan seemed shocked. "You're *sisters*?"

"As I have said to many people who try to pull the wool over my eyes, I'm not just a pretty face," Patty said. "People come to Scilly because they are either hiding from something or running away from someone." She regarded us with curiosity. "I'm not sure which it is with you two."

"We just came for the weekend," I said lamely.

"Bravo," said Margot, giving a slow clap. "Congratulations for working that out, but I'm sorry to say that you are veering off-piste here."

"Margot!" I exclaimed.

Patty seemed taken aback. "Excuse me?"

"Cui bono?" Margot said. "Who benefits from both Jago's and Lily's deaths? Certainly not my sister here. And even poor Alex . . . what would be in it for him? He already has a death sentence." Margot looked around the room. "No, I say look to yourselves and don't try to pin this on the outsiders."

My fury of moments earlier vanished. It was at times like this that I loved Margot to bits. She had never been afraid to speak her mind.

"How dare you!" Tegan was trembling with rage.

"Tell her about the life insurance policy, Evie," Margot urged.

"I'm all ears," Patty chimed in.

"Jago told me he cashed it in to repay the loan," I said.

"So you won't be getting any of that, Mrs. Ferris." Margot gave a dramatic pause. "And I bet that Mrs. Ferris still believed there was a policy in place. Something to start your new life with Alex . . . in Sweden!"

"Sweden?" Cador said. *"Sweden?"*

"Nice theory." Patty nodded. "Were you aware of this loan, Tegan?"

"No. At least I wasn't up until two days ago," said Tegan. "But what you are suggesting is deeply offensive!"

Patty regarded Margot with what looked like respect. "Your theories intrigue me, Margot. Go on."

"I'd like to speak now, please." Alex got up and walked to the center of the room.

"Alex!" said Tegan. "Please. Don't."

"I must." He took a deep breath. "I came to see Tegan un-invited. She begged me not to, but as you see, here I am. As Margot said, I have nothing to lose, and a man with nothing to lose is the most dangerous of all." He gave a sad smile. "But I can assure you, I am not a murderer."

Patty scribbled in her notebook.

"For pity's sake, will someone tell me what the hell is going on?" Cador exclaimed.

"Your mother and I fell in love when we were just seventeen," said Alex. "We were kept apart. Our letters were intercepted by Tegan's mother, who paid the postmistress—"

"Lily Travis," Margot and I chorused.

"Or Millicent Small, as she was known back then," Patty put in.

Tegan looked miserable. "Alex, please—"

"Shh—let me finish." Alex gave her a tender smile. "Tegan is completely innocent of everything. I just wanted to see her one last time. She has haunted me for the last forty-odd years. I just had to know if the torch I had been carrying for her all this time was a figment of my imagination."

"And was it?" Patty said softly.

"No." Alex reached behind him for a chair and sat down heavily. The exertion had exhausted him. "Not for either of us. It's still shining brightly."

There was an uncomfortable silence. Tears were trickling down Tegan's face and I felt a stirring of sympathy for her.

Cador's expression was stony. "So the portrait that Dennis was burning outside on the fire—is that something to do with you?"

"I didn't burn it," Dennis exclaimed. "I put it somewhere safe."

Tegan shot Dennis a grateful smile. "Thank you."

Alex took a deep breath. "Cador, there is something you need to know—"

"I can't listen to this." Cador jumped to his feet. "It all makes sense now. All of it." He spun away and marched over to the window.

"Right," said Patty. "Well, that sounds all very romantic, and speaking as someone who is no stranger to love affairs and broken hearts, all I can say is nice try, *Alex*—but I'm afraid I'm still going to have to ask you for your movements yesterday afternoon."

"Of course," he said. "Tegan and I went for a walk. I insisted she show me every inch of this little island. Of course I wanted to go to the lighthouse, but Dennis said that the footbridge had washed away."

"Meaning you would take the coast path?" Patty suggested.

"That's right. We went to the Galleon Garden and then on to William's Wood and the bird hide. Tegan had said that nothing had changed since that summer—even the décor inside this hotel takes me back all those years. It's like a time capsule here—"

"You can say that again," Margot whispered to me.

"Why don't you ask Evie?" said Alex. "She was in the bird hide."

"It's true," I said.

"Jago must have been following us," Alex went on. "He was very angry. Evie kindly tried to throw him off the scent, but of course he didn't believe her. Tegan left with Jago. I stayed and talked to Evie for a while and then she and I went our separate ways. I came back to the hotel. The causeway was closed, so I did not return to the Salty Boatman."

Patty frowned. "So where were you last night?"

"He was with me." Tegan sounded defiant. "I'm sorry, Cador, but it's true. Jago and I haven't shared a bedroom for years."

"Blimey," said Margot.

"Ssh!" I hissed.

"So the alibis you have for your whereabouts yesterday late afternoon are with each other?" said Patty. "Tricky."

We fell into another uncomfortable silence until Patty added, "Perhaps the knowledge that you had been reunited with your first love was too much for Jago. After all, presumably he and Alex had known each other from the past?"

"Known of, but not known personally," said Alex. "Jago was older. When you're kids, the age gap is huge."

"If you are suggesting he took his own life, he would never do that!" Tegan said suddenly.

"Evidence suggests that he did not take his own life," said Patty. "We're just trying—"

"My relationship with Alex has nothing to do with Jago's death," Tegan cried. "These *girls* are trying to throw you off the scent by putting it all back on Alex and me."

"That's not true!" Margot exclaimed.

Dennis cleared his throat. "Excuse me," he said. "I'd like to say something."

We all turned to Dennis.

"Mr. Jago paid the loan back in full in cash," he said. "I know because I was the one who delivered the money."

Chapter Twenty-six

"What?" Tegan hissed. "When?"

"Nine years ago. And yes, there was a receipt," said Dennis. "I suspect it is somewhere among Mr. Jago's papers, so you see—"

"Oh yes, we see all right," Tegan fumed, and again pointed an accusing finger at me. "You weren't even married to Bobby then, were you? If anything, the money belonged to Joanna."

"I realize that!" I exclaimed. "Why don't you ask her? After all, Joanna is your friend."

"You knew Evie's *husband*?" For the first time, Patty seemed off-balance. "But . . . how?"

"You weren't here at the time, Patty," Tegan said dryly. "You lived on the mainland—"

"Did I?" Patty thought for a moment. "Which husband?"

"Number two," said Tegan. "The vegan."

"Ah. Yes," Patty mused. "Carl the vegan."

"Evie's husband was married to my best friend," Tegan went on. "And since she's lied about working in Hollywood—"

"Evie doesn't, but *I* work in Hollywood," Margot protested.

Tegan ignored her. "How do we know that Evie isn't lying about everything else?"

"How do you know that Dennis is telling the truth—no offense, Dennis," said Margot. "I mean, if the money was paid back in cash—"

"You will just have to accept that I am telling the truth," said Dennis.

"What if only *part* of it was paid back?" Margot suggested.

"Jago showed me the receipt for the full amount," I said. "Remember?"

"Anyone can write that," Margot said with a sniff. "Jago could have written it himself."

"You make a good point." Patty nodded in agreement.

"Margot!" I gasped. "You're making things worse!"

But Margot seemed to be on a roll. "Have you ever considered the possibility that Jago killed Lily? He knew that he still owed the money and he knew that Lily had witnessed the loan. Evie turns up—catches him in the lie. Bingo. He has to take action."

Tegan didn't answer. She sat hunched on the sofa, hands clenched tightly.

"Another Hollywood theory," said Patty. "But please, do go on."

"It would have been easy to do," said Margot. "A quick climb up the fire escape. Lily always left the balcony door unlocked for her cat. Grabs a handy cushion."

"No! No!" Tegan was beginning to sound hysterical. "If anything, it was *Evie* who needed to get rid of the witness! You're staying next door. How convenient."

"Or you!" I threw right back. "The love letters that Lily had been keeping for all those years? Was Lily blackmailing you? Threatening to tell Jago about . . . about—" I stopped suddenly.

Tegan went pale. "About what?"

"Yes . . . about what?. . ." Patty looked over to Cador and then back to Alex, but she didn't say a word.

And then it was so obvious. Seeing the two men standing in the same room, the same height and coloring, vivid blue eyes and high cheekbones. I couldn't be the only one who had spotted it. The age would have been about right. What was Cador? Early forties?

Margot nudged me and leaned over. "Are you thinking what I'm thinking?"

I nodded and whispered back, "But let's keep this one quiet."

"Alex hasn't a clue, has he," she whispered. And I had to agree. "It's a bit of a *Star Wars* moment, isn't it."

No wonder Tegan had been hysterical. And now, if anyone had a motive to get rid of Lily, it was Tegan. It had to be. Lily had been the midwife. Lily would have delivered her son, and given her friendship with Tegan's mother, wouldn't Lily have guessed that Cador was not Jago's child? It sounded as though Alex and Tegan had enjoyed a passionate love affair, so when Alex went home to Sweden and Tegan suddenly married Jago out of the blue, the reason seemed glaringly obvious to me.

Patty finally spoke. My stomach clenched in anticipation. I felt as if I were witnessing a stage play, but instead she switched her attention back to me.

"Perhaps you can tell me what happened to your face?" Patty

pointed to hers. "A little scratch. It looks painful, but I don't think it will scar."

"I found Lily's cat outside on the balcony. When I picked him up he scratched me."

"What a perfect segue into the most thrilling part of our program today," said Patty. "Vicar? I believe you're up next."

I'd completely forgotten about the vicar, who had been quietly sitting in the wingback chair, stroking Mister Tig. Vicar Bill gently removed the cat from his lap and settled him back down before joining Patty in front of the fireplace.

"Perhaps you would like to enlighten our merry party," said Patty.

"Oh please," Tegan groaned. "Not Doctor Dolittle."

Vicar Bill cleared his throat. "As you all know—apart from our visitors—I am able to communicate with animals."

Margot let out a snort. "Sorry . . ." She snuffled into her hand. "It's just . . . wow. So L.A."

Vicar Bill seemed unperturbed. "I don't know why, but since the good Lord gave me the gift, I gladly do His bidding."

"And we're sorry for your loss, by the way," Patty said quickly.

"Don't worry. Millicent and I were never that close, but thank you." Vicar Bill surveyed the room in a way that I could just imagine would make him formidable in the pulpit. Then . . . he closed his eyes. "Just to clarify. I only see pictures. It is up to you to interpret them."

Patty had her pencil poised once more. "Go on."

"Mister Tig says that the woman who let him back into Lily's room was wearing pajamas. She walked to the powder room and started going through the cupboard above the washbasin."

"That's true!" I was amazed. "I was looking for Imodium—"

"Then the woman went through Millicent's scrapbook."

"Wait a minute," I said. "With all due respect to . . . Mister Tig, is he talking about the same woman as the woman in pajamas, because I saw Vanessa tearing pages out of Lily's scrapbook. She put them in her pocket."

Vicar Bill continued to keep his eyes closed. "I stand corrected. A girl with a tattoo went through Millicent's scrapbook."

"Wow," Margot whispered again. "That cat doesn't miss a thing."

"Do we know the significance of the scrapbook?" Patty asked.

"It's full of newspaper cuttings," said Tegan. "Lily was obsessed with celebrities, gory crime stories, anything scandalous."

"Now isn't that funny," mused Patty. "I would have thought her scrapbook would have contained names of all the babies she delivered on the island." Patty glanced over to Cador and then back to Alex again—a look that was not lost on Tegan, who had gone very still.

"I don't understand the relevance of this," Tegan said.

"Owen," said Patty, "why don't you go and bring down the scrapbook and perhaps look for a book that records all those little babies."

"Mister Tig says it's in a red leather box on the top shelf in the powder room," said Vicar Bill. "But you'll need the key. It's on his collar."

"What a helpful cat!" Patty said. "Carry on, Mister Tig. You make my job so much easier."

"Please don't—," Tegan whispered.

"And the woman in the pajamas took a photograph off the bookshelf," said Vicar Bill.

"I-I was going to mention that," I stammered. "I wanted to show Margot."

"And where is the photograph now?"

I felt my face redden. "I left it in one of the planters on the balcony."

"Now why would you do that?" said Patty.

I shrugged. "Honestly, I have no idea, but if Owen is going upstairs to Lily's room, he can look out on the balcony and it should still be there." I was beginning to get freaked out by Vicar Bill's psychic abilities. "Perhaps the vicar should ask Mister Tig what he saw earlier that afternoon?"

"All in good time," said Patty. "But for now, let's talk about this photograph that you hid in the planter on the balcony."

I took a deep breath. "It showed my husband and his first wife, Joanna, with Lily and Jago grouped around a sailing trophy."

"I took that photograph," said Tegan. "It was at the World Pilot Gig Championship around Scilly. We used to take part every year."

"That's why I wanted to show Margot," I said. "I had asked Jago if he had known my husband and if the name Millicent Small had meant anything to him. Jago denied it. I was putting the photograph back, but Tegan saw me out on the balcony and . . . the rest you know."

Vicar Bill cleared his throat. "There is something else that Mister Tig wants to tell you."

"We're all whiskers," said Patty. "Go ahead."

Vicar Bill adjusted his dog collar and licked his lips. He seemed nervous. "Mister Tig said that Mrs. Tegan and the foreign gentleman came to talk to Lily yesterday."

I remembered that vividly. It was just before I darted down the back staircase and bumped into Jago.

"What time would that be—Oh wait," said Patty. "The cat doesn't wear a watch."

"As I said," said Vicar Bill, "I only see pictures. But he told me that a rather nice bird landed on the balcony railing that looked fat and slow, so I assume it had to have been light outside."

"Good. Thank you, Mister Tig," said Patty. "And at least this solves the mystery of why the cat was stuck outside on the balcony. He was thinking of his supper." Patty flashed a smile. "Enlighten us on what Tegan and Alex were doing in Lily's bedroom, if you don't mind."

"There was an argument," said Vicar Bill. "Millicent was upset. Mrs. Tegan was going through her things—opening and closing drawers, searching for something—but they left empty-handed."

"What were you looking for?" Patty demanded.

"Our letters," said Alex.

"And where are these letters now?"

"We don't know," said Tegan. "But this has nothing to do with what happened to Lily."

"Perhaps we should ask Mister Tig what else he saw—before he was shut out on the balcony." Patty turned to Vicar Bill. "Well?"

The vicar closed his eyes once again, and after a few moments, he nodded. "Mister Tig saw someone dressed in a black waterproof hooded cape and Wellington boots."

I looked at Margot in dismay. "That was me," she faltered. "But I just was going back to my room."

"Not according to Mister Tig," said Vicar Bill.

Patty closed her notebook. "I think that's enough for now. Thank you to Vicar Bill and Mister Tig. If I want to question the cat again, I'll let you know. As for you non-Scillonians—as they say on the telly, *Don't go leaving the country*—although you won't get far. The tide is in."

Tegan let out a sigh of relief. "Then we're free to go?"

"You are, yes. But . . . Evelyn Mead and Margot Chandler . . . no."

"*Why* aren't we free to go?" Margot demanded.

"I feel I must caution you," Patty said calmly. "You have the right to remain silent. Anything you say can and will be used against you in a court of law. You have the right to speak to an attorney . . . I can't remember the rest."

"*What?*" I looked at Margot in horror. "Are we . . . are you *arresting* us?"

"Not exactly," said Patty. "I'm just reading the *Miranda* rights."

"*Miranda* rights?" Margot looked confused. "But . . . isn't that only in America? I didn't think they had them here."

"You are correct," said Patty. "But I've always wanted to say them and I thought you'd appreciate it." She smiled, but her eyes were cold. "I will be watching you, so consider it a warning."

Tegan smirked. "Dennis, make sure Patty has whatever she

needs. You can use the Ngaio Marsh room as a base. Dennis will bring up more coffee and sandwiches."

"Thank you," said Patty. "You are all free to go. Oh, Margot. Wait a moment, I have something for you."

"*Me?* Here?" Margot looked to me and shrugged.

"Aren't you the lucky one!" said Patty. "It's followed you all the way from Los Angeles via Kent and then St. Mary's. It must be important."

Patty produced a FedEx envelope.

All the color drained out of Margot's face. She snatched it from Patty's grasp and fled.

Chapter Twenty-seven

When Margot still hadn't come back to our room an hour later, I grabbed my Barbour and went out to find her. It had begun to rain.

As I reached the Galleon Garden, I heard the most terrible sobbing.

Margot was seated on a stone bench in an alcove partially hidden by a golden tiger figurehead on one side and a beautiful mermaid on the other. She was clutching the FedEx envelope to her chest. She was wet and shivering from the cold.

I slipped beside her and took her hand. "You'll catch your death out here."

She mumbled, "I don't care."

"Do you want to tell me what's wrong?"

She gave me the FedEx. Inside was a letter with an official letterhead from a law firm with about fifteen partners.

"Oh no," I said. "Is this a lawsuit?"

"Read it!"

I did as I was told with mounting bewilderment. "I don't understand. Brian is *divorcing* you?"

She began to rock back and forth, tears streaming down her face.

"But . . . I don't understand," I said again. "You were so happy!"

"I thought we were," she said bleakly, and started to cry again. "My heart is broken."

I put my arm around her shoulders and pulled her close. "Oh Margot, I am so very sorry."

Her grief was so raw I found myself in tears, too. I took off my coat and we snuggled under it together.

"Like old times under a blanket on Brighton beach," I said. "Remember?"

"Dad never liked Brian," Margot said flatly. "I should have listened to him. He said Brian was too full of himself. Called him a peacock."

"Dad didn't like Robert either," I reminded her. "He said I was marrying a geriatric and that I'd end up being a glorified nurse."

"All mouth and no trousers is what Dad called Brian," Margot went on. "Definitely no trousers in this case. He couldn't keep them on."

"I am so sorry," I said again.

"And I starved myself practically to death," she said. "I got down to a size two, but he still said I looked fat."

"I hate him," I said, and realized I meant it.

"I've been hungry for fourteen years."

It certainly explained why Margot had been eating for

England for the past twelve hours. "I was worried that you had a tapeworm or something. I've never seen you eat so much."

"Ugh. You are so disgusting." Margot gave a hollow laugh. "It's ironic. You marry a man who I was *so* sure would cheat on you. When I met Robert I thought, What does he want with my baby sister? He seemed too good to be true."

"We're not talking about me." I definitely did not want to have that conversation right now.

"It serves me right," Margot said ruefully. "I was so smug about Brian. I believed he was more likely to be a serial killer than a cheat."

"He did look a bit like Ted Bundy," I admitted. "He had that weird intense stare."

"Especially by candlelight. No," she said. "I told you it's because I'm fat."

"Margot!" I was appalled. "You are not fat."

"I got the boob job and then he wanted me to have a bum like Kim Kardashian. He said mine was too flat."

"Thank God you didn't."

She gave a weak smile. "Brian got hair plugs, you know."

Despite the seriousness of the situation, I had to laugh. "Like Elton John?"

She nodded again. "They were put in a bit too low. Now he looks like a monk because of his bald spot."

I gave her another squeeze.

"The pressure to be beautiful in Los Angeles is so demoralizing," she said.

"I wish you could have told me."

"No. You were stricken with grief—you and your wonderful marriage to the perfect Robert," said Margot. "It didn't seem right somehow. Besides, I kept hoping Brian would come to his senses." She wiped her nose on the back of her cashmere sweater sleeve. "Of course I knew something was going on—"

"Hence all the text messages and phone calls."

"Apparently he didn't want me to be taken by surprise. He wanted to warn me," she said. "I wish he was dead. No, actually I don't. That would be too good for him. I would rather he die a miserable death by poison or get mowed down by a car. You know you can hire people to do that kind of thing. It's pretty inexpensive."

"I know you don't mean that."

"Actually I do," said Margot. "I suspected, of course. There were the usual clichéd telltale signs that I chose to ignore. Brian was always working late and naturally he started dieting in earnest. There were other signs too."

"Go on."

"The front passenger seat in his car was always in a weird position. She's younger than him, of course. Sixteen years. *Jeniffer*, one *n*, two *f*'s and an asterisk over the letter *i*. I mean, who spells their name like that?"

"Aspiring actresses who are passionate about producers with hair plugs?"

"Brian told me he always had women throwing themselves at him." She took a deep breath. "I . . . I want to show you this text. That's why I ran off yesterday afternoon."

Margot retrieved her iPhone from her cardigan pocket and

scrolled up until she found what she was looking for. "You'll enjoy this. Look."

I read, *There's no nice way to say this, our marriage is over we're getting divorced.* I was stunned at Brian's cruelty.

"We never really know someone, do we," Margot whispered.

"Amen to that."

"It's ironic, isn't it," said Margot. "Here was I accusing you of putting your head in the sand and all the time I was doing that too."

"I'm so sorry."

"He said he kept trying to tell me, and maybe he had. When he said he needed a bit of space I just thought he wanted more time in his man cave. But what he really meant was infinite space from me."

"But the FedEx—"

"He said it was the only way I would accept that he was being serious."

"Brian must have sent it when you left for the U.K." I was disgusted. "What a coward. But . . . how did it get to Tregarrick? Did you tell him we were coming here?"

"Of course I did," she said. "He must have intercepted or rerouted it or whatever you have to do." She wiped her nose again. "He was so desperate to get rid of me."

"Bastard."

"And it gets worse." Margot gave me a look filled with so much pain I could hardly stand it. "He says there is no need for me to come back because he can get all my stuff shipped over in a container."

"Oh Margot. Why didn't you tell me?"

"Because you had such a perfect life. You were always the favorite—"

"That's not true!"

"Dad never seemed to approve of anything I did, even though I got top marks in school and was a prefect."

"Oh Margot," I whispered. "I feel terrible—absolutely terrible." How could I not have seen how unhappy she was?

"I thought moving to California would be so exciting."

"But it is," I exclaimed. "Look at your life! A house in Bel Air and a snow house in Deer Valley. Meeting movie stars, going to the Oscars—"

"Academy Awards, actually. We don't call them Oscars," Margot said. "That's the official name."

"Fine. Yes. Those. All the red carpet events! Compared to you I felt boring. You were brave and courageous and were having amazing adventures in California! I could never have done that."

"I was an impulsive idiot," said Margot.

"No you weren't! I admired you so much—still do, of course! Don't put yourself down. I love telling everyone about my famous sister in Hollywood."

"Oh Evie," Margot said miserably. "Gullible little Evie."

I bristled. "What are you talking about?"

Margot took a deep breath. "You see, there is no house in Bel Air or snow house in Deer Valley—"

"But that's not true," I protested. "Robert and I came to Utah that Christmas—"

"We were house-sitting for one of Brian's clients."

I was stunned. "But . . . what about all the amazing movies Brian made?"

"Since you never watch movies or TV, you could never have known that nothing ever took off," Margot said. "Sure, we got close to getting a movie green-lit a gazillion times, but . . ." She blushed. "I waited on tables at restaurants—good restaurants, I may add—just to pay the rent."

"The rent?"

"Hollywood is all about illusions," she went on. "We lived in a big house, but we didn't own it."

"You're kidding." I was struggling to make sense of all this.

"I wish I was." Margot gave a bitter smile. "They call independent film producers the bottom-feeders of Hollywood."

"Well, looking on the bright side," I said, "Jeniffer with one *n*, two *f*'s and an asterisk over the *i* is heading for a major disappointment."

"I called her, you know," Margot said suddenly.

You called *Jeniffer*?" I exclaimed. "When?"

"About fifteen minutes before you found me here this morning."

"But . . . it must have been the middle of the night in Los Angeles!"

"I know," said Margot. "And guess who answered the phone?"

"Brian?"

"Yep, Brian," said Margot. "One night I left my mobile switched on and put it under Brian's car seat when he said he was going out of town. I used my laptop to find my phone—you know, the app—and lo and behold, he was at her grungy little flat off Ventura Boulevard. I drove there, of course. Watched until the next morning, in fact, just to make sure. A part of me was hoping that it was all some horrible mistake and that his car had been stolen, but it was Brian."

My heart went out to Margot. What a terrible thing to discover. "Do you know how they met?"

"She'd come into the office months ago for an audition," said Margot. "That's how I got her phone number. So now you know everything."

"Thank you for telling me," I whispered. "I know it must have been difficult."

"I've missed you, sis," Margot said. "I'm so happy I could finally tell you. No more secrets. Promise? Let's make a pact never to keep a secret from each other again." She offered her hand. "Shake on it?"

For a moment I hesitated, but then I took her hand and said, "There is something I have to tell you."

Chapter Twenty-eight

"You are right about Robert and me," I said slowly. "He was still married to Joanna when we met—"

"God, Evie," said Margot with disgust. "How could you do that to another woman?"

"Just hear me out!" I protested. "Nothing physical happened between Robert and me until his divorce came through. I was never the other woman. It wasn't like that."

"What *was* it like?"

"She was always threatening to leave him!" I said. "When I met Robert, Joanna had moved in with a musician who was half her age. She asked Robert for a divorce."

"You never told me any of this," said Margot.

"You weren't living here," I pointed out. "The eight-hour time difference was terrible—and to be honest, the whole thing was so awful. The moment Joanna realized that Robert had actually fallen in love with someone else, she changed her mind and wanted him back."

I remembered the angry phone calls, Joanna turning up on our doorstep in the middle of the night and the way she manipulated their son, Michael. The hardest thing for me to understand was why Robert had felt guilty. To me it sounded as though life with Joanna had been a nightmare. She also made me out to be a home-wrecker, which was unfair and not true at all.

"Robert was very generous with her alimony," I said. "And of course Michael went to the best university. Despite that rocky start, we were happy, Margot."

"So Robert was a man of his word," said Margot. I wondered if she was being sarcastic, but I realized that she wasn't. "An honest man is hard to find. No wonder you miss him. I'm envious. I have always been envious of your perfect marriage, even though I thought you were mad marrying someone so much older."

"Nothing is ever what it seems, Margot." I took a deep breath. "On the morning that Robert died, I told him that I needed some time apart."

Margot's jaw dropped. "What? *Why?*"

"It was about having children."

Margot looked confused. "Robert suddenly wanted *children?*"

"No, but I did," I said. "I didn't just change my mind either. It was a dull ache that turned into a burning desire to have kids. You wouldn't understand since I know you don't have that gene."

"Hardly fair on Robert asking him to be a father again at his age," Margot remarked.

I was beginning to wish that I hadn't confided in her. "That's not the point. He said he was willing to try, but he hoped I wouldn't leave him if it turned out that we couldn't."

"And since you couldn't, it sounds like Robert's fears were realized."

"Let me finish!" I exclaimed. "Robert would never have been able to have fathered a child because . . . because . . . he had a vasectomy years ago."

"Holy cow! And he never told you?"

I shook my head. "Each time when I realized I wasn't pregnant, he pretended to be disappointed. He'd send me flowers, take me to dinner and just be so sweet and sympathetic. He kept saying that we could still be happy. Just the two of us."

"Didn't you have the children conversation when you first got together?"

"Of course." I nodded. "He asked me if I wanted kids and I said no because I didn't at the time. He should have told me then, but he didn't."

"How on earth did you find out? Did Joanna know? She must have!"

I took another deep breath. The memory was still very raw and what followed even more painful to relive. "I found out on Michael's thirtieth birthday."

"I thought Michael refused to talk to you."

"Maybe he grew up. Who knows?" I said. "Robert and I took him out for dinner. Michael made a casual comment about enjoying being the only son and heir and said he was happy that there could never be any more mini-Meads. That's how he put it."

"Mini-Meads? Funny." But Margot wasn't laughing. She was watching me with such love and concern I realized just how grateful I was to have her in my life.

"I thought about it and later asked Robert what that meant, so he told me the truth."

"Would you still have married him if he had?" Margot demanded.

"Yes, and I told him that, but I don't think he believed me."

"So why did you ask him for some space?"

"I . . . I just needed to think. I felt confused. His was a big lie, Margot."

"Not a deliberate lie," said Margot. "More of a lying by omission."

"I can't help wondering if I killed him."

"How?" she said. "Don't be ridiculous!"

"No. Listen. It was the morning after that fateful birthday dinner. Robert acted as if everything was back to normal. He couldn't understand why I was still upset and angry. I suppose it was then that I realized I needed some time away to think. I packed an overnight bag. He didn't try and stop me, Margot. He just sat at the kitchen table eating his bloody cornflakes and didn't say a word."

"In his defense, I am sure he didn't know what to do," said Margot. "You rarely lose your temper, but when you do you're impossible to talk to."

"He could have tried," I said lamely.

"Where exactly were you planning on going?"

"I hadn't thought that far," I said. "I drove around the countryside like a crazy woman, not sure what to do or where to go. And then I got the call from Nigel telling me that Robert had said I was divorcing him—which wasn't true. Nigel seemed really shocked. He couldn't believe it. He saw us as the perfect couple and said we should at least see a counselor."

"You never told me the details," Margot said quietly. "You just said he had a heart attack at breakfast, not that you weren't there."

"Nigel told me that Robert was in a terrible state—"

"Of course he was," said Margot. "What else did Nigel say?"

"He kept saying that life on my own would be difficult; that I'd find it hard to get a job—"

"Wow. So Robert must have believed you were gone for good. But what an odd thing for Nigel to say about you finding it hard to get a job." Margot sounded puzzled. "Did you tell him about Robert's vasectomy?"

"Of course not!" I was horrified. "That's private. I suppose Nigel couldn't understand why I would leave, and I certainly wasn't going to give him the details."

"What happened next?"

"About twenty minutes later Nigel called me again to say that by the time he got to Forster's Oast Robert was already unconscious."

"Awful."

"When I got back to the house the paramedics were loading his body into the ambulance." The image of that terrible morning hit me again. "My last memory of Robert is of him sitting at the kitchen table eating a bowl of cornflakes and reading the newspaper."

"Jeez," was all Margot managed to say.

"Don't you see?" I exclaimed. "If I hadn't left the house I would have been able to save him."

"But how?"

"CPR. I know CPR," I said. "Nigel tried, but it was too late."

"I thought Robert had a strong heart," said Margot.

"So did I. I knew he suffered from high blood pressure," I said. "But his heart was sound—maybe it was caused by the shock?"

We both fell quiet yet again. A flock of birds slowly flew overhead. The sun came out, making the raindrops glisten on the figureheads in the Galleon Garden. Everywhere was so quiet and peaceful. My old life seemed so very far away. Dennis had said that people came to Tregarrick Rock to escape from reality; that the tranquility of the island offered a sanctuary, a place for people to regroup and heal. I had thought it sounded so American, but now I realized what he meant.

"It's surprisingly lovely here when the sun comes out," I said finally.

"I was thinking the same thing," said Margot.

"We're both in a bit of a mess, aren't we."

"And broke," said Margot. "Brian doesn't have a dime and clearly neither does Robert. It's such a pity about this hotel. It's got a ton of potential."

"I know."

Margot thought for a moment. "Presumably Dennis must have given the cash to Joanna. It would have come in handy."

"Presumably," I agreed. "I doubt if she would have told Robert that she'd got it. If the date is right it was repaid in those months when Robert and I first got together." I had a sudden thought. "It didn't take her long to blow through it, though."

"How do you know that?"

I had been too embarrassed to tell Margot how Tegan verbally attacked me, but under our new promise, I knew I wanted to. "Tegan said that Joanna has nothing and it's all my fault that she's living in squalor."

"Tegan!" Margot scoffed. "Look at her with her Swedish lover! It's obvious that she pushed Jago off the cliff, but of course, the Scillonians all band together and it's the outsiders who become the suspects."

"I know."

"But . . . that Patty isn't stupid," Margot said slowly. "I think she knows that Tegan and Alex did it. She's just pretending that she doesn't so *they* don't leave the island. It's a classic police move."

"Do you really think so?"

"Guaranteed—especially now that she sees that Cador must be Alex's son. I wouldn't mind being a fly on the wall when Tegan has *that* conversation."

I thought of Cador's obvious distress in the Residents' Lounge and wondered if he'd guessed.

"And I thought our lives were messy," Margot said. "Let's go back to our room. I'm getting cold."

Dennis looked up eagerly from behind the counter as we entered the lobby, but disappointment flooded his face when he realized it was just Margot and me.

"Do you want your key?" he said, turning to the pigeonhole key cabinet.

"No, I have it," I said. "Still no sign of Vanessa?"

Dennis shook his head. "I think she's already halfway back to Penzance."

"What makes you think that?"

"Alex told me his hip waders were taken last night. She could have crossed the causeway at low tide."

"Why would she have done that?" Margot said. "Why run away unless—?"

"She didn't do it," Dennis insisted. "I know her. She wouldn't."

"Of course not," I said gently. The poor man seemed distraught, but in truth, how did we know she didn't?

Dennis shot me a grateful smile.

"Wait!" Margot exclaimed suddenly. "When you paid the loan back do you remember who you gave the money to?"

"What do you mean?" said Dennis.

"Was it a man or a woman?" Margot demanded.

Dennis seemed taken aback. "I took the ferry to Penzance and gave it to a woman. Why?"

"How did you know where to meet her?" Margot asked.

"Yes," I chimed in. "Did she call and make the arrangement?"

"Mr. Jago did that," said Dennis. "I'm not paid to ask questions."

"So no name," I said.

Dennis shook his head.

"Are you sure?" said Margot. "That's annoying."

"Sorry," said Dennis. "It was a long time ago. If you'll excuse me, I need to get on."

As we walked to the elevator to go up to our room, Margot said, "So it *was* Joanna."

"We don't know that—"

"It certainly explains the mystery of the handwriting on the receipt," said Margot. "Joanna could have easily forged his name."

I shook my head. "It doesn't make sense. Why would Joanna go to Penzance? Wouldn't Dennis have met her in London?"

"I thought you said she lived in Kent."

"She does, but . . ." I shrugged. "It just seems weird."

"Not unless Joanna didn't want Robert to know about the money," said Margot.

"Don't be silly. Of course Robert would have known about the money," I said. "Jago would have told him that he was able to repay the loan and with cash, no less. They would have had to have made a rendezvous."

We headed back to our room, glad to be in the warmth and even happier to find a kettle with tea bags and packets of powdered milk and sugar on a hospitality tray in the cupboard under the desk. For once Margot didn't complain.

"We need to call Joanna," Margot said suddenly. "Find out what she knows."

"Are you out of your mind?" Panic welled up in my chest. "I don't want any part of that. I'm definitely not going to call her."

"She needs to know that Robert's dead—"

"She has to know," I said. "I told you. I spoke to Michael the minute he landed in Sydney. He would have called his mother straightaway."

"Fine. If you won't do it then I will."

Margot kicked off her shoes and threw herself onto her bed.

I sat on the edge. She pulled out her iPhone. "I'll use mine. She won't recognize the number."

"I'm not sure I have her phone number," I said, knowing full well that I had. I'd always been so afraid of her calling me that I had found her number in Robert's phone and entered it into mine under the name Cruella. That way, I'd always be forewarned if she actually made contact. She never had.

"Come on, I know you have it." Margot snapped her fingers, so reluctantly, I obliged. At the very least it was a distraction from Brian's heartless texts and that awful letter.

"I'll put Joanna on speakerphone," said Margot. "The worst thing she can do is hang up on us."

Margot began to dial.

Chapter Twenty-nine

"Hello?" said a voice that sounded surprisingly like a young girl.

"Am I speaking to Joanna Mead?" said Margot in her most professional assistant voice.

"Yes. Who is this?"

"Please don't hang up, but I have Evie Mead on the line."

My jaw dropped. I shook my head vehemently. Margot shoved the iPhone at me and mouthed, *Big-girl pants!*

"I was expecting your call," Joanna said smoothly.

My heart sank. I braced myself for a flurry of insults, but instead she said, "Tegan tells me you are staying at Tregarrick Rock."

So Tegan had phoned her.

And suddenly I had to ask. "Did you know that Robert had a vasectomy?"

Margot was horrified. She tried to snatch the iPhone, but I jumped up and darted over to the window. My hands were shaking so much that I forgot to turn off the speakerphone.

Joanna actually laughed. "He didn't tell you?"

When I didn't answer she said, "I told him you'd want kids, but he insisted that you didn't."

"You discussed me?" I was appalled. For some reason this seemed even more of a betrayal than Robert keeping the vasectomy a secret.

"The hotel!" Margot hissed. "Ask her about the hotel!"

"So what exactly is this phone call about?" Joanna said. "Are you inviting me to Robert's funeral or is this about the autopsy?"

"What about the autopsy?"

"There seems to be some questions surrounding the circumstances of his death," Joanna said.

"Circumstances?" My stomach turned over. I had thought it was just a routine thing because Robert had died at home. "What circumstances? How do you know that?"

"Because the doctor is a family friend," she said simply. "And I am Robert's wife after all—"

"*Was*," I said firmly. "Was his wife."

"I'm surprised Harry—that's Dr. Barnaby to you—didn't mention it."

I felt stupid. I hadn't even thought to ask for details. I'd been too upset.

"The hotel!" Margot hissed again.

"Yes, Harry thought it was strange," Joanna went on. "Bobby had seen him for a thorough medical just three days before. He had never been in better health. That's why Harry talked about an autopsy. He couldn't understand why Bobby's heart had given out like that. Had he complained to you of any pains?"

"No," I said.

"But of course he wouldn't, would he," Joanna said. "A young wife! He wouldn't want you thinking that you'd married an old man."

Margot snatched the iPhone from me. "Hi, Joanna, this is Margot here, Evie's sister. Did you receive a hundred thousand pounds from Jago Ferris?"

"I have no idea what you are talking about," said Joanna.

"Robert loaned Jago Ferris one hundred thousand pounds and apparently he paid it back to you."

"Believe me, I would remember that," said Joanna. "I know nothing about a loan of any kind." She laughed. "What a pair you are! Is it not enough that Evelyn inherited all his worldly goods? You won't get anything from me because I don't have anything. Is that it? Do you have any other questions?"

"Wait!" I said, and took my iPhone back from Margot, thoroughly rattled. "There are no worldly goods. Robert died bankrupt."

"That's absolutely impossible!" said Joanna. "I heard about some of his less savory investments through Michael, of course, but Bobby had a lot of assets. He was one of the most enterprising men I'd ever met. He'd never allow that to happen. He was just too clever."

"So you did *not* sign a piece of paper saying you received one hundred thousand pounds?" I said to be sure. "And by the way, the money was rightly yours. This happened when you were married."

"How very generous of you to admit that." Joanna's voice dripped with sarcasm. "No. I did not sign anything."

"And are you saying that you never met Dennis Simmonds at Penzance?"

"*Penzance?*" Joanna laughed again. "Where? Let me guess. At the railway station, under the clock."

"Was it?" I demanded.

"I was being facetious," said Joanna. "I don't know a Dennis Simmonds."

"He works for Jago and has done for a number of years."

"Oh, *that* Dennis. I didn't know his last name," said Joanna. "Tegan told me Jago found him homeless somewhere. Invalided out of the army or something. I really don't remember."

It was becoming clear that Dennis had to have been lying about giving the money to Joanna.

"Dennis distinctly mentioned giving the cash to a woman," I said.

Joanna gave a heavy sigh. "Well, it wasn't me."

Vanessa, maybe? But why go through the charade of saying he met someone in Penzance if they were in it together?

Margot mouthed, *Oh my God! Dennis did it!*

Dennis had to have been putting on an act from the beginning to hide his part in stealing the cash. But there was a niggling doubt in my head that wouldn't go away.

"It sounds like you should be asking Dennis," Joanna said as if reading my thoughts. "Probably pocketed it himself by the sound of things."

"Did you know someone called Lily Travis?" I said suddenly. "Or maybe you would have remembered her as Millicent Small?"

"Yes, I remember her," said Joanna. "Always throwing herself at Jago and Bobby. Dreadful woman."

"When Tegan called you, did she tell you that Lily was dead?"

"Well, she must have been nearing ninety," said Joanna.

"She witnessed the loan document between *my* husband and Jago."

Joanna didn't correct me. "Oh, Millicent witnessed a lot of things. She used to keep it all in her little scrapbook, or was it her black book. I don't recall. I am sure Tegan isn't the only one to rejoice in her death."

Margot mouthed, *Why? Ask her why?*

"Why would you say that?" I asked. "Who?"

"I think we are finished now," said Joanna.

"Ask her!" Margot hissed, but I didn't.

"Joanna . . . I—"

"Good-bye! Thank you, Joanna," Margot shouted, and snatched the iPhone back. "Have a good life." She disconnected the call. "What a bitter woman. Ugh. No wonder he preferred you."

"I don't think that achieved anything." I showed her my hands. They were trembling. "That was horrible."

"I disagree. Now we know who killed Jago and Lily Travis— and very nearly killed you," Margot declared. "Dennis."

Chapter Thirty

"No," I said. "Why would he write a note pretending to be Jago and then not finish the job and push me over the cliff? Also . . . Tegan said it wasn't Jago's handwriting and Dennis stressed how pedantic he was about always writing the exact date and time. If he was forging the note, wouldn't he have made sure it looked authentic?"

"Good point," said Margot. "Vanessa and Dennis are in it together. He obviously followed you up there but suddenly got cold feet."

"He pulled me back from the edge of the cliff, Margot," I reminded her. "You should have seen how distraught he was over Jago. Plus—" I shuddered at the memory. "Jago's head was a bloodied mess. Wouldn't Dennis have had blood on his hands?"

"I'm just saying it's possible." Margot shrugged. "And Vanessa has disappeared—or has she? I think it's a ruse to throw everyone off the scent."

"I don't know what to think," I said.

"Dennis is the ringleader, I'm sure of it," said Margot. "And what about the mysterious Amazon delivery that he's been hoarding in his room?"

"It is a bit strange," I agreed.

"Who knows what Dennis has been buying off the Internet and putting in Vanessa's name? Jago found Dennis on the streets—he probably has some kind of post-traumatic stress disorder. No judgment, but war does funny things to people."

"I think that whatever Vanessa ripped out of Lily's scrapbook will give us a clue," I said.

"We'll never know," said Margot. "Vanessa has obviously gone with the wind. I can imagine her making a run for it wearing Alex's hip waders. I mean—did you see the size of his feet? They have to be a fourteen and she's so small. I can just imagine her flip-flopping along the causeway."

Margot began to snigger and then we both exploded into giggles that became more hysterical as she demonstrated with a gawky stride that would make a Monty Python's "Ministry of Silly Walks" proud.

"And what about the *cat*?" Margot went off in peals of laughter. "I wonder if he'll be called to the witness box!"

We fell into convulsions until Margot's phone rang. She glanced at the caller I.D. and froze. "Oh God, Evie. It's Brian. I . . . I don't want to talk to him."

"Then don't!"

"No, I have to. I hate this. Maybe he's changed his mind?" She leapt off the bed. "Brian? . . . Yes? . . . Yes! I got your bloody

FedEx—hold on." She hit mute and looked at me in anguish, saying, "I need to talk to him. I'm sorry. Just give me a minute."

"I'll leave you in private. I think I'm going out for a bit," I said. "Good luck."

The events of the morning had left me reeling—all the horrible revelations in the Residents' Lounge, to say nothing of being the prime suspects for Jago's murder; Margot's confession about the state of her marriage; and then the difficult conversation with Joanna. I needed to think and get my head straight. I couldn't just stay in our room. I was weary of theories and rehashing everything over and over again.

I dug out my Canon camera. It was an old model—I'd bought it way back in 2010—but I liked it. For the time being we were stuck on the island, so I may as well make the most of it. I'd brought it with me to photograph the birds, so that's what I would do.

Outside in the corridor, Lily's door stood open. I wondered what would happen to Mister Tig now that Lily was dead but got some comfort in knowing that he was the hotel cat. Hopefully someone would keep his Instagram account going.

Downstairs all was quiet. Dennis was standing at the counter as if in a daze. I just couldn't see him killing Jago or Lily. What would be the motive?

"Oh," he said with a frown. "You're going out again?"

"I can't go far," I said. "If it makes you feel any better you can call Patty and tell her I'm going to take some photographs—or I can if you tell me where she is."

"Cador took the police back in his skiff. Patty has a son—"

"She does?"

"Nice kid. She's a single mother so she had to sort him out with his grandmother. Then she's coming back this afternoon. Not much can happen until tomorrow. It's Sunday."

"So no need to tell her," I said.

"Mist is coming down again," Dennis said. "Best to stick to the west side."

And then I remembered something that Dennis had said earlier. "How old is Vanessa?"

If Dennis was taken aback by my question, he didn't show it. "Twenty-five."

Dennis told us that he had given the money to a woman nine years ago, so it couldn't have been Vanessa. She would have just been sixteen—unless he was lying.

"Why do you ask?"

"When you met that woman in Penzance, do you re-member what she looked like? How old? Fat? Slim? Blond? Brunette?"

"She was a little on the heavy side," Dennis said with a shrug. "Maybe around thirty."

"*Thirty?*" I was truly baffled. Joanna would have been in her fifties by then, so even if she had lied about not receiving the money, it couldn't have been given to her.

"Do you remember the woman's name?"

"I was just told to meet a woman under the clock on the main concourse at Penzance railway station."

Just a woman? Nothing else? "Why didn't you mention this earlier!" I exclaimed. "You must have got her age wrong."

"I was told that she would be wearing a navy raincoat with a *Harry Potter* scarf."

For a moment I wasn't sure if I had heard him properly. "A *Harry Potter* scarf?" I repeated. "You're sure of that?"

"I'm certain," said Dennis. "Because when I met her she was talking to some schoolkids who were wearing Hogwarts scarves. From the Hogwarts houses. I only know because Vanessa was obsessed with *Harry Potter* at the time too."

The only woman I knew who wore a *Harry Potter* scarf was Nigel's assistant, Cherie, and yet it seemed impossible that she had been the woman under the clock. But . . . was it? Robert had said she'd do anything for Nigel, anything at all. I felt sick.

"Are you alright?" said Dennis. "You look as if you have seen a ghost."

"I'm fine," I managed to say. "I just need some air." In fact, I desperately needed to get outside. I had to think.

Somehow I found myself in the Galleon Garden. I must have been walking on autopilot. I sat on the same bench where I had found Margot crying just hours before. Cherie—if it had been Cherie at the railway station—would never have acted alone.

Nine years ago would have put Cherie at around thirty, so she would have been the right age. Nigel must have known that Jago was repaying the loan, and personal assistants knew everything about their bosses. Maybe she . . . But I just couldn't avoid the obvious. Nigel had to have been involved. There was no other explanation.

I pulled out my iPhone to call Margot but realized that the

Galleon Garden was in the dell and that there would be no signal.

I had to get back to the hotel as quickly as possible. But wait, even if it was Cherie, what would that prove? That Nigel pocketed the money and forged the receipt? It had no bearing on what was happening right now on the island. Nigel was in Paris.

And then I saw a flash of black darting through the undergrowth. Someone was moving very quickly up through the terraces above me. It had to be Vanessa! She was still on the island.

"Vanessa!" I yelled out. "I see you!"

She stopped. And then carried on, taking the steps two at a time before veering to the left into a bank of trees.

I went after her.

"Vanessa!" I shouted out again. "Don't run! Wait! It's okay!"

But Vanessa stopped just long enough for me to catch a glimpse of her before she raced off again. When she started to ascend into the bracken, I found I had a phone signal and called Dennis. Let him come and sort out his niece.

"Is she heading for the coast path?" he said. The strain in his voice was palpable.

"I think so."

"Don't let her get that far, Evie," said Dennis. "I'm begging you. She might . . . she's tried before. I don't want her to do anything stupid. She's desperate. Please . . . just tell her to hold on. I'll be there as quickly as I can."

I tried to call Margot, but it went straight to voice mail. She must be still on the phone. There was no time to lose.

I hurried on.

Vanessa seemed to slow down once we were in the bracken, but not once did she turn around. I managed to keep her in my sights, all the while cursing under my breath. I had to at least try to keep her safe until Dennis came.

The crashing surf below grew louder as I drew closer to the coast path. I started the climb, stopping to catch my breath at William's Bench. Daylight was fading fast, but the view across to the neighboring islands of Tresco and Bryher was spectacular.

And then I reached the peculiar rock formation where Dennis and I had stood only yesterday.

Suddenly the gaping fissure seemed menacing, and a chill came over me. There was no way I was going to step through that without knowing what was on the other side.

"Vanessa?" I called out. "It's Evie. You're not in trouble. Your uncle will be here any minute. Come with me. I'm not going to hurt you."

She didn't answer.

"Vanessa?" I stepped closer to the fissure. "Come back with me."

"Hello, Evie," came a voice I knew so well. I stood quite still. Helpless. Paralyzed. Heart pounding. Then the hooded figure stepped out from behind the boulder and threw back its hood.

"Nigel," I whispered. "It's you."

Chapter Thirty-one

The shock was so deep that I couldn't speak. I didn't need to ask him what he was doing there. I already knew.

Wearing a black waterproof hooded cape from the hotel, Nigel had completely fooled me. How could I have been so stupid? Vanessa was half his size. How could I not have known that he was leading me away from the hotel like the Pied Piper?

Nigel regarded me with disdain. "I told you not to interfere. None of this would have happened if you'd done what I said. Nobody would have got hurt. This is your fault. You did this."

I clutched my camera tightly, mind reeling, desperate to run.

"You should see your face." Nigel actually laughed. "Deer in headlights, trying to work it out. Robert was right when he said you were a bit dense."

"Yes, I can't work things out, you are quite right," I said quickly. Keep him talking. Isn't that what they say in the movies? Dennis was already on his way. Patty and Cador were coming back to Tregarrick. I'd left Margot a message, too. Help was coming. I just needed to keep a cool head.

"Getting to Tregarrick is difficult enough when doing it legally," I said lightly. "How on earth did you manage it? I thought you were in Paris!"

"I was," he said. "But after our phone call yesterday I changed my plans. Do you know that it's only an hour and forty minutes from Paris to St. Mary's by private jet?"

"Gosh, I had no idea that you were that worried about me. I'm flattered." I tried to keep my voice on an even keel but the fact that Nigel had hired a plane filled me with horror.

"From there I borrowed a little boat called *Sandra*—"

"You sailed over from St. Mary's on a *Topper*?" It was a wild guess but judging by Nigel's expression, I was right.

"How did you know that?"

"How else could you have got across so quickly, especially with the tide," I said. "I'm impressed. You've always been a good sailor."

And then it hit me. It was Nigel who had pulled the Topper up on the beach, leaving the V-shaped trough in the sand. That's how he had got onto the island undetected. I had to keep calm. I had to keep *talking* to him. I had to play for time.

"The police are out looking for that boat," I lied. "It's been reported as stolen."

Nigel grinned. "Nice try, but unlikely. With a total of four police officers on Scilly I would think looking for an old boat would be a low priority. Besides, I'm going to return it."

I thought again. "And of course Cherie knew everything."

"Cherie will do anything for me," Nigel said.

"Yes. Robert always said she was in love with you."

"I liven up her boring marriage," said Nigel. "It's a nice arrangement."

"It was Cherie who met Dennis at Penzance railway station to get the cash, wasn't it."

Nigel seemed surprised. "How did you find out about that?"

"Dennis said the woman he met was wearing a *Harry Potter* scarf."

"Now it's my turn to be impressed," said Nigel. "An excellent deduction, Sherlock Holmes." He reached for my hand. "I think we should find somewhere sheltered to continue this conversation. I'm feeling a trifle exposed."

I stepped back and shook my head. "I'm not going anywhere with you," I exclaimed. "I trusted you!"

"Come on, Evie, don't be silly," he said. "I'll show you my little cave where I spent last night."

I shoved him hard and took off back the way I'd come, half stumbling along the coast path desperately not looking over into the abyss below.

I made it as far as William's Bench when Nigel brought me down in a violent rugby tackle, hurling me onto my back. I struggled, dropping my camera, but he was so much bigger than me.

"Nice try, but rather pathetic if you don't mind me saying," he said, catching his breath, his face just inches from my own.

"Please don't, Nigel," I said. "I've never done anything to hurt you. There has to be a way out of this."

Nigel rolled back onto his heels. He wasn't very handsome after all. His eyes were black and cold. There was a deep scratch down one cheek.

"It looks like that cat got you too." Nigel traced the scratch on my cheek and then his own. He was a vain man. He always had been.

"You spared the cat but not Lily?" I said. "Why?"

"I like cats," Nigel said simply.

"I don't understand," I said. "Why would you kill Lily?"

"Because she saw me."

"Where?" I exclaimed. "What do you mean?"

"I realized she had been watching me for quite some time through her little telescope. Nosy cow."

Of course she had. Lily had thought it was Margot roaming the grounds. Alex had thought he'd seen her and so had Cador. And all the time it must have been Nigel delivering the note for me. It was a miracle that the two hadn't run into each other on the island.

"That was pretty brazen of you." *Keep talking to him.* "But . . . how did you know where Lily was? Which room she was in? Which room *we* were in?"

"You told me when I called you. You were in hysterics, remember? All I had to do was get into the hotel, purloin some headed notepaper—very easy to find in such an old-fashioned establishment. It was in a blotter. Not many hotels offer that little touch anymore. Then I slipped the note under your door."

"How did you get into Lily's room?"

"I must say she was a little shocked when she realized I was not Margot," said Nigel. "But she invited me in all the same."

I could only imagine poor Lily's confusion.

"When she introduced herself I couldn't believe my luck,"

Nigel went on. "The fact that I'd found the one person who witnessed the loan was just icing on the cake."

"What did it matter if she witnessed it?" I said. "She probably didn't know that Jago had repaid it."

"I didn't want to risk it," said Nigel.

"She's old!" I exclaimed. "What did you do to her?"

"Let's just say she had a conversation with a cushion."

It was said in such a matter-of-fact way I was appalled. I stared in disbelief at this man that I thought I knew. This man who had come into our home for so many years, a man I had trusted implicitly.

"But you must have been interrupted," I said finally.

Nigel gave a slow smile. "Hmm. Not so dense, then. Why do you say that?"

"Lily's eyeglasses were smashed. You didn't put the cushion back, and of course, the dead giveaway—"

"Good turn of phrase—"

"Was that Lily was fully dressed."

Nigel laughed. "You are right. Yes, I was interrupted." He offered me his hand. "Up you come. You're going to get cold lying on the ground like that."

"I can get up myself." I threw off his hand and scrambled to my feet, stealing a glance toward the hotel. Where was everyone? I spied my camera lying in the grass. I'd leave it there. Then they'd know—someone would know I had come this way.

"How did you lure Jago out here?" I said. "I want to know."

"It was easy to *lure*—as you said—Jago to William's Bench."

"But . . . how?"

"The same way I invited you. In fact, the note *was* from you!"

"A note?" I didn't think another note had been found.

"Fortunately Jago kept it in his pocket. I tore it up when he made that rough landing on the beach," said Nigel as if reading my thoughts. "Clever. Yes?"

"It would have been, but you see . . . I didn't see that note from *you* until much later."

"I don't understand." Nigel frowned with confusion. "Then . . . what were you doing on the coast path?"

"I was already there when you slipped the note under the door," I said. "I was with Dennis. We found Jago together. The police were the ones who found your note." A tic began to pulse under Nigel's eye and I noticed a tension in his shoulders that had not been there before.

All too soon I realized what I had said. "But it's okay because no one would ever connect it to you," I said hastily. "No one knows that you are here. Even Joanna said she didn't know that Robert had loaned Jago any money let alone that he had repaid it."

Nigel stiffened and grabbed my shoulders tightly. "You spoke to *Joanna*?"

"Yes."

"When? When was this?" Nigel said sharply.

"Just after lunch today."

"What else did she say?" Nigel tightened his grip.

"Let go of me!"

"Tell me what she said!" he hissed.

"That she knew nothing about any money being repaid,"

I said again. "She never went to Penzance. That's when I worked out that it had to be Cherie—"

"No—not that," Nigel said impatiently. "What *else* did she say?"

"Nothing . . . why?" There was something in his eyes that I hadn't seen before. Fear.

"What about the doctor?" he demanded.

I was confused. "What doctor?"

"The family friend. Dr. Barnaby. Did Joanna mention him?" He shook me. Hard. "Did she? Did she mention the *doctor*?"

"Only that he was . . . was . . . surprised—," I stammered. "Because Robert had had a checkup just days before. That's why he wanted to have an autopsy. Why?"

"Christ!" Nigel exclaimed, and spun away. *"Damn!"*

And then with a sickening realization, I just knew. I couldn't believe it. I dared not believe it.

"What?" I whispered. "What did you do?"

Nigel didn't answer.

I felt numb. "You had something to do with Robert's death, didn't you," I said slowly. "He had a heart attack and you . . . you didn't help him. You just watched him die."

Nigel turned back and smiled again. He stepped toward me. "Yes, it was something like that."

"Why? Why would you do that? He was your friend. I was your friend. I've always liked you, Nigel."

For a moment Nigel faltered. "I don't want to hurt you, Evie. And I'm truly sorry. Really I am. If you'd only done what I asked and let me handle that letter none of this would have happened." Nigel stepped even closer. I began to back away.

"Why did you come here?" he demanded.

"For a weekend with my sister," I said.

"Truth, Evie."

"I am telling the truth," I said. "Yes, I admit I was curious. Who wouldn't have been? You had told me that I was going to lose my house; that Robert left me with hardly anything. But you are wrong if you thought I married him for his money. I loved him deeply."

He regarded me with curiosity. "You know, I actually believe you."

"The money would have been Joanna's anyway," I said.

Nigel looked at me with pity. "Seriously? You think this is only about one hundred thousand pounds?"

My mouth went dry. "Isn't it?"

"You really are dumb."

And then I saw with blinding clarity that Nigel must have been stealing from Robert for years. It explained Robert's slow, painful decline into bankruptcy. Nigel had been lying all the time about the health of Robert's finances.

Suddenly, I backed into hard rock. We had reached the boulders.

All the time we'd been talking, Nigel had been edging me farther and farther away from William's Bench along the coast path.

"It started in such a small way," said Nigel, who almost looked sad. "Borrowing a little bit here and there, but I always paid it back. *I always paid it back!*"

"Until one day you didn't," I said.

Nigel smirked. "I like you, Evie, and for the record, Robert loved you."

"I never doubted that he loved me, Nigel." And yet there was still something I just had to know. "That last day," I went on. "Was he upset about me leaving? You told me he was distraught, but he seemed indifferent to me."

"He was devastated," said Nigel. "You were the center of his world. He told me about the vasectomy. He told me you would leave him; that you were going to divorce him."

"I'm not Joanna," I said angrily. "I was in shock. I wanted to think."

"Robert was convinced," said Nigel. "I couldn't allow that to happen."

"So that's what all this is about." I was stunned. "A divorce from Robert would force the disclosure of his assets! You would have been found out. Everything would have been exposed."

And then it dawned on me with sickening clarity that Robert's heart attack had been no accident.

"What did you do to him?" I whispered.

For a moment I thought I saw a flicker of remorse in Nigel's eyes, but then it was gone. "Did you know that the symptoms of an allergic reaction are very similar to a heart attack?" he said.

I went very still. "Robert's nut allergy. You wouldn't . . . you didn't . . ." I shook my head, unwilling to believe such wickedness. It wouldn't have been quick. Robert would have died in agony. No wonder Nigel had panicked when he realized there was going to be an autopsy.

"I'd always known about Robert's allergy to peanuts," Nigel went on. "Just a smear of peanut oil on the rim of a water glass . . . that's all it took."

"I don't keep peanut oil in the house," I said as the full horror of Nigel's crime hit me. "Oh God. You . . . you must have brought it with you! You planned to murder your friend in cold blood."

"I'm a survivor," Nigel said simply. "So now you know. And now we're going out for a little sail."

"I'm not going anywhere with you!" I shouted. "Leave me alone."

Suddenly Nigel grabbed my arm and twisted it viciously behind me. "I can break this, you know."

And in that moment I knew he was going to kill me.

"You've got two choices," he said in my ear. "You can either go down the steps to the beach or"—he spun me round to face the cliff edge—"I can help you on your way."

"I'll come with you," I whispered.

The rock-hewn steps were slippery from the rain and uneven. It was all I could do to keep my balance. I kept trying to think of an escape. Could I outrun him on the beach? But my legs felt so weak I knew I wouldn't get very far.

Ten minutes later I realized there was no beach. The tide was in. Nigel had tied up the Topper to one of the rings drilled into the cliff face. I saw the name *Sandra* on the side of the hull and felt the first stirring of white-hot fear. This was it.

At the far end of the beach, I saw the half-submerged mouth of a cave. Nigel had mentioned he'd been hiding out in a cave. Wouldn't there have been some kind of ledge inside above the water level? I would beg him to leave me in there, yes—I would rather take my chances with the tide than go out on open water with a cold, calculating killer.

"Leave me in the cave," I begged. "By the time the tide turns you will be far away."

Nigel regarded me with amusement. "Really? You want me to?"

I nodded. "You'll be able to get away. Start a new life somewhere. Anywhere."

He hesitated for a moment. "Alright," he said. "But first, help me get going and then I'll take you there."

I couldn't believe what I was hearing. "Thank you, thank you!"

Nigel gallantly helped me step into the boat, which immediately tilted sideways under my weight. It had a shallow hull and felt so unstable that I leaned over to grab the side, fighting down raw terror.

The boat was so small. Waves were tossing the little vessel up and down as Nigel cast off. I clung to the side as the first bout of nausea hit me and I just had to lie down flat on the deck.

Nigel untied her and pushed off with his oar. When he snapped the oar back into one of the oarlocks, I noticed that the paddle was stained a deep brown red. Blood. He'd used it on Jago. I knew it.

Nigel deftly put up the mast and sails as I lay immobile and miserable. There was a bang as the wind filled the jib and we took off at speed, riding the swell away from Tregarrick Rock and, to my dismay, heading out to open water.

He'd never intended to take me to the cave at all. How easy I had made it for him to get me in the boat. He was surely going to throw me overboard. I knew it. I had to act fast while I could still see land.

Nigel was at the helm, tacking expertly back and forth as the Topper sped across the water. I just lay on the deck with my eyes shut, hands gripping the metal struts under the benches on either side.

And then suddenly the swell seemed to die down.

"Sorry if it was uncomfortable," said Nigel. "I just had to get out of that tricky bit."

I opened my eyes and saw my advantage.

Nigel was sitting at the helm with the rudder in one hand and his legs straddled over mine to keep his balance. Tucked under the bench was a life jacket.

I kicked one leg up with all the energy I could muster and caught him fair and square.

"Now who has balls?" I shouted as he cried out in pain and let go of the rudder.

The last thing I remember was the Topper whipping around, the boom spinning and striking Nigel on the head, and then . . . the numbing cold as I hit the water.

Chapter Thirty-two

When I surfaced all I could see was the upturned hull some twenty yards away. I heard this strange panting noise and realized it was coming from me. *Let go! Go with the current. Let go! Go with the current,* screamed the lifeguard as he frantically tried to paddle alongside me on his body board.

I was nine again on a beach in North Cornwall, caught in a riptide and being swept out to sea. Fighting for breath. Going under the surface. Silently screaming. Thrashing about. Drowning. And then I let go and allowed the sea to take me. Strong arms pulled me out and I knew I was safe.

But this time there would be no strong hands to save me. This time I was not on a crowded beach where lifeguards watched the waves through their binoculars.

This time I was going to join the eighty-plus galleons and those men who perished with them as the current took me to Windward Point and the lighthouse loomed closer and closer. Waves crashed at its base, sending spumes of water into the sky.

Let go! Go with the current. Let go! Go with the current!

So I did. And life felt peaceful once more. I didn't even register the speed at which the undertow was carrying me toward the lighthouse until a sudden gut-wrenching pain brought me to a violent halt.

I was wedged in between the ribs of what seemed to be the carcass of an old ship protruding out of the swirling water. It had to be the wreck of the *Athena* that Cador had told me about on Friday.

The brutal impact of the collision snapped me to my senses. I clung to a wooden rib for dear life as I tried to decide what to do. In the distance I could hear the haunting melody of the whistle buoy.

Terrified, I scanned the water for Nigel, but I couldn't see him anywhere.

As I clung there, watching the waves, I noticed a pattern. I'd made a mistake at the beach. The tide was coming in, not going out.

After five huge rollers there would come a lull. I watched the sequence half a dozen times just to make sure. It was an insane idea, but if I jumped at the right moment, I might be carried to the rocks below the lighthouse.

So I counted . . . and then I let go.

This time I was prepared and struck out for the lighthouse in my clumsy crawl, weighed down by my coat, but I caught the wave and felt myself being lifted up.

And then, with astonishing speed, the wave crested and spat me out. I hit the rock wall so hard I couldn't catch my breath, but I made a desperate grab for the jagged rocks and held on for dear life as the retreating wave tried to take me back with her.

Somehow I managed to drag myself up the rock face; bruised and with my nails bloodied from crawling, I tumbled over the lip and into a narrow gully. Exhausted.

I was alive, but now I thought of Nigel. Was he at this very moment able to right the Topper and sail to freedom?

As I lay catching my breath, it suddenly occurred to me that no one knew Nigel had been on the island. No one! Just me. He was going to get away with everything. Even if Margot suspected, there was no proof whatsoever that he had been here, let alone killed Jago and Lily.

I *had* to survive and stop him. For Robert's sake.

Slowly I managed to crawl up to the concrete apron and onto the steps in front of the rusty lighthouse door.

Dennis hadn't been joking when he'd said the wooden footbridge connecting the island to the lighthouse had been washed away. At one time there had been railings, but now there were just two or three posts visible only as the waves ebbed and flowed. There was no way I could get across until the tide turned, and even then, it would be incredibly dangerous.

Ironically, I could see the lights from the hotel twinkling in the distance on top of the bluff—so near and yet so far.

The water level was rising more quickly than I expected. Somehow I had to get into the lighthouse. I couldn't stop shivering. I had to get out of my wet clothes. But then I remembered the lighthouse was locked. Jago had demanded the keys.

Looking at the tidemark on the building, I realized that the water level often came well above the actual door.

I was going to drown. I had to get inside the lighthouse.

I turned to the door, dismayed to find it was an old-fashioned lock-and-key arrangement. I could hardly pick the lock. With rising panic I grabbed the handle and rattled it, when, to my astonishment, it opened. I darted inside and closed it behind me. I couldn't stop shaking.

Inside the entrance chamber, I was immediately struck by the gloom and creepy atmosphere. Other than the muffled sound of the waves pounding against the turquoise-tiled walls, it was eerily quiet and smelled of the sea, mildew and neglect. It was completely empty save for a thin shaft of light that filtered through a small window and caught the treads of a wrought-iron spiral staircase.

As I started to climb, my knees began to give way. My fingers were so numb with cold that I found it hard to hold on to the handrail. Staring up, I found the corkscrew view distinctly unnerving and yet beautiful. It seemed to curve all the way up to heaven.

Alex would have liked it.

I stepped out into the living area, where another small window showed a kitchen with fitted circular cupboards, a primer stove, a fridge and a small sink.

And then I saw it and my stomach turned right over.

On the primer stove stood a kettle. On the counter, a mug, a jar of instant coffee and an open carton of long-life milk.

Nigel had been lying about the cave. He must have been hiding out here all the time.

I viewed the upper floor with trepidation. The chances of him being here were next to none, weren't they? The boat had capsized. The swinging boom must have knocked him unconscious; most likely he had drowned. Or—an option that I dreaded to consider—he could have swum onto any one of the dozens of little islets and rocks that were scattered around Tregarrick.

And yet my skin prickled and I had the distinct feeling that I was not alone.

A screwdriver lay on the countertop. Why it was there I couldn't say, but it would do as a weapon. I grabbed it for courage and began to slowly go up the next set of stairs, conscious that my feet echoed on the iron treads with every step.

The next level revealed two bunks tucked into the circular walls of the lighthouse, piled high with blankets and moldy, damp pillows. Everywhere was coated with dust, and the smell was of decay.

But what stopped me in my tracks was a large full-length mirror and half a dozen or more giant faded satin cushions with gold tassels that were scattered on the floor along with moth-eaten beanbags. Candlestick holders had been fixed to the mirrors, where fresh candles still stood waiting to be lit, and empty champagne bottles were lined up around the perimeter on the floor. Stuck to the wall were a series of Polaroid photographs—two teenagers hopelessly in love. Laughing, goofing around for the camera. Tegan and Alex.

No wonder Alex wanted to come back and see the lighthouse again before he died. I wondered if Tegan had brought her other lovers here.

I grabbed a blanket and wrapped it around my shoulders and sank to the floor, clutching my knees to my chest in an effort to get warm. My iPhone was miraculously still in my pocket, but I knew that it would have been destroyed by the salt water.

I felt so cold, so tired. But I also knew that I couldn't allow myself to fall asleep.

It was then that I spotted a webbed handle peeping out from between the cushions.

It was a black canvas rucksack and looked vaguely familiar.

When I upended it onto the floor, I found a black tracksuit.

There was also a Swiss Army penknife, a bar of chocolate and a survival kit from a camping store.

I grabbed the clothing, knowing it would be far too big, but when I unrolled it, I realized it was meant for a woman! Not only that, wrapped in the leggings were the pages torn from Lily's scrapbook.

The rucksack was Vanessa's! She must be here. I glanced quickly at the newspaper clippings that had been taped to the pages.

With mounting astonishment I read:

Fake Pregnancy Stalker
Vanessa Parsons Wouldn't Take No for an Answer

A photograph of Vanessa's tattoo, *Dave and I Until We Die*, along with one showing her wearing a fake silicone belly "available on Amazon," accompanied the most bizarre report.

I read that Vanessa—a chef with a promising future—was so determined to win back her ex-boyfriend that she had claimed he had got her pregnant. The report went on to say that Vanessa's stalking efforts ranged from ordering unwanted pizzas and taxi services to hacking into her ex's computer, where she was able to cancel all his credit cards, including a nonrefundable holiday to the Seychelles with his new flame. It was when Vanessa turned to poisoning her rival with Visine eyedrops that she was caught, sentenced and served two and a half years in prison, charged with— And then I heard a sound from above.

"Vanessa!" I shouted out. "I know you're up there!"

As to be expected—there was no reply.

"It's Evie."

Still silence.

"Okay," I said, tossing off the blanket. "In that case I'm coming up!"

Chapter Thirty-three

When I got to eye level with the next floor up, I hesitated.

"I know you're there, Vanessa," I said again. "Please. I need your help."

I took one more step, and suddenly she was there, looming over me, holding an iron bar.

"Get away from me!" she screamed. "Get away!"

Startled, I stepped back and only just managed to grab the handrail to stop myself from falling.

"Whoa!" I said, and threw the screwdriver down. "Steady on. I'm not here to hurt you."

"I'll use this! I swear I will." Vanessa was wide-eyed with terror. "You killed Lily and made sure I'd get the blame—"

"What are you talking about?" I exclaimed.

"And Mr. Jago! You pushed him off the cliff, I know you did! Uncle Dennis said so!"

"I did not," I said. "A man . . . a man called Nigel did that. He almost killed me too."

"Never heard of him! Liar!" Vanessa screamed again. "I don't believe you."

I was fast losing my patience. "Vanessa, look at me! Don't be so bloody stupid! I am soaked through. Do you think I just waded across to the lighthouse for my own amusement? I nearly drowned."

Vanessa just stared. I must have looked a sight with my wet hair, soaking wet clothes and bloodied hands, shivering violently. I couldn't stop my teeth from chattering.

"I'm going down to the bunk room and I am going to change into some dry clothes," I said. "*Your* clothes."

"Don't touch my stuff!" she shrieked. "Don't you dare!"

I climbed down slowly backwards, not taking my eyes off her once. Stepping out of view, I peeled off my coat, jeans and sweater as quickly as I could and pulled on Vanessa's tracksuit. It was a little small.

I was perplexed. This was not what I was expecting, but I didn't care. I had to know what had happened to Nigel. I was convinced that if Vanessa had got on, then we could both get off. All we had to do was wait for the tide to turn.

I went to the bottom of the steps again.

"Why did you come to the lighthouse?" I asked. "Why did you run away?"

"I knew what it would look like," said Vanessa. "I knew I'd get the blame. Uncle Dennis told me to sit tight until things died down."

"Your uncle knows you are here?" I felt a burst of hope. "At the lighthouse?"

"Oh no," said Vanessa. "This was my idea. Lily told me

all about it once. Give her a few glasses of gin and she loved to talk. She told me that Mrs. Tegan was a tramp and that she used to bring all her lovers here because Lily watched her through the telescope—at least until Mr. Jago destroyed the footbridge with an axe."

So the footbridge had not been washed away in a storm after all.

"I found the keys in Mr. Jago's desk last night and took that photographer's waders so I could get across."

"Have you been here before?"

"Yes. Many times," said Vanessa. "I like to come here and think. Mrs. Tegan was so pretty when she was younger. You should see her photographs."

"Vanessa," I said, "I saw the pages from Lily's scrapbook about you and . . . your boyfriend, Dave." I struggled to find the right phrase and said very carefully, "The one who betrayed you?"

Vanessa hesitated. "He told me he loved me. He was going to take me to Paris for the weekend. He promised."

She was so young. I didn't have the heart to tell her it had probably been a ruse to get her to do what he wanted her to do. Instead I said, "I know what that feels like. My husband betrayed me too."

Vanessa appeared at the top of the steps.

I caught a glimmer of curiosity. "How?"

So I told her. I told her everything—right down to how Margot and I ended up coming to Tregarrick. I told her about being widowed; about Nigel's embezzlement and how he pushed Jago off the cliff top and killed Lily because she had seen him on the balcony on his way to deliver that note to me.

"I'm glad Lily's dead," Vanessa said suddenly. "She knew all the dirt on everyone. Why else do you think she lived in the best suite in the hotel for free?"

"I have no idea."

"Mr. Jago never liked me," she went on. "But the last laugh is on him! He's dead and Cador and I can be together, and you know what . . . he wasn't even Cador's real father! I saw Lily's black book once when I was cleaning her room. She forgot to lock it away."

"Ah yes," I said. "I heard about that black book."

"That's why she got the cameras installed," Vanessa declared.

"The *cameras*?" I said sharply.

"She had one of those spy apps on her phone." Vanessa nodded. "Little tiny cameras hidden around the room so she could spy on me. She wanted to make sure I wouldn't go through her stuff."

"The kitty-cam!" I exclaimed. "No, Vanessa. She was watching Mister Tig."

Vanessa looked incredulous. "Whatever for?"

"For his Instagram account, I assume." The idea seemed ridiculous, but Lily had been obsessed with that cat and she had shown me many funny clips that must have been recorded on her phone app.

I wondered who else knew about the hidden cameras. Vicar Bill—the so-called animal communicator? I distinctly remembered him asking for Lily's phone the night she died. He had put on a very convincing performance in the Residents' Lounge. In fact, he'd freaked me out and all the time it had been a party trick. Had Patty known about it, too? We'd all been fooled.

"That's why Lily got the Agatha Christie suite," Vanessa continued. "I used to hear Mrs. Tegan and Mr. Jago arguing about Lily all the time. They both hated her and yet I could never figure out why she still lived there rent free."

It all made sense now. Lily had held both of them to ransom—the loan he didn't want Tegan to know about in case she left him and the truth about Cador's parentage.

"Well, she's dead now," I said. "So you don't have to worry about her anymore."

Vanessa came down the steps and we both sat on the cushions. I was relieved to see her put down the iron bar.

"So you were never interested in Cador?" she said.

"Er . . . no," I said, reminding myself that I was dealing with a woman who was more than a little unbalanced. "I'm still coming to terms with what Robert did. Believe me, a relationship is the last thing on my mind."

"I would have dumped a whole bottle of Visine into his breakfast cereal," Vanessa said cheerfully. "I put some in your pie, you know."

"I gathered that." So that was what Owen had found in Vanessa's bedroom—Visine eyedrops. I remembered that it had been mentioned in the newspaper, too. "Only Margot ate it and not me."

"I wanted Dave to die." Vanessa thought for a moment and glanced down at her tattoos. "Will you tell Cador that I didn't do anything wrong?"

"I'm sure Cador already knows," I said, but of course I wasn't.

"He *does*?" Vanessa beamed with happiness, but then her face fell. "But what about Lily and all the horrible things she must have told him?"

I regarded her with concern. "What do you mean?"

"Why else do you think he didn't want to go out with me anymore?" Vanessa seemed amazed that I didn't know. "Lily told him about my tattoo. I don't think he liked me having a tattoo. I'm having it removed when I can save up enough money. She was such a spiteful old bitch."

"I can see that might have been a bit off-putting," I said carefully.

She frowned. "But the police will still think I did it, won't they?"

"They already know about your past," I said.

"Good." Vanessa visibly brightened. "Shall we eat the chocolate?" She jumped up to find the bar. "We can get back to the island when the tide is low. It's a bit difficult, but I can show you which posts are steady and how to walk along the frame of the footbridge. It will still hold even though the planks were chopped to bits."

"That's quite a few hours away." I glanced out of the window. The light was fading, but we still had a long time to low tide. "What's in the lantern room?" I asked.

"Nothing," she said. "It's just a room, really. All abandoned. Nothing up there except windows."

"No flares? A battery-operated torch?"

Vanessa shook her head. "There are some ropes."

I looked at the empty wine bottles—some with candle nubs, others empty. "Do you think there are any candles in the kitchen area?"

"Oh yes." Vanessa nodded. "I saw a box. I'll get them." Moments later she was back with a full box of wax candles. "And matches too!"

"Right," I said. "Let's take all the bottles and candles up to the lantern room, set them around the perimeter and light them. It'll be dark soon."

"Our own little lighthouse!" Vanessa said happily.

Above the sleeping quarters, we stepped into the area where I'd first seen Vanessa. Outside was an open deck. I didn't know the first thing about lighthouses, but I assumed that whatever was needed to keep the beacon going in the lantern room overhead would have been kept here.

We climbed the final narrow staircase into the lantern room. The windows were crusted with salt water. In the center stood the lens lantern, cracked and broken. There was something so sad about this room that used to be full of light, but once we'd arranged the empty wine bottles, stuck the candles in, and lit the flame, the glow shone warm and bright. I knew we'd soon be rescued.

I'd told Dennis exactly where I thought I'd seen Vanessa; I'd left my camera by William's Bench—from there, anyone would be able to see the light.

There was a bang, and a *whoosh* of cold air whistled up the vortex from below. Vanessa cocked her head. "It's Cador! He's come to rescue us!"

"Ssh," I said urgently. "It's too soon. Wait."

"But it's Cad—What? You mean—it could be *him*?"

I knew that not enough hours would have passed for the tide to have dropped enough yet. My heart started thumping in my chest.

Nigel must have survived. He'd made it. Deep down I always feared he would, and here I thought I was being so clever lighting all the candles. I may as well have written a sign saying, "Evie is here!"

When I whispered my suspicion, Vanessa's eyes widened in fear. But although Nigel assumed I was here, he did not expect Vanessa, too.

I had a plan.

Quietly we both crept down to the sleeping area. The staircase there was wider and Vanessa would be able to hide under the inverted treads. She retrieved the iron bar that she'd left on the cushions and crawled into the space to await my signal. I pushed several cushions in front to hide her.

For a moment I thought that he was injured. Maybe he made it to the lighthouse, but then came the slow footfall of heavy steps up the staircase, with no attempt at disguising the noise.

Silence again. Nigel must have stopped in the kitchen quarters.

The silence was excruciating. I looked over at Vanessa, who was crouched under the staircase—I could just see the whites of her eyes looking out. I gave her a thumbs-up, hoping that I seemed more confident than I felt. Every one of my senses was on high alert.

My ears strained to hear any movement, but there was nothing. Nothing at all, until: "Evie, I know you are up there."

Chapter Thirty-four

I looked over at Vanessa and gave her the nod.

"You are a silly girl," said Nigel. "I was never going to hurt you. The sea was too rough to drop you at the mouth of the cave. I was going to take you to the deepwater quay around the point."

I didn't answer.

"Come on. It's just the two of us, Evie," he said. "We can talk things over."

"Okay," I said. "Come on up, then."

Peering down between the treads, I saw Nigel remove an orange life jacket. He was wearing a dry-suit and must have shed the waterproof hooded cape when he fell overboard. He had to have surfaced under the Topper, where there would have been an air pocket.

Nigel's dip in the ocean had been just an inconvenience, nothing more.

"You're not going to do anything stupid, are you?" Nigel teased. "I won't come up until I see you."

I gave Vanessa the first signal and stepped onto the top of the staircase—and gave a cry of alarm.

Nigel was holding a small handgun and he was pointing it right at me. "Why don't you come down here?"

The gun was definitely not part of the plan.

"No, here is better," I said. "We can sit down. I don't feel very well."

"I'm not surprised. You must have swallowed gallons of seawater," said Nigel. "You really need to work on your crawl technique."

But to my relief, Nigel advanced.

My heart was hammering in my chest again. It was beating so hard that I felt sure he could hear it.

I was doing my part. Vanessa just had to do hers.

Slowly Nigel drew eye level with me. I was gratified to see a nasty cut on his brow. Nigel noticed me looking at it. "Just a graze . . ." But then his expression changed to suspicion. "Nice togs. Although a little tight and short in the leg for you."

How stupid of me not to realize that Nigel would notice. I prayed he didn't see the alarm on my face.

"I found them here," I said quickly. "This used to be Tegan's love nest. She left clothes. . . ."

Nigel's eyes narrowed as he studied the logo on the sweatshirt. I hadn't thought to look at it. I didn't even know what it said.

I remembered Vanessa's rucksack. Would Nigel see that, too? But I dared not move. Not now.

And then Nigel was there. I stepped aside and edged away from the staircase, hoping that he would follow me. It was the only way for Vanessa and me to be able to have the upper hand and keep the element of surprise.

Nigel moved toward me, scanning the room. "Pretty cozy up here. Ah, I see what you mean about Tegan's love nest. It's a bit *Arabian Nights* with all those cushions."

"Yes," I agreed, and looked over at Vanessa. The cushions had not shifted.

"Okay. Well, let's keep on going."

"What?" I said.

"Up. Keep going up." He waved the gun in my face. "Ladies first." He pushed me back to the staircase.

Vanessa did not move! I couldn't believe it. She was supposed to knock him out so we could tie him to the central column and wait for help to come. Why the hell hadn't she done that! But I had no choice. I had to follow Nigel's orders.

I did as I was told and stepped up into the empty room.

"Keep going," said Nigel. "We need to blow a few candles out, don't we?"

"Yes, yes, of course," I whispered. *It doesn't matter. Help is coming.*

We stepped into the lantern room. "Nice touch with the wine bottles and the candles—very clever. Funnily enough, if you hadn't lit them I wouldn't have known you'd made it."

"Well, I did," I said.

"But you thought I didn't," said Nigel. "Not so clever after all."

"You're stranded here just as much as I am," I pointed out.

"Blow them out," he said. "All of them."

So I did.

"What happened to your boat?" I said.

"She was easy to right," he said. "*Sandra* is tied up to the whistle buoy. It's not too difficult a swim for someone like me."

That meant he had an escape plan.

I felt sick.

Nigel wasn't going to let me go anywhere at all. He kept stepping closer—crowding me until my back was against the window that I now realized was in fact a glass door to another platform outside.

"And there is the widow's walk," he said. "Quite apt, don't you think?"

"I don't understand."

"Named after the wives of sailors who used to watch for their husbands' ships from the tops of their houses." Nigel cocked his head. "Really? You don't understand. It's a widow's walk and you're a widow."

And then I did.

"Open the door," Nigel said harshly.

"Please—"

"Then I will." He smashed the glass and kicked the wooden frame outward. A gust of wind came swirling inside, knocking several bottles over with a crash.

I glanced outside. The railing was so low—no more than a foot—and the platform so narrow. "Nigel—"

"How tall is this lighthouse?" Nigel mused. "A hundred feet, perhaps? Don't worry. It will be quick."

And then Vanessa loomed over Nigel's shoulder, holding the iron bar aloft. She'd climbed the treads so quietly I hadn't heard her approach.

Her face was set in grim determination and her eyes were

black as coal. A quick nod and gesture and I knew what she had planned.

Nigel regarded me with curiosity. "What, Evie? What's going on in that little brain of—"

Vanessa screamed, "Duck!" I fell to the floor just as Nigel spun round and the iron bar made contact under his jawbone. There was a sickening crunch of metal on bone, followed by Vanessa shoving him backwards with all her might—out of the doorway and over the railing to plunge onto the rocks below.

Horrified, I raced to the edge just in time to see Nigel's broken body being washed out to sea. I was appalled.

"I thought my plan was better," Vanessa said mildly. "Shall we light the candles again?"

Chapter Thirty-five

Two hours later, Vanessa and I were wrapped up in blankets sipping hot toddies in the Residents' Lounge.

Patty finished a phone call and came over with a smile. "Cherie's being arrested as we speak," she said. "Apparently she can't stop talking. Nigel had an offshore account in the Cayman Islands."

"That's amazing," I exclaimed.

"And let's not forget Sandra. She's ecstatic that her husband is getting his boat back."

Margot, who had not let go of my hand once, said, "So much has happened since you were lolling about in that lighthouse."

"Hardly lolling," I said, taking a deep draught of hot toddy.

"Patty found the black book that confirmed Alex was Cador's biological father—"

"And the love letters between Tegan and Alex," said Patty. "Thanks to Mister Tig, who told us exactly where to look."

"In the powder room—the red leather box?" I suggested. "Yes. I need to talk to you about Mister Tig's powers of observation."

Patty looked me straight in the eye. "I'm sure I don't know what you mean."

"Who cares about the cat!" Margot's eyes were out on stalks. "Cador already *knew*!"

I looked to Patty and she nodded. "It turns out that Jago told Cador when he was seven years old that he wasn't his biological father but that he would always love him like his own. It takes a man to admit that."

"Jago made Cador promise not to say anything," said Margot. "He told us that Jago didn't want anyone else to know either. Lily held that over his head. She really was a nasty piece of work."

"Even Tegan?" I said.

"Especially Tegan," Margot went on. "Jago believed that Tegan was only staying with him for Cador's sake."

"That's so sad," I said. "No wonder Jago freaked out when Alex turned up. He knew exactly who he was straightaway. His fear of losing Tegan was very real. And Alex? What did Cador think of Alex—and Alex of Cador?"

"You know . . . it was like a real Hollywood movie," said Patty with an exaggerated sigh. "Quite lovely. The only thing missing was the music."

Dennis came over. "Is it alright if Vanessa goes to her room now?"

"No problem," said Patty. "Just keep an eye on her."

"What's going to happen to Vanessa?" At first I hadn't

wanted to say that Vanessa had pushed Nigel over the railing, but given her mental condition, I had had second thoughts.

"She won't be charged with murder, but I fear she'll face charges of manslaughter—"

"But she was protecting us. It was in self-defense!" I protested. "Nigel had a gun!"

"That's for the judge to decide. As you know, her track record is a little dodgy and she's already given her phone number to Kip here and asked him if he has a girlfriend—which does not bode well for Kip because he does." Patty shook her head. "No, Vanessa needs help and Dennis understands that. She'll be on her way to a psychiatric facility first thing in the morning."

I had to admit I was relieved.

"As for the pair of you: I knew that both of you were talking a load of bullshit—pardon my French—when you arrived. Although I will say that given Margot's Hollywood connections I was almost convinced with the *Pirates of the Caribbean* ploy."

"So we're not in any trouble?" I ventured.

Patty grinned. "Not yet. Now if you'll excuse me, I have a date tonight."

Chapter Thirty-six

The letter from Tregarrick Rock arrived on a Friday morning when Margot and I were finishing packing up the last of the moving boxes at Forster's. The bank had repossessed the house. Everything was going into storage until Robert's estate was settled, which could be months, if not years. In the meantime, Margot and I were moving into a dreary furnished flat in Tonbridge that was all we could afford.

"Open it!" Margot exclaimed.

It was written on the familiar hotel stationery with the logo of Windward Point Lighthouse, and I read the contents with increasing surprise.

"What?" Margot demanded. "You've had your mouth open for the last two minutes—not an attractive look, by the way."

"It's from Tegan," I said. "Apparently Alex is a good candidate for a revolutionary new drug at a private oncology clinic in Germany."

"Gosh," said Margot. "That's good news for them."

"She asked if we would be interested in leasing Tregarrick Rock from the Ferris family trust—look."

I handed her the letter and her jaw dropped, too.

"You're never going back to California," I said. "We're both homeless and broke. It'll take a long time for whatever money I am owed from Nigel's shenanigans—"

"But a lease is temporary," said Margot. "I mean . . . how long?"

"That's up to us," I said. "Anyway, isn't everything in life temporary?"

"Don't you remember the weather out there?" Margot grumbled. "It was awful."

"It was November and apparently not normally like that. Now it's spring," I said. "The daffodils will be out."

"I've always loved daffodils," Margot said wistfully. "Okay. Yes, let's! Call her!"

After promising to keep Dennis on and ironing out a few details—including taking care of Mister Tig—I put the phone down in a daze. "This is madness."

"And Cador really doesn't want it?" Margot broke into my thoughts.

"Apparently not," I said. "He's focusing on his marine salvage company."

"So he's staying on Tregarrick?"

"Yes, why?" I noticed a gleam in Margot's eye. "You're *interested* in him, aren't you."

"Maybe." She shrugged. "I'm not completely dead from the waist down, you know, even if you are."

I pulled a face. "You have such a way with words."

"I might write a screenplay there," she said. "Two girls stranded on an island in the dead of winter with a serial killer on the loose. I've still got my Hollywood connections."

"Not *Scilly Pirates* then, but *Scilly Sisters*," I said dryly. "There is a snag, though. We're responsible for everything—maintenance, upkeep, repairs—"

"Good!" Margot nodded excitedly. "We can start by getting rid of all that awful 1970s stuff—sell it on eBay or something. I know we can get the hotel up to scratch. We'll have a luxury spa, put in a helipad . . ."

"We won't be able to afford a helipad."

"I know what I'm talking about, if we want to attract Johnny—"

"Please! No Johnny Depp!"

One week later, Margot and I were back on Tregarrick. It was the most beautiful day, with a cobalt-blue sky and barely a breeze. I'd even enjoyed the short hop by helicopter from Land's End Airport to St. Mary's Airport. I had to admit that I was warming to Margot's helipad idea.

Patty met us at the arrivals lounge.

We waved, but she looked grave and asked us to follow her into a small room. It was painted in gunmetal gray and held just four plastic chairs grouped around a Formica table.

"I hope you're not planning on doing a strip search," Margot joked. "I'm not wearing matching underwear."

"No." I laughed. "We're not smuggling anything in."

But Patty did not smile. "I'm afraid you'll have to get back on that helicopter," she said. "There's been a horrible mistake."

Margot and I looked at each other in dismay.

"But . . . I canceled our rental," I said. "We're homeless."

"Just kidding." Patty broke into a broad grin. "But hear ye this . . . if you misbehave I will find out."

Margot and I exchanged puzzled looks. "How?" we chorused.

"Because . . ." Patty tapped the side of her nose and winked. "The cat will let me know."

Acknowledgments

When my sister's close friend Gill Knight told me that she had lived and worked on Tresco, one of the five inhabited islands on the Isles of Scilly, I knew I had to set a mystery series there.

Located just twenty-eight miles off the southwest Cornish coastline, the 142 islands and islets have always fascinated me. Described as England's "enchanting archipelago," each island has its own beauty, but it was Tresco that caught my imagination.

Measuring just 2.2 miles long by one mile wide, the diversity of the terrain is astonishing. At one end there are sandy beaches, azure waters and the stunning Abbey Gardens, with a mesmerizing array of subtropical plants. At the other, wild, rugged cliff tops covered in heather and old castle ruins. The surrounding seabed is home to dozens of shipwrecks that date back to the fourteenth century. But what I love most is that there are no cars, no hospital, no streetlamps and, best of all, no police presence! I couldn't think of a better location for a mystery series.

At this point I must stress that my island is a place of fiction. Tregarrick is a topographical mash-up of Tresco and Burgh Islands near Bigbury-on-Sea in Devon. I loved the idea of a hotel being close enough to civilization but accessible only by a tidal causeway. That's the wonderful thing about being a writer—we have the freedom to create our own imaginary worlds. So a massive thank-you to Gill for so graciously sharing her experiences and inspiring this one.

As always, there are people without whose help this book would not have been published. I'd like to thank my amazing editor, Hannah O'Grady, for her guiding comments and keen editorial eye; to the interior designer, Michelle McMillian; to Rhys Davies, for making my illegible hand-drawn map into a work of art; and to Mary-Ann Lasher and David Rotstein, for the exquisite book jacket. I am happy that my adored feline friend, Mister Tig, is immortalized on paper.

I'm grateful to my wonderful agents, Dominick Abel and David Grossman, with a special thank-you to Dominick, for his friendship, guidance and candor.

Heartfelt gratitude goes to Claire Carmichael, a terrific teacher and friend, from the UCLA Writers' Extension Program, where I first began my journey to publication.

Thanks to my long-suffering boss of twenty years, Mark Davis of Davis Elen Advertising, for his enthusiastic support of my writing "hobby."

No acknowledgment would be complete without thanking my kindred sprits in the writing community lifeboat—Rhys Bowen, Kate Carlisle, Elizabeth Duncan, Mark Durel, Carolyn Hart, Jenn McKinlay, Clare Langley-Hawthorne, Andra St. Ivanyi, Daryl Wood Gerber and Julian Unthank, who loves the Isles of Scilly just as much as I do. Thank you to Linda Sterry D.O., for helping me find a medically creative way to commit murder.

And finally, to all my family who have always encouraged me to follow my dreams, with a special thanks to my much-missed dad, for passing on his sense of humor; my daughter, Sarah, who keeps me organized; and to the canine gods for sending me my muses, the Hungarian Vizslas, Draco and Athena.

Read on for an excerpt from

DANGER AT THE COVE —

the next mystery by Hannah Dennison,
coming soon in hardcover from Minotaur Books!

Chapter One

"Do you mind moving those plants into the potting shed before you run my errand, Ollie?" I pointed to the flimsy trays of plastic pots filled with geraniums, begonias and lavender that stood next to the empty cast-iron urns along the flagstone terrace. "There's another storm forecast for early evening and I don't want them to blow away."

I put down my fork and trowel and got to my feet, dismayed at the stiffness in my legs from kneeling. For the past two hours I had been weeding the flower borders in preparation for the upcoming grand reopening of the Tregarrick Rock Hotel.

"Anything for you." Ollie, our newest hire, gave me a gold-capped smile. "I'll get the wheelbarrow."

It was a crisp spring day in March with a light breeze. Birdsong mingled with the muffled sound of waves breaking against the distant rocks below. White clouds drifted across a blue sky, but far away on the horizon, toward the Atlantic Ocean, an ominous band of dark clouds was building.

Over the past few months, the Isles of Scilly had been struck by a number of ferocious storms that were working their way through the alphabet. Tonight we were promised Storm Iona. Though all the islands had taken a battering, nature had given Tregarrick in particular one extraordinary surprise. The violence of the weather, coupled with extreme spring tides, had shifted the seabed, and three days ago the wooden ribs of what remained of a nineteenth-century schooner had surfaced from the deep in Tregarrick Sound.

Shipwrecks were not uncommon around Scilly. In fact there were over eight hundred wrecks scattered all over the ocean floor. Still, it was impossible not to get caught up in the mystery of what had happened to the old schooner and what treasures might emerge from the deep. Unfortunately, Cador Ferris, the one person who would really know, was off the grid in the Bahamas on a marine salvage expedition himself. As heir to the Tregarrick island estate, Cador was our landlord. He'd already left for Nassau when Margot and I moved in three months ago, and despite repeated attempts to get ahold of him to discuss repairs to the hotel, we'd not heard from him for weeks.

In the meantime, thanks to a supermoon, combined with a phenomenon called syzygy and the vernal equinox, we were eagerly awaiting tomorrow's once-every-eighteen-years chance to actually walk on the seabed out to the wreck at low tide.

"You mentioned you were seeing your girlfriend after you've picked up my package from the courier," I said to Ollie.

"Yeah, that's the plan."

"Just be mindful of the time and the tide. Don't leave heading back to the last minute like you usually do. And yes," I added firmly as Ollie gave me an eye roll, "I know you're an excellent skipper and I know that the crossing only takes twenty-five minutes from St. Mary's, but I'm serious. Can't you meet Becky another day when there isn't a storm forecast?"

"Nope," said Ollie. "Her dad has finally agreed to see me. It's time to talk to him man-to-man."

"Well, good luck," I said. He was going to need it.

Ollie's infatuation with young Becky Goldolphin, the only daughter of one of the founding families on Scilly, seemed to be all-consuming.

"Just because I don't wear a suit, old Cyril thinks I'm not good enough for his only daughter," Ollie went on. "Idiot."

I regarded our twentysomething handyman-cum-gardener with amusement. With his dark shoulder-length hair tied back into a ponytail, gold-capped front tooth, body piercings and both arms heavily tattooed with skulls and mermaids, Ollie could easily pass for a pirate.

My sister, Margot, and I had yet to meet Becky, who by all accounts was classy and intelligent and just as obsessed with him—enough to change her mind about going off to study medicine at the Imperial College London so that she could stay close by Ollie.

Margot sided with Becky's father. Even though we'd never met him, we'd heard that Becky was the center of his world. I could understand Becky's fascination with Ollie, though. He had an insatiable curiosity, committing to memory everything about the history of the Isles of Scilly, including where to catch the best sunset or watch for a rare migrating whale. He had a wicked sense of humor and was the epitome of a bad boy with a heart. He was also an excellent seaman.

"You'll have to ask Dennis for the boat key to the *Sand-piper*," I said.

The *Sandpiper* was a twenty-four-foot cabin cruiser. Margot and I had bought her secondhand from Cador and had her re-painted a vibrant turquoise. It was our latest in a rather long line of acquisitions—including new laptops and new appliances—that Margot had insisted were necessary to make running our fifteen-bedroom boutique hotel smooth and efficient.

Although we would continue to use the trademark "sea tractor" to ferry visitors across from Tregarrick at low tide, having the cruiser gave us the freedom to get off the tidal islet whenever we chose.

"On second thought, I'll be fine in my old dinghy," Ollie said suddenly.

"You told me the dinghy had a slow puncture," I said. "I really don't want my new camera equipment sinking to the bot-tom of the ocean and you with it. Take the *Sandpiper*."

"I didn't know you cared." Ollie grinned. "Okay. I will. Do you need anything else while I'm on St. Mary's?"

This was another thing Margot and I had rapidly discovered as we'd adjusted to life in the Isles of Scilly. Apart from a gen-eral store and a post office, the Salty Boatman pub, St. Paul's church and a cute little gift shop on Tregarrick itself, all the shops and social services were on the main island.

"Thanks, but there's no need. We've got a grocery shipment from Tesco tomorrow." Then I thought again. "Actually, there is one more thing. Would you mind checking our PO Box at the post office?"

When Margot and I first moved to Tregarrick Rock, we decided to rent a postbox on St. Mary's. We rarely used it, since it turned out that the inter-island postal service was surprisingly efficient for regular mail, so we often forgot to check it.

"Dennis can give you the key for that, too," I said.

Ollie pulled a face.

I regarded him with dismay. "I thought you and Dennis were getting along better now."

Ollie shrugged. "Sort of. He's just so . . . particular about everything. He lives by his watch."

It was true. As a former marine, our hotel manager, Dennis Simmonds, was obsessed with punctuality and dependable to a fault. He was the complete opposite of Ollie, who preferred to "go with the flow" and had a propensity to tell Dennis to "lighten up."

Ollie picked up the handles of the wheelbarrow and, with me following, set off for the potting shed.

"No point unloading the plants," I said as Ollie maneuvered the wheelbarrow inside the small space. I closed the old wooden door behind us on our way out and looped the padlock through the hasp, but as usual I didn't lock it.

"Don't forget to take your waterproofs," I reminded Ollie. I pointed to a mug with a pirate on the front that he'd set down on the fence post. "And please take your mug back to the annex."

He rolled his eyes again. "Anything else?"

"Make sure your phone is charged in case I have to call you."

"Yes, Mum."

I laughed. "You bring out the maternal instinct in me." It was true, he did. Ollie didn't like to talk about his past—I knew he had grown up in care somewhere in Cornwall—and I never pressed him. He seemed happy to be working for us and I was pleased when he said he felt he was part of our little family.

Behind the potting shed was a narrow path flanked by a laurel hedge that led to an ugly green prefab annex. Accessed down a short flight of steps, it was used to house six seasonal staff. At the moment it was home to Ollie, and temporary accommodation for Sam Quick, one of the two electricians who were currently rewiring part of the hotel.

Ollie picked up his pirate mug and headed for the annex, reappearing five minutes later dressed in waterproofs. He brandished his iPhone. "Call me if you think of anything else." He hesitated, then took a deep breath. "Any chance I can have an advance on my paycheck this week?" He gave a sheepish grin. "Becky's twenty-first birthday is coming up and she's seen a bracelet she really likes."

I wished he hadn't asked. Ollie was lucky we paid him weekly—and in cash—but he'd asked Margot already for an advance this week and she'd said no.

"Ollie, I'm sorry, but not this time," I said.

The problem was that Margot and I were strapped for cash, too. My sister's divorce settlement was still not final and the small life insurance policy from my deceased husband, Robert, had all but gone. I'd even had to sell a Rolex Comex Submariner from the watch collection that he had—by sheer luck—transferred into my name before he died and that thankfully his creditors couldn't touch. Perhaps it was just as well that Robert had died before he knew the full extent of the damage his business manager had done to all his hard-earned savings.

Then, just two weeks ago, an electrical fire had started in the kitchen. Fortunately, Dennis had put it out before it had taken hold. We subsequently discovered that the hotel wiring hadn't been updated for over forty years and that it couldn't support most of our new appliances.

By some miracle, we managed to find a local electrical company, Quick & Sons, who agreed to rewire the one branch circuit that mattered until we could afford to do the rest, but the process had been incredibly disruptive. Right now the kitchen, reception area and Residents' Lounge resembled a building site and, with the open house just over a week away, I was worried we'd never be ready in time.

"Speak of the devil," muttered Ollie just as Dennis, a burly man in his fifties with closely cropped hair and a military bearing, strode toward us. He was wearing his civvy street uniform of formal black jacket and red polka-dot tie.

Dennis had worked at the hotel for years and stayed on when Margot and I took over. He had been fiercely loyal to Cador's father, Jago, and it was only during these past few weeks that he had warmed to us as he realized we weren't planning on making drastic changes to the spirit of the hotel.

"I thought you'd like to know that I just got a call from Cador Ferris," said Dennis. "He received my email about the wreck and is on his way back. If he makes all his connections, his ETA will be between sixteen and seventeen hundred hours on Sunday afternoon."

"That's great news." I was pleased, as the list of things to discuss with Cador was growing longer by the day. Gesturing to Ollie, I added, "Ollie needs the keys for the *Sandpiper* and PO Box. He's running an errand for me."

Dennis's hazel eyes narrowed. "But I gave him the key two days ago."

"Oh right, yeah. You did." Ollie flashed a smile. "I think I left it in the glove box on the boat—"

"Then you'd better go and get it," said Dennis.

"Can't you just give me the spare?" Ollie demanded. "I'm in a bit of a hurry and by the time I've gone down to the causeway and—"

"Just give him the spare, Dennis," I said. "Ollie will give both boat keys back to you when he returns. Right, Ollie?"

"Cross my heart and hope to die," said Ollie with a grin.

Dennis gave a grunt that implied he was not amused. "Margot is looking for you. She's in reception."

"Will you let her know I'm out here?"

Dennis nodded and strode away, with Ollie hurrying to keep up with his long strides.

My thoughts automatically turned to Cador.

Following Jago's death and the decision of his mother, Tegan, to live in Germany with her first love, who was undergoing treatment for cancer, Cador had inherited the island of Tregarrick. Luckily for us, he wasn't interested in running the hotel, which was why Margot and I had been able to lease it for a peppercorn rent with the proviso that we handled the miscellaneous "repairs." Unfortunately, those repairs were proving to be far more expensive than either of us had predicted.

The enormity of what Margot and I had taken on hit me afresh. We had jumped at the opportunity for a new start far away from her old life in Hollywood and mine in Kent. Although we still loved this corner of paradise and were determined to make it work, I knew that Margot had been having second thoughts, and I'd be lying if I said I hadn't had them, too.

We were no strangers to the hospitality trade. Our parents had run a guesthouse in Hove for years before they both died; I had worked at the Red Fox art gallery in Soho until I married Robert, and Margot had moved to Los Angeles with her producer husband, Brian, where she'd run an independent film production company and rubbed shoulders with Hollywood celebrities.

And then, all of a sudden, everything changed. Robert died and Brian divorced Margot and a few months later, here we were running a crumbling Art Deco hotel twenty-eight miles off the southwest Cornish peninsula.

We must have been mad, I thought. But then, as I perched on the edge of a stone planter, I took in the magnificent views and remembered why I had fallen in love with Tregarrick Rock in the first place.

It was no more than an islet, connected to the island of Tregarrick by a tidal causeway that took about fifteen minutes to cross on foot or by sea tractor. For an islet so small, the topography couldn't be more diverse.

On one side, broad terraces of subtropical plants, lofty California pines and holm oaks crept up the hillside to meet William's Wood, a dense forest of evergreens that provided a shelterbelt to the eastern elements. There was also a Bronze Age burial chamber set into the hillside.

William's Wood overlooked Tregarrick Sound toward the neighboring island of Bryher. Below was Seal Cove, aptly named for the seals that loved to bask on the rocky outcrops. On the same side was the Mermaid Lagoon, a saltwater swimming pool cradled in a natural rock formation and accessed down a steep flight of stone steps from the rear of the hotel.

Moving to the center of the island was a dell, or grassy basin. Enclosed by lush plants, it was laid to lawn and dotted with a handful of topiaries in exotic shapes. A box hedge archway opened onto one of my favorite places—the Galleon Garden of ships' figureheads. Many of them had been salvaged from the surrounding ocean floor.

Beyond the dell was a lake, bordered by tall pampas grass and reeds that hid a wooden bird hide. Scilly was a well-known stopping place for migrating birds and a paradise for bird-watching—something I had recently discovered and loved to do.

To the west stretched a rugged coastline blanketed with gorse and bracken that reminded me of the Scottish Highlands, complete with a ruined watchtower that perched majestically on the bluff. It had been a place of refuge for the Royalists seeking sanctuary during the English Civil War.

Finally, there was Windward Point Lighthouse right on the northernmost tip of the island—the perfect logo for our hotel stationery.

The beauty of our new home, and all the renovations we had made so far, had helped diminish the harrowing events of the past few months. The loss of my adored Robert was becoming more bearable.

For the first time in years I had taken out my camera again. It was one of the many things I had enjoyed doing before I had married, and had willingly—though unconsciously—put aside in favor of spending time with Robert. Now I was on a voyage of self-rediscovery and although there were times when my sadness was overwhelming, the magic of Tregarrick Rock had become my sanctuary.

Unfortunately, the same wasn't true for my sister. She was impulsive and headstrong, and I'd been worried about her abrupt decision to quit Hollywood and move here. I knew that she missed her life in Los Angeles, and any day I expected her to announce that she was going back to California.

"Hey, sis. There you are!"

I hadn't heard Margot's footsteps as she approached. Wrapped in a cherry-red cashmere shawl, she waved a clear plastic folder at me. "Kim's magic checklist!" Margot picked up the kneeler, carefully balanced it on the planter next to mine and took a seat.

"You shouldn't sit on a cold surface," she scolded. "You'll get hemorrhoids."

"That's an old wives' tale," I said.

"Maybe." She grinned. "But is it worth the risk?"

I regarded my big sister with relief. Her eyes sparkled and she actually seemed cheerful.

Margot had evidently spent the morning touching up her roots—she was not a natural blond. I had wondered what she had been up to and was pleased at this display of vanity. Margot—usually high-maintenance—hadn't bothered with her appearance for weeks.

"Good job with the hair," I said. "That explains what you were doing."

"Well, that, and finalizing the plans with Kim for our open

house." Kim Winters was our new super-efficient cook-cum-housekeeper-cum-marketing guru. With her obsessive attention to detail, she and Dennis had turned out to be the perfect team to manage the hotel. "Take a look."

Under the heading *Open House, Saturday, March 28th, ten p.m. to six p.m.* was a long list of items, including hiring a calligrapher, writing the labels for the arts and crafts exhibition, setting up the garden furniture on the terrace and confirming local sponsorships for the finger foods and beverages. Most items had been ticked off as completed, except for three major jobs—sorting out the flower beds and planters on the terrace; rewiring and repainting the kitchen, ground-floor reception area and Residents' Lounge; and hanging the art we'd sourced from local artists.

"I think we're nearly there," Margot declared.

"I think 'nearly there' is rather optimistic," I said gloomily. "Have you been in the Residents' Lounge today? You can't just slap on new paint. It will need to be completely replastered first. Quick & Sons are definitely not living up to their name. They're so slow!"

"Well, Kim suggested a painting party," said Margot. "What do you think?"

"A painting party?" I regarded her with amusement. "I don't think I've ever seen you hold a paintbrush."

"There's a first time for everything," she said. "And I know that Louise won't mind."

"Louise?" I said. "Who is Louise?"

Margot looked uncomfortable. "Now, before you freak out, let me explain . . ."